Loose Associations

Loose Associations

❖

Fritz Wolf

Library of Congress Control Number: 2018905069
ISBN: Hardcover   978-1-9845-2003-6
                 Softcover   978-1-9845-2002-9
                 eBook   978-1-9845-2001-2

Print information available on the last page.

Rev. date: 05/11/2018

To order additional copies of this book, contact:
Xlibris
1-888-795-4274
www.Xlibris.com
Orders@Xlibris.com
776515

CHAPTER 1

One bygone relative ate soap, and one talked with rocks that talked back. They'd been in the old country, maybe County Clare. There were other weird family members, and he tried to bring them to mind. Faces, names, recollections, remembrances, rumination from his parents—mainly rubbish, hard to sort out.

The actual name Laughlin meant "stranger" from a Scandinavian word. Maybe they had been from Norway or Sweden originally. In the late 1700s, some Laughlins came to New York and more moved west. Some of them had weird children who didn't talk until there were eight or nine years old; apparently they had suffered from chewing windows sills coated with lead paint. One only sang, and one had white hair as a child. There was a surviving scrap of a marriage chest carved 1763 for a Missouri woman named Annie. She and Mr. Patrick Laughlin had eight kids, three died of scarlet fever all at once and one was killed in an Indian-French war. A next-generation survivor became a bookkeeper and lived way out west in Chicago, and one played violin in Kansas City.

There was another Laughlin who swore he was from Scotland and married a German woman named Gerta in 1788. They had seven live children, two of them having died of diarrhea. They lived in Pennsylvania and knew Benjamin Franklin. Two of the grandsons robbed a bank in Colorado like Jesse James and were killed in the process. The rest were quietly living and dying in The War for Independence, the War of 1812, the Mexican War, the Civil War, the Spanish-American war, and so on down all the wars in the twentieth century.

One Laughlin family made it to Lansing, Michigan, and ran a dairy farm and by 1871, some were growing and picking apples, and by 1913 many went to Detroit to work on Henry Ford's production lines

These were his people, the motley ones, according to his father, Eliot, who imbibed in manhattans with the whiskey adulterated with vermouth and bitters. He liked the sweet, sticky taste and the maraschino cherry, which he said reminded him of better times. Stories changed depending on his alcohol titer but always had to do with New York and lots of children surviving and dying. His father would laugh at the story of the uncle's wife who ate soap and curse at the gamblers who lost everything rather than leaving him money. He didn't care much for anything, including his own son or Detroit, and preferred lamenting about past losses.

Does being a drunk classify as a medical illness or an addictive personality or the ubiquitous indulgent asshole? Drinking, his face curdled into sour hate for his son. He was crazed. When working, he was a policeman until he stroked.

On his mother's side, he heard from his grandmother Pauline, who would read him fairy tales and tell him he was a prince. She told him that a distant cousin Hessian hero from way back fought with Washington, and another later generation helped with the underground railroad. That family moved west too. In one branch, there were thirteen kids, and they farmed all along the central states in the 1850s. Sometimes they ate weeds and had to kill all their chickens to survive. Two grew up and moved to Arizona, and three brothers went to Montana to ranch, giving up farming.

Regarding his own immediate branch, his mother's grandparents came from Germany in the 1830s. A great-grandfather who everyone said was romantic like Goethe, wrote poetry, and had died of tuberculosis. Maria only knew about a few others from what her mother, Laughlin's grandmother Pauline, told her, who was too busy cleaning house to talk about the past, merely saying, "I'm glad you got off the farm and made good as a teacher." She did mention there had been a great uncle on his grandfather's side who hanged himself

with a horse bridle and one who had a "calling" that took him off on
Lake Erie in a row boat. No one received a report about the calling
message, and he was considered dead and gone.

With ambivalence, Maria also admitted maybe there had been a
Wobbly in the family, and he was trying to remember what an aunt
Harriet had done that had been kept from him while he was young.
His mother's own brother, Helmut Meer, practiced carpentry until
he was drafted. He wrote once to his sister, saying his tools in the
garage were for her kids if she ever had some. He never returned.
The discharge from the Navy was in San Diego after the Korean
War, and he wrote he was going to Alaska. There was no further
information on his whereabouts. No one used the tools until James
bought his own house years later. His mother had saved them for him.

What could he say about his mother? Was she just a normal
suffering wife or a masochist? Whatever, she was there for her son.
His mother taught school and patience for his father's behavior.

Laughlin reconsidered, thought maybe it was starch, not soap
that some family member ate. Lots of Southern people ate starch
and clay. How do you chew soap? And a bridle would be hard to
hang from. Maybe it was a lasso like in the cowboy movies where the
coiling rope hung from a gnarled tree. Holding his lower lip with his
teeth, he reviewed his family's mental health with chagrin and spots
of pride. He had become a sheriff to please an unappeasable father
and now was on a job that provoked these recollections.

*   *   *

Among the scattered skyscrapers and squat malls cluttering
Los Angeles, near the downtown bronze-colored Metropolitan
Transportation building, sat the pale Twin Towers Jail. Two
dumbbell-shaped buildings with multiple slivered windows extruded
from the cement gray Men's Central Jail like bullae. They did not
bulge out alone. Wedged between them was a diamond-shaped
reception center and, strung along their periphery, the usual parasitic
bail bondmen's offices lit with thin neon signs and the dinky fast-food

stores bereft of franchise chain names but stocked with Twinkies and Budweiser cans.

About a half mile away in the crowded Philippe's restaurant, Laughlin stationed himself upstairs to wolf down a French dip sandwich and potato salad at a thickly varnished wood table surrounded by brick walls. Around him were office types with ties or heels, everyone gobbling and gabbing. There was no way to spot the crazies for sure.

He was on another assignment and wanted to add a good job to his record. Of course, he got ribbed unmercifully about getting another weird case. The murder case at the zoo had caused all sorts of banter about his being an animal familiar with such behaviors as howling. Not very original stuff but constant.

The new case was about the disappearance of a man who belonged to the LA County Jail staff, a mental health administrator working to help crazies. There was a wariness about investigations in home territory. The other detectives, assigned cases dealing with battered, beaten, and finally dead women or robberies gone astray to murder, expressed testy suspicion he might investigate their own as well as the mental health staff at the jail. At report Bob Shepard and Rich Litman joked about the assignment really being a subterfuge to assess the mental condition of Laughlin.

"You know I tried to think of anybody in my family who was mental. There was Randy, my cousin. He went berserk on PCP. My mom, she screams at my dad, but that's not really crazy, like off the wall," Shepard decided.

"Me, my grandpa went bonkers in the head after a stroke, but he died fast. Let's see, and I had an aunt who married four times. Is that crazy?" Litman speculated.

"What about back further?" Shepard asked.

"Oh, there was a distant cousin three times removed who jumped off a freeway bridge. Some figure he was trying to fly, not kill himself, but who knows, he was a big whiskey lover," Litman replied.

"I figure if you go back far enough, some crazy has to come up," Laughlin interjected.

"Yeah, especially in your family, buddy," Shepard shot back.

"Yeah, yeah. Thanks a lot. Well, it's my case and I'm going to try to make good."

"Just keep sane, Sheriff," Litman said, and the two detectives walked off to their cases.

There was this missing, presumed dead, as the line goes, mental health administrator. Who knew what that job was about? Who did that? There were very few facts in the complaint, and Laughlin had to start at the beginning.

So far, nothing was known about him except his wife finally called to say he had not come home for months and she wondered if he was still on a fact-finding trip. The FBI had gotten involved after the wife called the sheriff. What kind of man the missing person was or what a mental health administrator in the jail did was still unknown.

The sergeant finished his bread with the last swipe of the salty brown gravy, wiped his mouth with its trimmed mustache, and resolved to find out. Cleaning his hands off and downing his Coke, he walked out onto the treeless sidewalk. The September sun made a bright blank screen of air for the moving cars. He crossed over the asphalt and scarred cement to go under a morose bridge where the debris of paper cups, butts, plastic bags, and pee collected. At the other end was the jail.

Stalking him was the memory of being a new deputy in Men's Central and herding the marching color-coded inmates. Big as he was, jail cut him down to size and poked at his resolve to fit in. After training, all he wanted to do was to survive in the jail, his primary goal. He took it one day at a time and was thankful if he made it through the maze of inmates and paperwork. The mentor message had always been these inmates are the enemies, and they will kill you if they can. That was how he began his time as a sheriff's deputy. It was hard few years, a tentative time, when he had no other experiences to guide him. The thick, sick paint-colored bars held flight-and-fight emotions for both inmates and their keepers. In that sense it was very much like the zoo. Unpredictable beings able to kill.

All these guys, the same age or younger than he was, caught and stuck. He on one side of the coin, and they on the other. There were hundreds of them in electric blue jumpsuits at the processing area lying on or milling around white-sheeted bunk beds stacked everywhere.

Then they were moved deeper into the unknowns of the building to await court dates or serve their time. They were mostly black-haired Hispanic or African American heads topping the uniformity of the new jumpsuits, stepping, stepping, stepping forward. They were marched around for one reason or another through cinder block halls, always in lines forming blue and dirty orange-colored centipedes.

In their final destinations, he remembered the massive metal of the dark cages woven together in bars and platforms. He'd watched the inmates while he walked the sealed in gangplanks suspended over the two tiers of cells, six or more to a cell spending days in the gray steel. He hoped there would be no rocking agitation, no swearing or screaming, no blatant masturbation, no banging of bodies. He'd hoped they would all lie quietly, read magazines, talk, do their time peacefully, nonviolently, waiting for trials or release days.

Mental health services were kept apart. The really orange-clothed crazies were sent upstairs to small single rooms with slits in their cell doors used for talking and slipping meal trays in and out. The doors were thick steel and painted a sickened mustard yellow, scraped and beaten with years of abuse. Sometimes a mental health staff member would take a loony guy out of his safe haven, and they would sit in the hall on a steel screen black bench. While they talked, Laughlin would stand about guarding. Alert to any sudden actions. The conversations were usually inane or insane, and the staff would look down at their clipboards or flip through a chart, and that would be the end of it.

The inmate would shuffle back and, when he was safe once more, yell through the slit for his mother or a drink or to look out for the end of the world or to beware the coming of the bad guys, wherever they were. Laughlin remembered how glad he had been to get downstairs again to the bad, not mad.

Now he was back as a detective to investigate a missing man in the mental health department and the old and new complexes held foreign auras. Like everyone else, he'd had a natural avoidance of the crazies who took care of the crazies. He would come face-to-face with it all. It was another test of his mettle. He reminded himself he could not cower now. There was no need. He was a sheriff.

Outside the buildings, there were the usual five or six men milling on the corner, and one slumped down against a lamppost. Three brown-haired women, all with tight slacks containing their robust butts, were in front of him, laughing and sipping fast-food cups of some fizzy drink and munching chips. Two of them turned to look at him and nodded in approval. One offered him some fries, but he put his hand up, gesturing no thanks, just as a small scarf-covered figure with two babies pushed a stroller slowly out of the visitor's entrance and separated him from what he guessed were three of the mental health staff.

To the left was the familiar gray monolith jail, but to the right were the beige brick buildings finished for years but never occupied until now. The hope for better care and decreased tension prompted the transfer of inmates. This year, 1998, Laughlin was assigned the case. Women and the mentally ill inmates had already filled up the twin towers. He'd interviewed one woman for a previous case and hadn't been back since. There was no drain to hospitals to decompress all the mentally ill and their numbers rose, swamping the pristine but inadequate modules on all seven floors.

This was a new operation to him, and he was going to interview the administrative assistant to Franklin Mo, the missing mental health administrator. The man had been gone for months before anyone reported it, and that in itself was a strange aspect of the case. Why was the department involved? There had been blood found in the missing man's car.

He made his way to the Central Jail non-secured area, past the pictures of old sheriffs and the new sheriff and his staff, to an open blue painted room with multiple cubicles partitions like a maze. All were unoccupied except for one in the center.

The secretary or administrative assistant II, which was what her desk labeled her, was Florence McBride. She squirmed in her chair and continued to do so throughout the whole interview. The chair squeaked as she swiveled and wiggled back and forth and her shoulders rose up and her nose twitched like a distracted rabbit with each squeak.

"Mr. Mo, he didn't tell me nothing. I thought he was on another fact-finding mission. That's all I can say."

"What are your responsibilities to him?"

Her face turned a darker shade as she coughed and reached for what Laughlin thought were candy corns. "Listen, I do what I'm told to do. Been here eighteen years but only with Mr. Mo for three. Sometimes I types up a notice or send an e-mail. I also picks up the mail and things. Oh, and I files and things like that."

"Did he appear different or mention any stresses the weeks before he left?"

"Not that I noticed. Like always, he was gone a lot and stuff."

"Any strange calls?"

"I can't say," she replied and pulled out a drawer, fussed with some papers and shut it. She wiggled some more and her chair banged up against the desk.

"Were you looking for something to give me?"

"Can't say that I was. I had some gum and stuff in here, but it's gone."

"Can you give me a picture of your boss, his style, you know."

"Picture? Why in the world would I have a picture of that man. He was mean to me and didn't give a flying you-know-what about me or my troubles. To tell you the truth, I was in raptures when he was gone. He don't mean a thing to me, so no pictures of him, for sure."

Startled by the response, Laughlin answered, "I guess I meant can you described how he acted. How was he mean to you, for example?"

"How's I to know? He acted like an asshole, never did anything for all the good I did, copying his stuff and keeping quiet. Even that time when I was up for a promotion to the next grade administrator assistant, may have made an extra fifty bucks, he didn't have time to fill out a recommendation and just said he was too busy to bother with me. Imagine that. I did all his dirty work and he couldn't even sign a paper for me."

"What dirty work did you do for him, the stuff you kept quiet about?"

"I'm supposed to tell you now. Jesus, how can I trust you?" She shook her head. "I ain't saying nothin' else. Maybe I'll get me another position, and I don't want to risk it. You understand, huh? I don't know what was okay and what was not, copying charts, filthy photos and stuff. Why did that guy love all kinds of things between legs, I mean really, it was enough to make you puke. Nasty, nasty."

"I guess you were put in an awkward position, Ms. McBride, trying to please your boss and get ahead," Laughlin sympathized but realized too late, he should have kept his mouth shut and let her continue her monologue.

"It's Mrs. McBride, but you're right on, knocked it out of the park with that one. You can understand how I'm shutting up right now, okay?"

"It must have been stressful. I hope you can let me know more about it all when you feel more secure." He never knew whether to risk addressing women with the Ms. or Mrs. title now that miss was out of favor. He backtracked and offered, "You probably know best whom to talk to. I'm interested in any other staff who know him. Can you arrange for them to meet me?" Laughlin handed her his telephone number and waited.

"You'd best be going over to the Towers and meet them there. They don't come here, and he don't go there if possible," she explained, while fussing with her hair, repositioning a big multi-fanged clip on her head and restoring her composure.

"They're the ones knowed him best?" The comment was met with a shrug. "Please have one of them meet me here ASAP," Laughlin insisted, and the administrative assistant bunched up her nose but complied.

CHAPTER 2

It took a whole hour on the phone until anyone of the senior staff was located and made it over to the cubicle where Mrs. McBride had directed Laughlin to sit and wait. Restless and irritated, Laughlin had walked up and reexamined photos of past sheriffs, each enshrined in their own framed place on the long hall. Finally, he slumped down on a plastic chair, and Mrs. McBride brought over a broad, husky man with graying hair and ashen face.

He sat across from Laughlin and sweated and sweated more: sweated until his forehead looked strung with clear beads of sweat. His neck glistened like a greased pole sitting on a stuffed crash dummy. He was a fat frightened man. His pink shirt and baby-blue tie were partially covered by a black wrinkled suit, which puffed at the shoulders when he sat down.

Freddy Poplar, psychologist at the outpatient inmate modules, didn't seem to think he should betray Franklin Mo with any talk and asked to be excused as though he had to piss. He probably did, Laughlin surmised by the way the guy was clapping his legs together and holding a bent briefcase against his crotch like a four-year-old. Laughlin told him to come back after he was done relieving himself, and when Poplar did return, he was still sweating and tense. Diarrhea was what Laughlin predicted next but he proceeded with the questioning.

The man talked about his pressures as the head of the men's clinic and how hard it was to control any of the staff. They were gone for hours, and when they returned, they passed by the cells, questioning further only if an inmate didn't answer when his name was called. The still perspiring psychologist clutched his thin briefcase, pressing it over his supposedly empty bladder, and partially released it only when dipping into his pockets for tissues, pulling out wads of wet shredded stuff.

"Mr. Mo is very much in charge and didn't like we program chiefs to contradict him. He threatened to fire me at least three times after Dr. Weber came because we tried some of her suggestions on how to evaluate patients.

"But I really have to get back to my office for a meeting. I really have to meet with the deputies about the seventh floor."

"What about?"

"I can't say. Just that the seventh floor is for the psychotic inmates, and we're trying to figure out what to do so they don't hang themselves and how much toilet paper they can have without stuffing down their throats to suicide. They have to get therapy out of their cells and that's the problem. We have to watch them. I've gotta get a drink now." He coughed into his sleeve, got up after a nod from Laughlin, went to the drinking fountain and returned still coughing.

"How do your staff get along with Mr. Mo?"

"Oh, I try really hard to get along with everyone."

"I'll come with you to the meeting," Laughlin suggested, trying to appease the agitated man.

"Oh, I don't know. Did you get clearance?" the worried, impending heart attack asked. "I can't be responsible. I have too much to do."

The two men walked across the street and up a stairway into the hall. Poplar, breathing heavily, paused and wiped his brow. Long hallways were lit with incandescent lights penetrating even the cracks in the tile. The sally port door slid open and they stood inside. Laughlin got his permit, and then another one of the many doors slid open, and they were on their way. The way was through a myriad of doors again, into an encased fifteen-by-fifteen-foot shimmering steel elevator and to Dr. Poplar's office on the fifth floor. The psychologist kept pausing, wiping, and looking back at Laughlin to make sure he kept up. He didn't have to worry. They entered the office together.

The sequestered, dismal room held four plain-clothes staffers on folding chairs and two sheriff's men leaning at the door. One of the standing uniforms was a round-faced, maybe twenty-five-year-old deputy, and the other was a brawny, black senior deputy named Williams, who knew Laughlin and greeted him with a quick nod.

Poplar lumbered in, put his brief case on one of four mismatched desks of either beaten steel or scratched wood, and offered, "So sorry I'm late. Sergeant Laughlin is here. We were looking into Franklin's disappearance. Anyone have anything to add?"

A slight, frowning man began to talk. He had a dark copious mustache and beard. The hair surrounded his large lips, which squirmed like pink slugs, as he whined, "I, for one, think we better solve this therapy situation. We need more deputies up on seven. Now, it's just unsafe." He looked around for approval. "I don't think any of us should go in when the inmates are out of the cells, and I certainly won't," he opined and then clasped his hands over his belly.

"This is Dr. Marks, a psychologist. Peter, what about Franklin?" Poplar retorted.

"What about him? He never told us anything. What are we supposed to know? Did he have enemies? After Dr. Weber left, most of us didn't see him anymore, except at the general meetings. I don't know what we're supposed to do, Freddy. Why aren't you helping us? We need protection. I used to ask Franklin to please intercede, and he would nod, and tell me how obstinate the sheriffs were. He never told me why. It was frustrating. He got to go to all meetings with the sheriffs, but nothing ever came of them. He'd complain about how incompetent the deputies were. I didn't think that. I just wanted more of them up there on seven."

An opulently endowed woman, budging in her front and rear, barely held in by a red knit dress and black boots, leaned forward on her desk and said, "We didn't even get told he was missing until Wednesday. I mean, weeks had gone by. As a staff member, I felt discriminated against."

"Well, Dr. Forester, this sergeant is investigating, and we should help him if we know anything."

"Like I said, he told me nothing. He shined me on with smiles and ignored me. I had that run-in with that patient threatening me. I was really scared when the time came he might be released. Franklin didn't tell the sheriffs about the threats." The distressed woman swore quietly and continued, "Word got back to me that he said I was overreacting, black woman thing. I was pissed, but when I confronted him, he just said it was a misunderstanding, and I should lock my front door.

"What kind of protection was that? He was never our advocate."

The group nodded in agreement but remained silent. One large-eyed staffer with the name tag Brad Eagleton, MSW askew on his stripped shirt, gently scratched his scalp throughout the exchange and played with the recovery until he flicked it on the floor. He then dug in his ear. Finally, he said quietly, "I didn't get to know him well. In fact, I can't remember him up here since, maybe, six months ago, when I came back from my vacation. He was hanging around with the women's staff and not here much. Was he going to get us more help ever?"

The last of the staff, a social worker named Lattice Ling, concurred on the illusiveness of the missing man before he was officially missing. "I did report the case overload, and he said he'd look into it, but that was months ago. Nothing happened, and he discarded two of my memos," she complained. She herself was following "too many" cases. "Another thing, Brad and I had really hoped the new sheriff's doctrine of more educational programs would be started, but Franklin said the sheriffs wouldn't listen and to let the inmates watch whatever TV reruns were available. I wonder if he even brought it up at the meetings. There was no follow through." She paused and then gave an earnest plea for extra staff help to set up the programs they'd developed. "It's just sad that we can't get more done," she concluded. Fussing with her multiple files, the slight woman with large glasses slipping down her nose, shook her head and sighed.

There was a series of nods and chairs scooting up to desks and then the report began, and Franklin Mo's disappearance disappeared from the group's attention.

The organization of Tower I was stacked against mental health— that is, the more disturbed were sent to the higher floors. The third floor was the medical ward and offices; the fourth floor was for stable men usually not on medication and getting ready for discharge or held the coveted homosexuals module, desirable because there was less chance of being beaten up by your cellmates.

The fifth floor housed the inmates who were considered relatively stable mental health outpatients. They were lined up for medications and occasional occupational therapy, which consisted of learning something about computers, and then going back to watching *Gilligan's Island* reruns. The sixth floor men were similar but a little less stable, on new medications, needing some observation to see if there was any progress. They were the graduates from the upper floors. Topping the least mentally healthy were the inmates of the seventh floor, the subject of the present meeting.

Freddy began sweating again and reading out names, which were matched to certain behaviors. Laughlin listened to the cases being presented. They consisted of inmates screaming, feces throwing, head banging, soporific, catatonic, suicidal, paranoid, murderous, delusional as Christ, designing devils or the CIA, and pure indiscriminate haters. He heard the latest plans for another set of Velcro clothing to prevent hanging, decisions about how much toilet paper to give out to prevent stuffing it down throats to asphyxiation, when showers could be taken, etc. These were the decisions made by the sheriffs but problems the staff had to deal with.

Not much was said about the actual treatment of patients on this top floor until psychiatrists examined the inmates, and more psychiatrists could be hired to examine them sooner and give their recommendations. Laughlin understood that this particular staff was there to check patients periodically and wait for dispositions. A few other personnel wandered in and out of the stuffy office and, when in, stared at their fingernails or wrote in little pads for their eyes alone. No one added any relevant information to the whereabouts of Mr. Mo.

After getting permission, Dr. Poplar suggested they go down to the cafeteria for some coffee. Laughlin agreed, and they sat together with Deputy Williams.

"This job is a lot of work, but I was hoping for it to make things better."

"How'd you come here?"

"Oh, I finished my degree, and another child was on the way. It seemed like a good secure position. I never thought I'd become a program head."

"What is the program anyway?" Laughlin asked, looking a Freddy.

"That's a good question. The jail is a hodgepodge of illnesses. To control behavior is most important. It's hard. Program heads manage staff for groups of men and women inmates. Many of these inmates are like kids, teenage kids." He gulped his coffee down and then a glass of water. "We try to get them to behave and finally get back to Men's Central if possible or out altogether. Of course, some of them can't understand much, knocked in the head so many times or dumbed down by drugs. It's enough if they follow the rules, and it's really good if they take their meds. Sometimes we try to train them a little in computers and even just plain arithmetic. Socialization is done in small groups. The hope is that they learn to get along once they get discharged."

"Looks like you have your hands full."

"I tell you, Detective Laughlin, I don't know which is harder, my own teenagers or the inmates. Seriously, though, I appreciate your understanding. I'm fifty-four years old and, this is where I'm going to end up, nowhere else to go and I'd sure like to make it better than it is. We need more room and more staff and more supplies. But who cares? It's frustrating to say the least. The county has so many other demands."

"Budget problems all over," Laughlin sympathized.

"Isn't that the truth. You know the staff we have, they get burnt out. It's a never-ending shuffle in and out of sick men, arrested for whatever and back again in no time."

"And Franklin Mo?" Laughlin tried again.

"Franklin. I don't know what to say. He was in administration and managed evaluations. I saw him only if there was a complaint from somewhere. That was torture because there was no explaining the problems to him. He's just say fix it or keep it quiet." The distressed man looked at his watch, excusing himself. He apologized profusely to Sergeant Laughlin for having to leave him to head for another meeting.

After their coffee, Laughlin toured the seven floors with Senior Deputy Williams, who was as amiable as he remembered from past years.

Each tower floor had a central flat area, which branched off into the contained module beyond the guard station or the visitor/lawyer meeting rooms. Williams strolled into the seventh floor. Laughlin's uneasiness surfaced when he entered the infamous module, even though inmates were behind locked doors with glass panels. Cells had narrow enclosures ending with vertical window slits to the outside, like the walls were squinting. Tensing, he turned quickly at the slightest noise. These caged men were the severely mentally ill, unpredictables of the city. He didn't know what their agenda was. It wasn't necessarily stealing, drugs, rape. In them there were the inner commands whose resultant actions couldn't be foreseen.

Three inmates out of their rooms were sitting at the steel tables, talking calmly with two brawny deputies and Brad, the social worker, from the meeting. The inmates were writing with stubby pencils on half sheets of paper. Williams explained they were either writing letters or filling out varying complaints, usually about food. At that moment, all three were lucid and in control. Laughlin and he went up to them and asked how it was going.

"It's fucking shitty in here if you're interested, sheriff guy. Worse than prison. I hears them teasing me to kill myself. Why dinnit they let me burn, only broke a few windows getting out on that there playground?"

"For me, it's good to be out of that cell. There were bad spirits in there, sliding around, around me and my head. I couldn't even jack off. How do they seep through them windows anyway? I wants to kill them."

The third man just stared at the air and stroked his throat covered with tattoos of guns. He marked his paper with multiple x's, big and little. That was all.

A few of the still enclosed inmates began screaming. It was hard to make out what they were saying. One man threw himself against the door and banged his head. A deputy went up to him and shouted, "Bobby, don't bang your head. Stop hurting yourself! Calm down, man. What's the matter?"

"We have to call the extraction team up here when some guy can't be controlled. If anyone can calm him down, Deputy Kincade can. Do you want to see the histories of these guys? I doubt if they can tell you anything about Franklin Mo."

Laughlin figured what the extraction team had to be and concurred with leaving. He didn't want to provoke the head-beating guy. They went down a floor.

"The thing is, these guys can be calm one minute and kill the next. The two talkative ones are in here for trials. One beat up a kid he grabbed, saying his was the devil's spawn and set fire to the preschool with torches. The other one rented a hotel suite and tried to hang his wife out the window for trying to poison his dinner with spirits, and the quiet one is in for robbery of a pharmacy, beating up the owner badly, saying God send him messages that told him to stop people getting pills, shit like that."

Laughlin understood. Unpredictable beyond most people was the conclusion.

The homosexual unit's inmates startled him with their delight at the visit, their myriad of physical states due to freewheeling estrogen effects, and their willingness to talk. There were men ranging from plucked eyebrows to full breasted, penis intact strutting types to timid, tiny types afraid of being attacked. They knew nothing about Franklin Mo except to offer, "He sometimes took a honey to interview for a few hours." The group laughed knowingly and added, "He was a pencil dick."

"How would you know that, Pat?" Williams asked a smooth skinned, spiked-blond-haired man. Pat gawked mockingly. He blew the deputy a kiss and sealed his lips with a little finger extended with an inch of nail. Then he slid in among the entertained group.

Williams and Laughlin moved on as did the insinuations.

The other modules held what seemed like more docile and older men than in Central Jail, mainly chronic schizophrenics and the brain damaged according to Williams. Surveying the mental health staff, Laughlin found it consisted of unruffled psychiatrists, many gray-haired. They were assessing the mental states and refilling meds. They kept to themselves wearing their reading glasses slightly down on their noses, and saw only charts, never spotting or acknowledging any intrigue among the personnel. Inmates would line up and sit patiently for their interview.

When consulted, Dr. Parker was puzzled about Franklin Mo missing and responded with "The guy was never around as far as I was concerned. He spent more time walking back and forth as far as I could see and never did me any good regarding supplies or transfers of the inmates I thought should be moved faster. It was pretty much a given that he wasn't worth talking to, and that left us all bitching to each other as far as I could see."

"I'd say we were left alone, and, considering all the work, that was okay by me," a Dr. Norman added.

"Yeah, that's true. What we really need is more staff, psychiatrists especially, to sort through the inmates faster," Dr. Simpson chimed in. Then they all turned back to the card tables of charts and lines of patients, which left Williams and Laughlin standing by as observers.

A few psychologists tried to run a group or two, while social workers tried to help with discharges back to Men's Central or to the street. They were the same ones Laughlin had seen at the meeting. Inmates would shuffle out into the day room, and Laughlin could hear the group leader coaxing comments from resistant group members sitting in folding chairs, patiently waiting to go back to the module. He could hear the social workers take elaborate histories from eager inmates wanting to get out and promise new beginnings and be busy writing rather than talking.

None of the staff revealed squat about the illusive Mr. Mo, and Laughlin wondered what this guy really did in jail Mental Health.

"So, Williams, what's your take on this guy?"

"I don't have one. In my observing him, all I saw was he'd bustle in and out like a bumbling bureaucrat, taking some notes and nodding to himself in profound frowns. Some of the staff are solid and try to be helpful to the deputies but this guy seemed always to take offense at anything the deputies asked of him. It was basically assumed he was an asshole. I guess that's my take on him too."

"A consensus, I gather," Laughlin concluded.

Senior Deputy Williams, aware of the dearth of information about Franklin Mo, suggested the sergeant talk with the women's staff. He led him to the Twin Tower II. "They're a mean bunch of bitches toward their own, I tell you that, but Franklin Mo and them hung out together. Like lunches and long meetings. Nothing salacious as I could tell."

Laughlin thanked the deputy for the offered information during the tour aside from the missing man being illusive if on the job. After introductions, Williams dropped Laughlin off at the second tower and left.

CHAPTER 3

In the women's section, white lights melded the halls and tile into a bright illusion of order. Dr. Mary Mason, psychologist on call that day for the new patients and apparently on call the last day anyone saw Franklin Mo, gave the sergeant a cursory nod and led him down a hall to a small room. She was like the new Geico gecko ad, thin with wide-placed eyes and arms that moved in an undulating fashion as she reached for charts. She didn't have the lizard's charming accent, and she held Laughlin at bay long enough to establish who was in charge. He waited patiently while sizing up her little office way off to the side of the module for the incarcerated women. There were a few photos, fake flowers, one telephone, a few pamphlets, and no books.

Laughlin reflected on the men's mental health jail being full and empty at the same time: jammed with the scooped-up mentally sick and void of shared purpose other than put the inmates out on the street again. A never-ending supply waited. Maybe the women's tower would be different.

Finally, she turned to him swiveling her gray desk chair, and rolled up her sleeves to reveal thin, stark arms and hands with clipped white-painted nails.

"Well?" she asked as she strapped her arms across her chest.

"When was the last time you saw Franklin Mo?"

"Look, Franklin Mo is a friend of my husband's and mine. He took care of me when I first came here and showed me the ropes." She fluffed her hair with both hands and looked at him. "I have no idea where he is."

"Why weren't you worried? Especially when he was not around for so long. No communication from your boss, no letters, no e-mails, no calls. Wasn't that strange?"

"Well, I . . . well, I, I just knew he was all right. He'd tell me he had to go on trips to check out other mental health facilities, and he'd send me postcards and things. I even got to go on one with him to Arizona, and we got to party a little after the meetings."

"Party?"

"Oh please, calm down. Franklin and I understood each other from the get-go. He really likes to take someone with him to evaluate places and talk to patients. He is a big schmoozer and could really work a room of administrators since he came from this big-time place. He'd send postcards about the visit."

"So you did get something recently? When was the last time you got a postcard?"

"Oh, about a month or so ago. I don't know why he didn't take me this time."

She wasn't giving up anything unless asked, and Laughlin disliked her reticence. "Where was it from?"

"Right here, I think. Anyway, the postcard was the Hollywood sign. He said he was having a wonderful time, if you must know."

"Do you still have it?"

Without answering, Dr. Mason opened a desk drawer, poked around the papers lying quietly in their dark bed, pinched a few in her left hand, and said, "Guess not." She closed the drawer quickly and put her fingers of her right hand on her left wrist, took her pulse, while she stared at her watch.

"Was it sent to the jail address?"

"Oh, let me think. Maybe not." Her beeper went off, she dialed a phone number and offered, "I'll be there in a minute. Hold on."

Ignoring Laughlin, Dr. Mason wrote a number on an index card, picked up a file, and started for the door.

Laughlin stood up and followed.

"Oh, wait here if you like. I have to see this inmate."

"No, I'll come along." That was that.

They walked down a polished tile floor between more clean white walls, and through a sally port door unto the cement floor with a few card tables on it and then stepped into an inmate module. The silence between them was not a truce. Laughlin didn't understand why the power plays, but he decided to play pacifist and wait on any assumptions.

The module consisted of curved mute walls holding two tiers of rooms with railings of PC pipe fitted together to contain the walkways and thick glass doors to the bunks. A baptistery with no salvation. The female inmates were in the downstairs day area, sitting on the little seat pods sprung up from the round steel tables, baby mushrooms around a mother.

With her chart across her chest like body armor, Dr. Mason stood waiting for a deputy to accompany her between the tables of perched inmates. The deputy was a muscled black woman named Jefferson, with a wide belt for gun and other accoutrements that canceled out her curvaceous build. As they moved in, the women, appraising the sergeant and at times stretching out a hand but never touching him, did not speak a word. Laughlin felt on display. This overt evaluation was different from walking into a party or a concert and getting attention. This was more like an auction and he was admired meat.

Mason did nothing to allay the pervasive anxiety, thick with threats.

One table had collected a clot of women's backs. Smack on the center of the tabletop was a singing hulk.

Approaching the table, a short inmate with blunt-cut hair and a purple cheek scar perpendicular to her upper lip came over to Dr. Mason, pleading, "You got to do something here, you got to. Mother Tobias is breathing bad. I told you that last night, and you don't do nothing."

"Go sit down, Lorene, and let me talk to her. Hear me, go sit down now," Mary Mason said abruptly, blowing her cover of control and irritated by the reminder that she had been told of this trouble before.

Lorene retaliated with "Don't go bossing me, you bitch. Act like the doctor youse supposed to be, you fucker, faker, filthy slut."

The deputy raised her arm and pointed to an empty seat and Lorene nodded in compliance. "Get a fucking doctor in here, mind me, I'm telling you, get the paramedics and a doctor in here now!" she screamed and sat down.

Laughlin went over to Mother Tobias. Breathing like bellows, her breath screeching in and out, she was singing "I am woman, hear me roar" over and over. He took her pulse, saw the distended neck veins, felt the quivering in her back with each desperate breath, noticed the ankles like red elephant legs, and looked at Dr. Mason.

"I think the woman's got it right. Mother Tobias needs medical care now," Laughlin offered. The distressed singer looked at him as her eyes began to water, and she put her hand on his shoulder. "Boy, don't touch me. That's assault unless I agree to it." She coughed loudly, and then began her song again, "I am woman, hear me roar. But, sheriff man, I likes your caring for me."

Dr. Mason stood aside and leaned in a confidential manner toward Laughlin to explain, "This inmate has been medically cleared in the IRC, Sergeant. She's manic-depressive. We get at least one woman a month singing Helen Reddy. Always acting up. Preaching to the other inmates about justice and how their boyfriends use them to run drugs and whore. Gets real dramatic. I think we can handle this one."

"Doctor, this woman's in heart failure and maybe pneumonia. You don't have to be a genius to know it. Look at her labored breathing, distended neck veins, swollen ankles. She's in trouble," Laughlin persisted.

"I am the word of truth, fat woman, ugly woman, crazy woman, black woman, goddess woman, listen to me and divine the truth. You girls must save yourselves and not be imprisoned by the greed of men. Don't burst forth from his seed with more trouble. Don't be led by the carrot of his dick down the path of crime, drugs, murder," Mother Tobias expounded and then stopped suddenly. She opened her eyes wide and a wet rumbling cough spewed forth a green jelly of mucus directly on Dr. Mason's white arms.

Dr. Mason gasped in horror, tried to brush the clinging visitor off with the unscathed chart, and scurried out of the module's port, pushing the deputy aside.

"Dr. Mason," Laughlin called as he followed her and the deputy. The door closed behind them, and they left the singing cougher. "Dr. Mason," Laughlin tried again.

"I've got nothing more to say!" she shouted and fled down the hall to the bathroom.

Laughlin stood outside the door with Deputy Jefferson, waiting for her return and some action. None came.

"Who's in charge here anyway? I want to see another doctor now," he told the calm but agreeable deputy.

"Sure, I agree with you. Tobias is in trouble. That loogie was impressive. Let's page the psychiatrist on call," she replied.

Approximately twelve minutes after Deputy Jefferson explained the request, a petite full-faced Asian woman stepped off the steel elevator onto the gray cement. Laughlin was still looking for a physician.

The woman, dressed in a white coat, light blue blouse, black slacks and shoes that gently clicked on the cement came up to the two sheriffs, nodded, and said, "Let's go see the patient now."

"Sergeant Laughlin, this is Dr. Banting. Doctor, Detective James Laughlin, investigating Franklin Mo's disappearance," Deputy Jefferson said politely. She added, "As a psychiatrist and, therefore, a medical doctor, she can decide whether to send the inmate to medicine."

"Beatrice Banting, Sheriff Laughlin." The doctor reached out her hand and shook Laughlin's with a firm, tight grip. It signaled confidence and helped him allay any doubts about her competence.

Returning to the module, the inmates immediately parted for the three of them and with less than a minute of observation and permission to listen to her lungs, a decision was made. Mother Tobias would be taken to the medical inpatient ward at the jail and probably transferred to the county hospital. The wheelchair arrived with attendants and Deputy Jefferson gave them the transfer orders.

"You must have had some medical training, Sergeant," Banting said as she walked toward the offices.

"Some," Laughlin responded but was distracted as Mother Tobias sang as loudly as her weakened breath could allow. Then she was swallowed up by the elevator.

While the deputy went to the security tower to visit with some buddies, the psychiatrist and Laughlin sat down at a small table outside the module. Dr. Banting wrote rapidly in the chart. Her hand was small and smooth. Laughlin studied her face, which had an impeccable complexion he's only seen in babies. Somehow the women he'd been with always had busy skin along with their passions. While she wrote, the woman's black straight hair suddenly slid over her face, jarring his musing.

"Do you have any ideas about Franklin Mo's disappearance?" he began, hoping to get her to turn her face up toward him, and offer some of her observations. She had decided to work for the county because her husband had been promoted to a bank vice president relocated to LA, and she was still deciding what kind of a psychiatric practice she wanted in this unique city. Dr. Weber and Dr. Brandt had been encouraging, and so she signed on.

"I think I'm doing some good in a really dispirited place."

She patiently explained the differences between psychiatrists, all trained in medical school and then in residency, and psychologists, some at least university trained in psychology programs and others with "Psych Ds" given at other types of schools. Everyone gets to be called doctor.

"It's a very diverse group as far as background training and it shows. I was shocked at how little anyone knew or cared about the inmates. No one understood any medicine. Things are beginning to change, but it's scary. Don't get caught in jail especially when you're sick."

"And Franklin Mo?"

"I think he was one of the people who the county thought might help bring some order to the place, but from what I understand, he merely avoided any trouble by blaming the sheriffs. They thought he was inconsequential. I was privy to some conversations, so I figure it wasn't his being Asian as much as his being a bull slinger."

"You didn't like him?"

"Oh, I didn't have much to do with him. He hung around with Mason and the gang in women's. After Dr. Weber left, the rift between staff got worse and I try to stay out of it."

"The rift?"

"Well, the idea was to get a better quality of professionals here since it is the largest facility of its kind. People got mighty defensive when new demands were made. They'd coasted all those years when no one cared what happened in the jails. Now more focus, the Department of Justice, and a new compassionate sheriff have made things heat up. I can't say that Mr. Mo being here, or not being here, has made any difference that I noticed. He was a person who I essentially avoided. He would invite me to lunch. Rumor had it that lunch was not lunch and such, but I stayed away from him. I'm not sure if that irritated him, but he knew not to mess with me."

Laughlin thanked Dr. Banting and told Deputy Jefferson he wanted to go back to Mason's office.

Dr. Mason was at her desk and had a few pill bottles lying on her papers. She looked at him and said, "Now you see what we have to deal with. I'll be damned if I want to be exposed to TB or AIDS. These women are even dumber than the men and more vicious too."

"Tobias was very sick. Why didn't anybody care enough to check her?"

"Are you deaf or something? I told you she was cleared at the inmate reception center by the medical doctors as she came through, even before transfer here. She was just being shitty to me, that's all."

"Does this thing happen often?"

"We are dealing with criminals, you know, and they have no respect. I'm going to get myself checked over right now," she decided and began to pack up her pills in a bulky purse covered with buckles and snaps.

"My guess is that these inmates get little respect as well," Laughlin suggested.

"Oh, take their side, who cares? My pressure is up and I'm going to get myself checked." Walking out with Laughlin behind her, she met another staff member and told her to answer Laughlin's questions. Dr. Mary Moreland was a psychologist who had worked at the county for four years. She had a pleasant demeanor, which was a relief from Dr. Mason's, and she offered to sit down with Laughlin in her small office down the hall. A plain office with a beige tint like its occupier, Dr. Moreland had one poster of the Cardinals and acknowledged fondness for her home state. There were a few charts carefully piled on each other to cover a plain Formica desk and a cup full of sharpened pencils topped with Bart Simpson erasers.

She readily explained the coverage of the women's modules and thought maybe that Mrs. Tobias was admitted over a week ago. After willingly pulling the records to check, she confirmed the date of admission. The older woman had pending arraignment for passing bogus checks. Somehow the hearing hadn't come up yet and her court-appointed lawyer had missed two meetings.

The file was meager and only a few lines of notes were apparent other than "doing well," "eats well," "coughing sometimes," for the medical assessment by random staff. Dr. Moreland read the notes about the inmate's behavior, which were limited to comments about helping other inmates and being belligerent at meals.

"It's hard to keep up with all the chart writing as well as talk to all our patients during shifts. If we have any trouble, it's over makeup and getting hair done. Most of the women are here for soliciting and it's usually with the undercover cops. We've got a couple drug pushers but mainly users who get caught with their boyfriends dealing." She spoke with familiarity, and her round face, framed by straight blond streaked hair, ended her observations with a smile.

"How'd you wind up here?"

"Oh, I finished my Psych D degree online and decided to stay in California, and they, the county, was glad to have me, even though

I hadn't gone to a university, so I took the job. It's different being in Los Angeles."

"Did you get special training for these types of patients?"

"You mean the inmates?"

"Yes, the inmates."

"I don't know if I'd call it training. I went around with older staff for a while and watched them interview. That was it. Everyone seemed to like my notes."

"And Franklin Mo, how was he involved?"

"I'm not sure what you mean? You're a detective, right? I heard that Mr. Mo was missing."

"Yes, he has apparently been missing for at least a couple months."

"Mr. Mo went to lunch almost every day. He was here with the staff. They would go to Chinatown, the Golden Dragon. I went at first, but it took too long, and I had too much to do. He took a special interest in helping Dr. Mason, who had some physical illnesses. He was kind to her. She was the program head for women here at the jail and had stress all the time. I heard she was thinking of leaving and he talked her into staying."

"Did you get along with him?"

"Sure. Why? Did he say something about me?"

"I wondered because it appears many people had problems with him not doing his job," Laughlin tossed out the teaser.

"You know, he was a little too sophisticated for me. You know, wanting to have drinks and dinners and stuff to discuss policy and stuff, but he was gone enough of the time so that it wasn't too much of a problem and stuff."

Laughlin heard the repeated use of the word "stuff" as an indication of some trouble with the subject matter. How to approach her to get a more candid opinion, earn an honest answer, was part of his learning to interview. He rephrased the question, "Did he and you see things differently?"

"You know we did. Of course, he was the administrator and I was just staff, but I thought some of the inmates could be transferred out to better situations and he . . . he just wanted to keep them 'cause they didn't make trouble."

"How was that resolved?"

"It really wasn't. I got scared. I think he copped a feel once and after he suggested we have lunch at his apartment, I begged off and didn't bring it up again. I said my boyfriend was waiting for me. His invitation didn't seem right and stuff, but I wasn't going to get in trouble with him. I shared my concerns with Dr. Mason and she said to forget it. He was more experienced than me, and besides, I already knew he could spread rumors that were not nice and stuff like that could hurt."

"Rumors?"

He would report on staff, and it got back that he would kinda exaggerate about faking hours, taking unapproved time off and stuff. I was late once and was really scared he would make sure I was docked a whole day. He didn't, but he said I owed him. I know he reported lost supplies blamed on a staff nurse who left after that. All she had done was give the antibiotics the way they were supposed to be given, not skip doses. Anyway, now he's gone for a while and that's a relief. That's all I can say. If it's all right, I think I'll go now. I have some new evaluations. Should I show you to the elevators?"

Laughlin thanked the young woman, the interview concluded, and the detective was left to speculate as he descended to the long hallways and sally port out. Franklin Mo was missing, but some parts of him were being filled in without much redeeming of his character.

Laughlin wondered about the vulnerability of the staff. Here was a setup wherein power was authorized, accepted, condoned, and, like an infection, misuse spread from the lowly inmates and their pecking order to the deputies, mental health staff, and administrators. Now the Department of Justice was nosing around and calling into question the program, but was it calling into question the intimidations, undercover operations, incompetency that could squirm around in between rules and regulations like . . . like what? Like streptococci he's seen in science programs, giggling and jiggling, or like fungus spreading fuzz over fallen fruit, or white worms of flies eating flesh.

He wasn't sure what images fit but felt the crawling, the chaos, the feeding on fools and captives. He was only told about the surface, and it was grating enough. How would the new Sheriff and the head of Mental Health deal with this all? Franklin Mo was Laughlin's focus, and he had to remember that.

Outside was glorious, covered in blue sky and fresh air, maybe polluted but not controlled air-conditioning. Traffic yelled freedom and he beat it through the lanes to the beach just in time for the sunset.

CHAPTER 4

Laughlin's partner, Senior Deputy Joseph Max, was returning from taking a day off and would help with interviews at the jail. There were still quite a few administrative and office staff to see.

Deputy Max would continue with the men's outpatient inmate staff, and Laughlin would cover the jail hospital ward and Dr. Conner. Chase Conner, MD obviously worked out to buff out his average height, and his intense blue eyes challenged all he encountered. He showed Laughlin into the ward chart room with its long counters and rolling chairs.

"I don't have a true office 'cause I'm on the ward when I'm here. I keep my stuff in a locker and at home," he explained. "This is going to have to do."

"No problem. Did you have much contact with Administrator Mo?"

"Can't say I did and can't say I missed it. He tended to avoid this area. We've got sick people here—diabetics, hypertensives, surgical recoveries, and all disturbed mentally."

"How did you find out he was missing?"

"I work ten hours a day and so I hear plenty of scuttlebutt."

"Why that schedule? And what were the rumors?"

"That gives me a forty-hour week in four days. I can earn enough money to finally get out of debt and buy myself a house. My wife and I are trying to save. She's a nurse at the county hospital. We want out of this shit city with its smog and traffic. So I work hard. When I'm not here, I work at the inmate reception area, medically clearing new admissions," he said and took a swallow of creamed coffee. He'd also offered Laughlin a cup but the sergeant declined. "Regarding the rumors, they ran along the lines of cheating the county to murdering inmates he didn't like."

"What do you mean?"

"I can work extra hours moonlighting. Like I said, we're after money to get out of here and back to a smaller town to raise kids. School loans are a bitch."

"The cheating and murdering?"

"Let's walk around the ward and talk as we go. You sure you don't any coffee?"

"No, I'm okay."

"There are individual rooms here with thick glass so everyone is observable. You can see we have agitated patients. This one here, the AKA amputee, decompensated. He mumbled and screamed about seeing his buddy get taken away when they were out on the street and he never saw him again. Apparently, he—the buddy, that is—had spit at Franklin and complained he'd been approached inappropriately. Of course, the story wasn't very clear and nothing came of it. This man, being so-called paranoid, was arrested for stalking Franklin Mo. How you stalk someone from a wheelchair was beyond me, but that was the claim."

"Why is he here?"

"Oh, he got some cellulitis of his other leg and we're treating it while he reconstitutes on psychotropic meds."

"Shouldn't he be in a real hospital?"

"If his infection indicated the need for IV antibiotics, he would be in a more intense treatment area at the county hospital but they're full up too. So far, he's doing fine here with oral meds. I watch him." Dr. Conner walked on and sipped his coffee. "This man was beaten up in Central and has to be observed for possible bleeds. He complained about another inmate harassing him. He's got this pterygium, and his roommate didn't like his evil eye. His eye has this growth on the white part that looked spooky. It's really harmless, caused by exposure to the sun, called a surfer's eye. Somehow it set someone off. It's not clear whether that inmate took him on or deputies handled it. Franklin Mo had apparently interviewed him just before the incident and ticked him off. The guy said Franklin told him he was going to hell, scolding the guy for his drug habit and warning him the devil was watching—a little off even for Franklin Mo. I never figured Franklin as getting religion. Why that happened, I don't know, and why Mo was even interviewing, I don't know either. Anyway, it didn't end well."

"How'd you hear about that?"

"A deputy brought the inmate over post-concussion after the negative skull work up, and we were talking. Many of the staff have tried to calm things down after Franklin's proselytizing. He goes on these tirades periodically, telling inmates to reform or burn in hell."

The patient came to the thick glass door and traced his finger along it. He appeared dazed and scratched at his bandaged head.

Conner tapped on the door and shook his head. "Don't do that. Leave it be, Burnell."

Burnell looked at him, smiled and nodded his understanding. He went to his bed and sat down, looking at his hands.

"How does he have license to preach? Is he authorized?"

"There are chaplains here and they hold groups. They come and go, and sometimes Franklin accompanies them. I don't know. It seems to me better if the guy is not around than when he is."

"Do other staff agree with you?"

"I guess it would be best if you talk to some of them directly. I've got to change a dressing anyway. Go on back to the chart room and talk with some of the staff. Good luck," Conner said and held out his hand for a cursory handshake.

Laughlin walked around the winding ward hall that led him back to the staff chart room. There were three nurses writing up notes and a clerk filing.

The nurses and clerk all admitted Franklin had asked them to lunch and they had avoided him and the invitation. They wouldn't say anything else. A male nurse just shrugged and said nothing.

Dr. Conner returned, wrote some notes in a tattered chart with a metal cover, and asked if Laughlin would like to go down to the IRC. "It might help to understand how things can get hectic. That's where the last Franklin incident took place. Today's watch commander is a buddy of mine."

They wound up going down a long plank and into a hallway. Overlooking the guard enclosure were a long series of boxy rooms. Men of all ages lined up waiting to be processed while locked in cement rooms like research lab cages.

Conner showed him the giant hull-like parking area where the "fish" were unloaded from those white and black buses and, then, the shower rooms and the medical clearance lines before admission. The doctor waved at his cohorts and signaled to the nurses he'd be back that night and asked Laughlin if he'd like a break. They went to the cafeteria.

Laughlin trailed after the briskly walking doctor. Images of hundreds of caught men milling around in sealed rooms and being shuffled through the process lines wouldn't leave him. It was like fish in nets.

"Yup, sometimes a thousand guys a day. Of course, the women have to be kept in a separate area. They lift their tops up or pull them down to start a riot."

"Even when the men are in the cells?"

"Oh yeah, they try to break down the doors. Once, they got a woman and she was dead before the deputies could separate out what the hell was going on. The other women just watched, glad it wasn't them, I guess. I heard that the plan is to transfer women out of here all together, put them in the old Sybil Brand facility out of the way. Franklin Mo was involved with that because he wanted the women to stay here."

"Why would Franklin Mo be down in the Inmate Reception Area?" Laughlin asked.

"Beats me. But of course, he could do pretty much what he wanted as long as he didn't get in the way of the deputies." Conner ate a big slice of pie and had some coffee. "For me, I'm more concerned about the medical staff. There are some old-timers here who know zilch medicine and just punt everybody and anybody to mental health or the county hospital if they can."

"Don't they have to be trained medical doctors?"

"Sure. The question is when they were trained and their motivation. Anyway, that's all I can really tell you. Franklin Mo roamed around but mainly he was absent. A typical administrator in my book."

"And the murder rumors?"

"There were questions about placing vulnerable inmates with gang members, skinheads, bullies if they caught Franklin's eye and didn't like his diatribes. It's easy enough to provoke tough guys even in the mental health modules, and we'd get the consequences in our medical unit."

"Didn't the other doctors object?"

"Sure. Lots happen here, especially at night. Sometimes the deputies don't know about Franklin and the mental health people just do as he says. Staff tries to keep up, but it doesn't always work out that way. Well, I'm going back. Sorry I couldn't be more of a help."

Laughlin thanked Conner and made his way back to the sally port and out. He called Max and they decided to meet at the station. Driving slowly through the rush hour traffic, he saw a big black-and-white bus with bars on its windows. He knew those buses shuffled captives back and forth from the jail to prison to court to wherever. He recalled the full bus terminal under the IRC for unloading. His thoughts traced the operation storing people in local stations and moving individuals through the enormous system processing in the jails. The new buildings were already full up with the mentally ill. A deputy called it the last necessary sewer.

Franklin Mo could do as he wanted and it didn't sound like he did good if he did anything at all. He was inconspicuous. A depraved dropping in the city's myriad machinations. Laughlin felt uneasy. His understanding was unclear. What conclusions had he made to share with Max?

There were the administrative assistant's stories about photos, the women staffers recalling multiple suggestive invitations, strange issues of proselytizing and selecting inmates for punishment and for undefined nefarious reasons. Most of all was his absentee status, supposedly under the guise of inspecting other jail mental health facilities.

CHAPTER 5

Black birds eat meat. The raven, a black blot on the road, hopped about, gathered speed for takeoff and flew into the hot, clear air. Ten minutes later, he appeared again and landed on Burt Small's picnic table fifty yards from the road. The bird was distressed and made strange coughing sounds, and when Small's helmeted thirteen-year-old daughter came out of the house to get her toppled bike off the driveway, the raven looked at her and waited. She could see something coming out of the beak, dark and mangled. Then, as the bird opened its beak and tried to regurgitate, something else caught the light and sparkled. Struggling again, trying to dislodge the thing by scraping with its claw, the animal became oblivious to the human.

Throwing her bike helmet on the gravel, the young girl ran back into the house and minutes later, she and her mother, in blue sweats and barefoot, reappeared with a big cardboard box. The bird was shaking and its marble black eyes stared intently while tuffs of feathers above its beak undulated in the slight breeze. It hopped and staggered and then fell off the table. Trying to right itself and hop away, it bumped into the broad leg of the table and stood stunned.

The girl approached the stricken thing, talking in soft tones, "It's all right. Take it easy," while the mother covered the bird with the box and slid a lid under to seal the animal inside. They could hear it scratching around in the dark, and, with the mother holding her finger over her mouth to signal "no talking," they carried the box to the car.

"I saw something shiny but also some pink stuff, Mom. It's creepy."

"Well, let's see if we can help the bird. I hope it doesn't die. The zoo is the best chance to save it. Quiet now, let's not scare it."

After a loud exchange with the ticket-taker guard, the rescuers where led to the office behind the gift shop. Within ten minutes, Gerald Diamond got out of a little blue truck and limped down the rest of the asphalt path to meet them. The old vet was in good humor and figured another city pigeon had met with another window but would recover.

After taking the patient and treating it, Diamond reported the incident to a plump but mustached deputy. "What can I tell you? It's like I said, I removed the thing that was blocking the raven's throat, stuck probably as it tried to eat the tissue, and there it was, a human finger with this ring, a pinkie ring, I figure," Diamond speculated.

"Thank you for the address of the people who brought it in. I'll report it and have the sergeant get in contact with you," Deputy Daniels responded.

"The bird's okay. Merely a little weak. We'll let him go after a little R and R. Marvelous birds. Clever."

"Well, sir, I wouldn't know."

"Of course, you wouldn't know but weren't you at all curious?" Diamond paused and then continued, "Raven: Corvus corax. Fan tail, not wedge like crows, life span nineteen years or so, perches above to view nests, cull eggs, and inadvertently create better hiding nests for other birds. They feed like gulls at the beach, drop things to open them, can say words, territorial while breeding."

"Thanks, sir."

"Okay be off with you. Care more about the dead finger than the live bird, huh?"

"Well, sir, this is weird, to say the least. I'd better get back. Come to think of it, maybe you should wait to release it. You know, it might lead us to a body."

"Possibly, possibly. By the way, say hello to a detective James Laughlin and a Joseph Max. I know them," Diamond called and then watched as the deputy ran to his car with the specimen held out before him. He gently laid the box of evidence on the back seat, got in the car, and moved slowly out of the parking lot. Diamond mused that the deputy carried on like he had a bomb.

The vet returned to his little truck and made the following note: "The specimen found at a home fifteen miles from here. There was what appeared to be a fifth digit, proximal phalanx, no sign of the distal, of a human, ring attached, wedged in pharynx; extraction successful without sedation. Bird is doing well and is an alert, grateful fellow. Will keep for a few days and then release at original site of capture. The ring is some diamond-studded thing, not from a high school or college."

CHAPTER 6

Franklin Mo's wife called The Missing Persons Bureau, after her husband had been gone for two months. Now it had been close to three more weeks and still no word. She claimed she delayed reporting him missing because he was "always traveling" around the country. His car had showed up in front of their house the day she did call, and there was dried blood on the seats, front and back.

The wife had handed over her husband's hairbrush and his mental health badge with a picture that had fingerprints all over it. Forensics reported the DNA blood was not Mo's, but the only fingerprints on the car inside and out were his.

So far, Laughlin informed his deputy, Joseph Max, that interviews of family, friends, and staff at the jail's mental health section had yielded zilch. Yes, there might have been motives attributed to such as Dr. Weber, some even to jail staff and inmates, maybe his wife and mother-in-law, but it was all very unsubstantial.

At Deputy Daniel's suggestion, DNA matching was done but no match of the lonely finger and Mo's DNA was made. Strangely, the finger matched the blood in the car. Further search of the area of the raven and the Small's home had not turned up anything yet.

With that information, Laughlin rang the ornate copper inlaid doorbell on the outside gate of the Mo's home in San Marino. The very tony community had become primarily the home of Asians moving up from the cities of Alhambra and Monterey. The Sycamore trees' blotchy thick limbs and unwavering, angular leaves covered the entrance and created a somber immutability.

A tiny gray-haired woman, wrapped in a neck-tight black shift and white socks with sandals, opened the front door, shuffled to the gate, and peered quizzically to see who was disturbing her tranquility.

Laughlin introduced himself, "I'm Detective Sergeant James Laughlin of the sheriff's department. I was here a while ago when Mr. Mo's disappearance was first reported and I need to talk to Mrs. Mo again."

The woman was silent, turned with a gesture to come along, and shuffled up the path jutting in and out of azalea bushes and lemon trees. He followed.

Nothing had changed in the entrance hall, and he sat on the same hard maroon bench as he had done when he first interviewed the wife. Peeking in the living room, there were still pastel art paintings of ballet dancers clustered together on green walls, and there were old iron weapons, even a crossbow mounted next to them. Framing a carved door were two standing screens with long-legged birds painted on them and wooden chairs with little tapered wings on the tops. Bright gold and dark green stubby chests stood against the walls. The decorator or Mrs. Mo had strange or very modern taste, Laughlin concluded.

Through the carved door, Mrs. Mo appeared with a lovely smiling face, a graceful woman, who laughed spontaneously about her husband's trips out of town; each time she opened her mouth, she revealed one gold canine tooth with a diamond-like stone in its center to match her decorated fingernails.

They had learned very little from her other than her husband had gone on frequent trips for study of other facilities like the one he worked at and that the couple had been married for thirty years via an arranged marriage. She came from a wealthy family of import-export dealers and the parents had been worried she was not interested in marriage even after the age of twenty-nine.

The distain and disregard for her husband was evident and she did not try to hide it. They had one child, a boy, called Aaron, and he was thirty and out of the house. The wizen, door-answering woman was the wife's mother, and she had lived with them some twenty-three years after her husband had died. She nodded, and slid away.

Mrs. Mo came up to the hall with her hand held out to shake the detective's in greeting. "I hope you don't have news of him. I'm so happy free of obligation," she said and swept her hand around toward the decorated green room. "Come in, come in."

She ushered him into the room with red mahogany furniture constructed in filigree wood designs. She had been carrying a small book and placed it in one of the chests, closing it gently with the door's brass handle.

He could see there were many bound leather books tucked in the shelves. There were spikes of jade flower branches in vases on all the round table surfaces. Separate from the ornate benches and down two stairs there were couches upholstered in fabric of bright orange circles and emerald green pillows. Plump red pillows lay on the floor near a tiled fireplace and a small stone fountain.

"Don't be shy, tell me what's going on. I want to go to Hong Kong. So much is happening now. I'll be leaving in a couple weeks." She plopped down on a couch and put a small electronic date book in her lap.

"Well, Mrs. Mo, we have no more news on your husband, but a bizarre finding has led me back to you for more information," Laughlin began. "Do you recognize this ring?" He pulled out a small photograph from his pocket and handed to her while still standing.

"Oh, do sit down, officer. Do you want a drink of some sort, tea or whatever?"

"No need, thank you," he replied and stepped backward to sit on the other couch near where the woman had settled.

"Poor quality, possibly onyx with minuscule diamonds. Nothing I would want."

"Have you seen it before?"

"I can't say. The photo is so dark. It may be the ring of an acquaintance of my husband's—Jeffrey."

"Do you have a last name?"

"Jeffrey Trainer is all I know, why?"

"This ring was found with blood on it," Laughlin explained, deliberately leaving out the found finger, "the blood matches the blood found in the car."

"Really? How fascinating. Is that why you're calling it bizarre? Maybe it was when he got his hand caught in the door."

"That information wasn't in the earlier interview with you. When did that happen?"

"That isn't in the earlier interview with me because it wasn't relevant to my reporting my husband gone. I have absolutely no idea when he might have bled in my husband's car. I was merely speculating. Now do you have anything to tell me about Franklin or not?"

"We're still working on it," and he added defensively, "the FBI hasn't anything either."

"Well, I assume the interview is over. Thank you for the update," she said with a glance at her date book.

"Jeffrey Trainer . . ."

"Just see yourself out, please." With that, Mrs. Mo glided out of the living room through another carved door and was gone behind its gentle closing.

Laughlin stood up and shoved his notebook into his jacket pocket and turned to go to the hall and out the door. Suddenly, in back of him, silently scrutinizing his movements, the grandmother swept her hand across her face as though swatting a fly, and bade him follow again as she clip-clopped away. She was crumbling with age, and he followed her more out of respect than hope for some relevant information. This time, they went into the kitchen. It was all stainless steel with green marble counters and a skylight that traversed the whole room.

The guide patted a stool near a counter full of bottles of liquor Laughlin was familiar with and then some he'd never seen. Twisted, green, bright red, and clear containers sat next to them.

"What's your pleasure?" she said in perfect English.

"Pardon?"

"What's the alcohol you like to drink? It's all the same, really, so I'll drink anything you like with you. I'm Bowed Flower," she said and smiled broadly, showing perfect white teeth.

After a quizzical pause while watching her eager face raising its eyebrows to encourage an answer, Laughlin replied, "Thank you very much, Mrs. Bowed Flower, but I can't drink on the job."

"Oh, how regrettable, well, take a bottle with you and pick out one for me to drink. I've got to tell you some things. I can't wait any longer, in case I drop dead or something."

He looked for some sherry but when he presented her with the bottle, she turned her head back and forth. He tried some cabernet, same response. Champagne. No. She then put her hand on his and moved it over to the bottle of Jack Daniels bourbon and nodded.

"It's like a Philip Marlowe case, only you're much more handsome than Humphrey. He died of throat cancer. Too bad. Are you healthy?"

"Yes, I guess so," Laughlin answered respectfully.

"Look, you can't believe any of them. They're major liars. I know I've lived among them as they say. Franklin, he didn't really live here, thank Confucius, God, Jesus, Abraham, Mohamed, Buddha, Vishnu, and all the rest. Franklin was a sly twerp. He convinced my husband that it would be best for my daughter to get married and get married to him. I was one of those follow-behind wives until my husband died. I didn't want my daughter Emerald to be like that. She was smart and emancipated here."

Laughlin watched the woman, hunched over like a vulture, pour an inch-high drink, go to the fridge, get a Coke, put a splash from the can in the glass, and drink it down like a true guzzler. He listened to her banter halfheartedly. The day had been drawn out and nothing had come of it except this Jeffrey Trainer name. A potent drink was very tempting.

"Sir, are you listening? We're all disguised. The United States is as dangerous a country as there ever was, so I pretend I'm a foreigner who can't speak the language, and I get by all over town. I carry my Bullock's shopping bag, and that's all. I tell you I've let you in on my chosen name of Bowed Flower because I own Disney stock."

Frowning but trying to mask his doubts with concern, the detective asked, "What is it you want to tell me?"

"I told you, Franklin never lived here. He had some place in South Pas, his secret place. You didn't know that, did you?" With great satisfaction, the intense little figure poured two inches of bourbon this time and added a tinier splash of Coke. She began humming "Zippidy do da, what a beautiful day" and downed her drink before continuing, "I want to help the law, so I've exposed the real me to you. Don't disappoint."

"Wouldn't we have known about a South Pasadena apartment through our investigation of his records, like credit cards, phone, Mrs. Mo's information?" he asked rhetorically.

"Yes, that is if he kept a record of it, but he paid cash up front, I know. I would see him take it from Emerald's stash. I could never tell her. It would have hurt too much since he already was a bastard."

"What's the name he used?"

"Ah, you are smart. I told you we were all disguised. He used the name Dolmar. I don't know why, maybe he misspelled Dahmer, the cannibal. I found the receipt in his car, the one he finally left here. I clean everything before the maid comes."

"Did his son know about the apartment?"

"That's not his son. My daughter had an affair with a man who lives in Hong Kong. They loved each other, and Franklin didn't object about it because he liked things just the way they were."

"Who's this Jeffrey Trainer?"

"Who knows about him? He came here to hang around and once or twice to borrow Franklin's car, but lately, he'd just brush me off as an old woman."

Laughlin looked a Mrs. Bowed Flower carefully. She'd given him real information, more than he'd collected in these long days searching around for something vital to the case. Could she be believed or was she a delusional, lonely woman? The only way to find out was to track down the leads. Max was going to be happy with something to do. The description of the lost finger man was unremarkable, medium height, medium build, medium hair.

Laughlin gently took the grandmother's hand to shake it, and she raised it for him to plant a kiss on before he left her on the stool in that stainless kitchen. She smiled and said, "Come back to let me know how things are going, won't you? I'm a good guy or gal as they say."

"I'll give you a call."

"Oh no, the white phone is bugged. I don't talk much on it. Come by. I'll be here even when Emerald goes to Hong Kong. I am in the process of summing up the meaning of my life and have to stay at my desk most of the day. I'll be here, merely ring the bell. Give me your card too."

He nodded and left her, walked resolutely to the front door, strolled out into the fragrant garden, thought of her words about summing up the meaning of her life, smiled, and decided to get himself some barbecue ribs.

CHAPTER 7

Following up on Mrs. Flower's gossip, Max had scouted out the Pasadena locales finding names Duncun, Dutton, Dollar, Dupart, Dollup, and then struck gold with one apartment complex mailboxes. The apartment was under the name Frank Dolmer not Dolmar, but Bowed Flower had been close enough, paranoid or not. It was in a pink building with an arched entrance. Inside were a courtyard with a dry tile fountain and separate green doors to each apartment downstairs and a winding staircase with flowered tiles pushed into the risers. The staircase pavers led all the way to the second story and the apartment, whose entrance faced the courtyard. Laughlin and Max had the key from the manager who was a snarky, potbellied guy patching some stucco in the back and didn't want to go up the stairs. He said he hadn't seen Mr. Dolmer for at least three months and that he'd paid for the whole year. Laughlin didn't bother asking if the guy had pocketed the rent money.

The door opened easily, and the place smelled of incense or pot or both. The living room was sparsely furnished with a tan couch and three spoke-wheeled chairs around a bathroom shaggy rug, but in the bedroom was a different story. Like some disturbed teenager's den, the room was draped with black cloth and glowing stars and planets on the ceiling and blown-up photographs on the walls. Every one of the photos was of the missing man, naked or reclining on the bed. There were small photos on a dresser that showed a group of people at some sort of Christmas party and one that Max pointed out of a conference with the missing person and three others.

There was a six-foot bookcase of a vinyl record collection of everything, from Stan Kenton to Ella Fitzgerald to the three Bs. Most of them still sealed in clear plastic with their designed covers unmarred. There was no stereo.

"How come he can afford these records? I want them," Laughlin complained.

"Work harder, man. We aren't getting big enough payoffs, I guess," Max replied, laughing.

"But where is the record player? This is strange."

"Carry on, and let's not try and figure out this guy yet."

"Okay, I'll get the dresser while you get the closet, Max," Laughlin indicated and pulled the top drawer of an elegant carved antique. Immediately the two men looked back to each other in surprise. The dresser and the closet were filled with beautifully arranged clothes. The detectives listed their observations to each other: cashmere coats, tweed jackets, twenty hangers with gabardine slacks, silk handkerchiefs matching each tie, and immaculately stacked silk shirts, handwoven sweaters, and satin briefs of red and white.

"Man, this guy liked his tailor," Max remarked with understatement.

"No mistake about that. What the hell was this all about anyway? Did the guy live here?" In the bottom dresser drawer was one other strange object, a silver framed photo of Nora Weber, MD, wrapped in a bookstore bag. The address of the bookstore was in Santa Monica.

Laughlin shared this finding with Max. They agreed she was better-looking than most psychiatrists and didn't have a goatee. Then they looked into the bathroom where silk robes and perfumed aftershave greeted them. No pills.

Both the men went into the kitchen, which was the only other room, and found a stainless-steel refrigerator and wine cooler stacked full. A Wolf range with a hood vented next to the sliding door reflected its compatriots. The old refrigerator that came with the apartment was huddled next to a scarred stove on a pathetic balcony overlooking the alley.

"It's got to be a love nest, rendezvous kind of thing," Max guessed.

"Well, let's get on it. Long day ahead for forensics and us. I've had it after this. Follow up on size of clothes, tailor, dry cleaning, stove and fridge delivery, hairbrush and toothbrush DNA, etc." Laughlin recited.

"Why all this leg work and no action work?" Max complained.

"You expect too much, Max. This is an investigation, not an action movie," Laughlin offered and then went back to the photo of the psychiatrist who apparently had run in with Mo. He'd follow up with the bookstore.

CHAPTER 8

That night, to help organize the case, Laughlin drove around listening to some clarinet solos, ate at a big Italian restaurant, and went to hear some music at Harvell's before going home. What he really wanted was some classical piece with a cello to get things in perspective. No one knew he liked the music his grandmother always played for him: she of the bookstore excursions and the paintings.

In his driveway, he doused the car lights. Immediately, the night smothered his street like a collapsing corpse. His home, an angular hump in the row of houses, was barely visible. Streetlights out again, he cursed. Crossing the grass, he did his usual survey and noticed movement on the porch. A regular rocking broke the fuzzy dark and creaking traversed the railing. As his eyes adjusted, he climbed the steps slowly and found a crouching body on the slatted wooden deck to the side of the welcome mat.

"Hello," the little lump said. "Long day, huh?"

"Never mind about my day. Who are you and what the hell are you doing on my porch?"

"Mr. Winkler of Broadhurst, that's who, and stop being so cranky. I was tired and I had to sit down, out of the way and all. Without the streetlights, it's hard for me to see. This your place? It looks kinda empty, although the wood's well maintained. Lord, I was one tired traveler."

"Don't you think you should go home, Mr. Winkler?" Laughlin began and followed up with "Do you know where your home is?"

"Oh, not that again—address, city, state, county, country, hemisphere, planet and the like. Calm down, I won't hurt you. Help me up, damn it. Where are your manners? Fucking youngsters."

Laughlin bent down, tucked his hand under the lump's arm, and lifted him straight up. The wisecracker weighed close to nothing and slipped around in his jacket like a Popsicle in its wrapper.

"I'll get started again when Rosie comes back."

Laughlin turned on the light, which surrounded what was an old man, puffy around the eyes with a nose lost in jowls, a scraggly mustache and displaced whiskers like two commas separated by a dark dash of smile. A wide-eyed lemur came to mind.

"Damn, that hurts the retinas. Turn it off, turn it off," Mr. Winker instructed loudly.

Laughlin quickly responded, "Okay, okay."

There was a little shuffling and Winkler leaned heavily on the railing.

"Get some chairs out here, will you?"

"Look, I've had a long day. Time for you to get going before I—"

"Don't threaten me, buster. I only came up for a little rest. Chill, as they say."

Laughlin couldn't help but smile at the retort. He reexamined his find. "I'm just going to turn on the hall light to see better. Don't worry, not the porch light. Chairs are over there."

Winkler was neatly dressed in a green suit, three or four sizes too big but cleaned and pressed.

"Rosie, Rosie, come on. This jerk is yelling at us."

"Hey, it's been a long day."

There were only the crickets in the night air and no Rosie appeared. Laughlin waited and then opened his front door and walked in, leaving the old man leaning against the railing. With beer bottles clutched in his fingers, he lifted two chairs over with his wrists and settled the newly found lump into one and he in the other.

"I'd love that beer. You weren't going to have two, were you?" Winkler said innocently.

Laughlin handed him a bottle and raised his for a toast.

"Now you're being more hospitable, young man. I thank you for that and the Budweiser. I'm puzzled why I haven't met you before. This is my neighborhood, been here for forty-seven years and three months."

"Well, I have long and strange hours."

"What do you do? You're a big man, relatively handsome I'd say except for your caustic manner."

"I'm a sergeant in the sheriff's department."

"No way. Never met one of you guys before, although I read about your fucking antics all the time."

"Why so vulgar?"

"Compared with you and your generation, I'm a virgin."

"So how often do you park yourself on other people's porches?"

"More often lately. Rosie's in a spring mood even though it's fall, and so we're out a longer time. This spring had too much rain for her."

"I'm going for another beer, you want one?"

"No, I'll stick with this one. You know, this is the first time in my life when I really can't gauge how I feel, definitely and unquestionably. All the articles on health and cancer and heart disease make you monitor yourself and feel unsure if this or that is just normal or something dangerous. When is the bullet coming for me? It's like Russian roulette, what's going to kill you, and every time I feel a little tired, I have to ask if this is it. Damn."

"Want some food?" Laughlin asked.

"No, merely feeling age. 'And so from hour to hour, we ripe and ripe, And then from hour to hour, we rot and rot, And thereby hangs a tale.' Shakespeare said it all."

"Shakespeare? Profound for one o'clock in the morning."

Ignoring the hint, Winkler asked, "So what do you do in this life, my dear host?"

"I told you I'm in the sheriff's department."

"Ah yes, you did. I assume you are a detective. Robbery, homicide, vice and the lot. Now what's the case. Maybe I could be your Meyer," the now more assured visitor offered.

"Meyer?"

"Let me deduce from that question. You don't know much literature, whether it be the Bard or John D. MacDonald. A shame for such an obviously bright fellow. Meyer was Travis McGee's friend and consultant, really MacDonald's alter ego. He himself was a degreed economics graduate."

"Mr. Winkler, thank you for that information, but I think we should call it a night. I've got to get up and follow some leads tomorrow—"

The tenacious guest interrupted with, "Oh, how wonderful! Tell me about it please."

"Look, I'll walk you home, and we'll do this some other time. Lead the way." Laughlin's patience had left with the last swig of beer. He stood up and took the bottles back inside, and when he returned, Winkler was up and held a big black cat in his arms.

"This is Rosie," he announced with pride. "Please carry her for me while we talk and walk."

As they ambled down the sidewalk, Laughlin began summarizing the case as fast as he could, quickly listing findings: missing administrator, not reported to authorities until about two months after last seen at work and at home; wife not interested; wife's mother more informative; stepson not in the country; blood from another man found in missing man's car, and this man last seen when he came to give a workout session; finger found in a crow's mouth; mental health jail personnel frightened and close-mouthed; missing man had lots of enemies including psychiatrists; an apartment with extravagant clothes paid up through the end of the year.

"Well, James, I think you've made a crucial assumption," Winkler said in deep tones.

"Are we at your place yet?"

"Not yet. The rather erroneous and stupid assumption is that the trainer's name was Jeffrey Trainer, the women only labeled him that for clarity of the character role, not the surname, and here we are. Be more careful, Detective," he admonished. "Good night."

The old man took the docile cat, scampered up the steps, and began talking to a figure in the door, "Rosie, Rosie, wife of mine, I had to wait for Rosie the cat. Don't yell."

The door shut and the porch light went off, and Laughlin was alone.

Afterward, at the corner, he had to orient himself to the streets because he had been concentrating on the case, holding the heavy cat, and letting the old man lead him along.

CHAPTER 9

First thing in the morning, Laughlin called Mrs. Mo and asked for clarification on the last name of Jeffrey *the* trainer. Mrs. Mo laughed and said she didn't know him by any other name, but maybe the gym bag he left in the garage might help. The canvas bag was a blue Nike with JF initials, two pairs of Nike sweats, and dirty laundry. The prints from the big plastic bag full of old socks identified him in the system as Jeffrey Faulk, a one-time felon for burglary and drug possession, hospitalized for amphetamine-induced paranoia, who had been living in a board and care on the westside, according to his PO.

"Let's follow up on this now, Max. Who knows, maybe Jeffrey is there. All the blood in the car and the finger, a red herring."

"Board and cares are like rooming houses," Max remarked. "Why would he be there, with all the expensive gear in that bag?"

"Yeah, I guess they don't do any interventions like halfway houses. I think some of them give out medications though. Let's get on it."

"He must've had money to buy stuff like the bag."

Max and Laughlin paid their visit. They drove down the cluttered street tunneling under massive electrical wires and pulled up on a driveway that led nowhere but to a wall with big yellow graffiti initials blaring across it. The Rosewood Board and Care was sandwiched between flat-faced stucco apartment buildings. There was an iron gate for a door, bordered by morose plastic palms in concrete planter boxes, and open to an old-style motel courtyard. In the center was an empty swimming pool with torn lawn chairs in the deep end. Surrounding the cement rim were two tiers of doors and walkways.

Silence and cement were the only residual of an aquamarine and glamorous palm tree life, probably late '50s, Laughlin guessed—a dead time. Now a crazy haven, more of a prison cellblock wedged in where it wasn't welcome.

A few men, smoking and leaning about, watched them as they walked to the back where the well-marked office was tucked in. A cough echoed around the dull gray enclave and then it was quiet again. Max kept peering into open door ways before moving on. The stillness didn't give off tranquility. Anticipation of danger hung over them like some stinging thing. They both became mute and hesitant.

Before the detectives reached their destination, five more men with an eerie clairvoyance stumbled out of open doors to stare unimpressed at the visitors. Their eyes showed no evidence of care in "board and care," only menacing boredom. Suddenly, cutting the stale air, a somber young woman with torn denim shorts leaned over the upper walkway and yelled, "Hey, guys, come and get me! Don't bother with the dumb shit manager." She cleared her throat with a guttural sound, spit, and, holding tightly with both hands to the one iron railing, carefully made her way down the stairs.

Except for her outburst, the enclosure was still sodden with fumes, BO, and listlessness.

Trying to maintain composure, Max mumbled how dismal the place was and decided, "No wonder people were mentally ill if they had to stay here."

"I guess this is better than the streets," Laughlin suggested.

"Maybe, but you won't catch me in one of these. I rather live in my car."

"You have to have one, that's the thing."

Just then, the girl made it down the steps and fell into Laughlin's arms rather than over the side of the swimming pool.

"Whoa, that was close. Thanks," she purred and waited to be carried.

A bulky man attendant, identified by his white shirt with the board-and-care logo, grabbed her. "Come on, Cindy, time to take a nap," he directed, and without another word from her, pushed her toward a room on the lower level. A doughy woman in a bright red wig peeked out of a doorway and yelled for the girl to stop her drinking and to come in and fix her hair.

Laughlin stood and watched and then moved on with Max. "What the hell do you make of her?"

"She was bombed all right and the guys here were not showing any interest. I wonder why?" Max observed.

"Don't mind Cindy. She's a little suicidal when she'd been drinking. You know, booze is a depressant. Skips her medicines and sells 'em to get cash. She'll crash after you leave. We had to take her even though we don't like them that young," a stubby man explained, leaning out of the office door. His hair and tie, both stringy, were plastered against his balding head and wrinkled shirt, and his belly lapped softly over his thin belt. "So what's your business?"

"Jeffrey Faulk? Is he here?" Laughlin asked as he peered into the office.

"Hey, come on in. Name's Lobbler, Frankie, been manager here for seven years."

The office coated with grime and smoke held gray file cabinets, a marred wooden desk, and newspapers. There was a door leading to a room with a refrigerator and shelves of medicines. Lobbler shut that quickly and locked it with one of his many keys. He gestured to the vinyl couch rammed against a wall, while he shuffled behind his desk and piled some loose newspapers on top of one another. "You the police?" He lit a thin cigar and waited.

"Sheriff department," Max answered. "We're looking for this guy."

"What'd he do? We haven't seen him for a month or more. His conservator still sends us his money, so we figure he's coming back."

"We need to talk to him. Where's his room?"

"Warrant or not, no problem. We run a good place here. I'll take you to his bed."

The three of them walked back toward the front. The sheriff's men were alert and aware of followers, and Lobbler acted nonchalantly, ignoring the troops. Those that followed seemed more curious than threatening. One beanpole man, one sniveling and stumbling one, and the last with rolled-up sleeves exhibiting tattoos and a swagger.

"Any of you guys know Jeffrey Faulk?" Laughlin ventured.

"Ah, Jeffrey, yeah. Faulk his last name, huh? What he done?" the gaunt, tall man with a black Grateful Dead sweatshirt asked.

"Fucker was always after my belt and my radio. I know he got his, didn't he?" the sniveling man asked, pinching his nose and wiping the results on his pants.

"Just looking for him, mister," Max answered.

"He was a fucker, thought he was better than me, that's what. Can I have his boom box, Frank?" the brawny man asked.

"Look, beat it. Leave us be. Go get your snack, and let me take care of these gentlemen. Come on, guys," Lobbler ordered. The three followers stopped, shrugged, and disappeared in open doorways.

"This is Jeffrey's. Come on in."

They entered a small dingy room with the brown-patched plaid drapes like a route 66 motel almost covering two windows. Adjusting their eyes, they saw three mattresses pushed up against the walls on the floor and a coffee table with mugs and stains stationed in the center of the room. Lying in one of the beds was a thin white man with a long disheveled brown beard. A sheet was strangled around his legs.

"Gene, Gene, put your wanger away. Gene, stop playing with yourself and tell me where Jeffrey's stuff is," Lobbler instructed. "Gene and Jeffrey, they're buddies."

Gene turned his head toward the voices but kept sawing away. He took his left hand and pointed toward the mattress under the window.

"Gene, these here men are the sheriffs. Put your dick away now," Lobbler reiterated.

The preoccupied Gene covered himself with a rumpled pair of his pants and the sheet, became a moving mound, and kept going. Laughlin and Max went over to Faulk's mattress. There were a purple sheet and a brown blanket lying abandoned on the stained striped mattress, no thicker than a mat. There were a few books shoved in the corner. Laughlin picked them up. They were fitness books and one Crumb comic book.

Max stood looking over the whole sordid findings and then lifted the edge of the mattress. He found three cards, a yellow legal pad, and a few pills. The find consisted of a Gold's Gym handout, a conservator's, and Franklin Mo's business cards.

"How come you get his SSI money, Mr. Lobbler?" Laughlin said offhandedly while pushing the mattress around and checking a small trunk at the end of Jeffrey Faulk's territory. The boom box was gone and there was nothing in the opened trunk.

"Oh shit, I done did it again, sinner, sinner. Lord, have mercy on me. I spilled my come in the desert," Gene yelled, got up and ran out the door.

"Get him, get him. He'll jump," Lobbler screamed and ran for the agitated masturbator.

Laughlin and Max swung around and were out the door just in time to see Gene fly off the rim into the pool. He landed face down and rolled to the deep end, bumping and rocking the chairs. Max made it down to the deep end first and retrieved the limp man.

"Goddamn son of a bitch!" Lobbler yelled and went back to his office.

Laughlin and Max examined the stretched-out Gene. His left cheek was abraded to a rough sandpaper consistency. His eyes were wide open and full of tears. He could move all his extremities. Holding the injured side of his face and twisting his head back and forth, he began mumbling, "God, I'm truly sorry. It come over me like a demon. Forgive me." He looked at Laughlin and began crying.

"Whoa, listen, Gene, we all got needs. No big deal. Take it easy," Laughlin responded. "Can you sit up?"

The tormented man made a small effort to raise himself with the help of the two sheriffs. Laughlin thought the whole sinner speech bizarre and somehow false. He always felt crazies couldn't really believe the things they said so earnestly. Gene spoke clearly, with no slurred speech. Probably no drugs onboard. He had a long straight nose that parted his arched brows as his hands smeared the scrapes, tears and blood that dripped down one side of his face to his beard and blue dirty shirt.

Max told him to stop rubbing the bleeding skin, and the man obeyed.

Then Cindy broke out screaming. Leaning over the stricken man, she yelled, "Gene's done it again. Gene went over the side. Wow! Gene, you are an Olympic diver, man. Yea, Gene." The attendant went after her again to get her into her room. Laughlin could hear her cursing and laughing. "What the fuck, I didn't do nothing. Come near and I'll hit you. Come on, shithead, come on."

"God will damn me. The genes are spewing. They're evil. They're planning to kill. The seed eviscerates my goodness. Fortitude is forgotten. Help me," Gene pleaded, grabbing Laughlin's arm and turning back and forth to look in his rescuers' faces. Laughlin became aware of the man's hand. The thumb was gone at the first joint.

Max stuck his arms under Gene and lifted him to a lounge chair by the entrance. As the moaning man settled, two police came through the entrance.

Lobbler ran up to them and said, "Get him, needs to be on a hold. The asshole jumped again."

Laughlin and Max exchanged information with the LAPD guys and they took Gene away, gingerly lifting him into the squad car.

Lobbler stood at the door and turned to go back to the office. Then he saw Laughlin and Max again. "Hey, this guy is nuts. The police, they take him to county hospital and keep him for a 72 hour hold, but damn, if he doesn't beat probable cause and be back here again right after that. I tell you, one more time and he's outta here for good. I can fill this place faster than a whore's cunt."

"Does this go on all day?" Max asked.

"Nah, most times it's quiet here," the manager said flippantly. "I see to that."

Like the other docile roommates after all the commotion dispersed, the two sheriff's men followed the manager back to the office along with a few others. Lobbler dismissed any stragglers and explained that this was the second time in three months Gene had gone off the deep end. Pun not intended. There were board and cares all over the county. It was usually a relatively good business, he opined. Most of the people were on SSI, disability insurance, and had their checks sent to him to subtract the rent and keep their little extra money of about ten or so dollars for spending when they wanted it. Of course, there were the drugs both prescribed, pandered, and purloined, but Lobbler came to the conclusion that that could happen on the street as well.

"At least they had a roof over their heads here and reasonable food," Lobbler offered. "Remember, they closed all the state hospitals about thirty or so years ago and thought they could help the Genes of the world with local mental health clinics. The support hasn't made it though. At least I'm doing something for these sickos."

"Did Faulk have all his fingers?" Laughlin finally asked.

Lobbler grimaced and said, "Far as I know. Maybe you're meaning Gene. Last thing he cut off was his thumb to stop himself from masturbating. Didn't work though, did it?" The manager laughed and lit a cigarette.

There wasn't much more to get out of the guy. He never saw Gene or Faulk get any visitors or phone calls, and he had no idea about Franklin Mo. When they left, they had the conservator's card and no other lead unless they could get back to Gene.

Max was silent until Laughlin shrugged and came forth with, "What was that smell? Sweat, pot, cigars, hopelessness. The place was fucked."

They settled in the car and pulled away from the board and care to the loaded street of supposedly rationale drivers.

"The place is like storage for the mentally ill. How could families leave them like that?" Max questioned and aimed the car for the freeway ramp.

"I don't know. Who really cares?"

"You're telling me. Lobbler, he was like that short, great actor guy in *Taxi*, what's his name? Didn't really give a damn about any of them. The truth is I can't ever get tolerant to really mentally sick either."

"What do you do with these strange people?" Laughlin felt hungover with aversion and yet, "I feel sorry for them, and I can't understand them. I want to get away from them is my first reaction. It would be weird to have one of them in your family. Get them labeled and put away, I guess. How does the mind get so mixed up? How do they get around in the world?"

"Poorly, I guess, that's why they wind up in places like that."

"How do they live or don't live. Those mattresses were gross. It's enough to drive you crazy too. I wonder how Jeffrey Trainer Faulk had such a stylish gym bag and socks, associating with Mo, and still living at the board and care like a man without anything."

"You finally getting to that, Sarge?" Max asked.

"My guess is Franklin Mo gave it all to him, but why? They weren't related."

"What do families do with these types—guys who lost their minds? Looks like they dump them and let the rest of the world take care of them," Max wondered as they made it back to the station. He had a headache as they arrived.

"Yeah, could be families can't handle them." For some strange reason, Laughlin thought of the lost boys in Peter Pan. Embarrassed to say so to Max, he wondered if these board and care men had fallen out with drugs and drink and banged brains, not baby carriages. This time there were little girls too. He thought of the times he'd been hit and his brain was still working. His mother had stood by him.

They had no answers.

Chapter 10

"Here I am in my seventy-seventh year but why fool you? It's rather my seventy-eighth or seventy-ninth year, and I keep disappearing, morphing into the infamous 'tip' of the iceberg. I have had to have a mammogram, a sonogram, a CAT scan, a PET scan. All to preserve me even though I don't own animals, yet no one can see anything but the lumpy upper layer of an old woman with gray icicle hairs in spicules crowning her head. No one sees the thinking business owner, the mother, the orgasmic woman, the galloping girl, the big sister, the little sister, the daughter, the first-generation American.

"They are interested in the 'case' and the lesion, the lump, the calcium they may find, and whom to write the report to. It is aggravating. and then you come along, dear Sergeant James Laughlin, to brighten my afternoon and ask me questions about intriguing issues, about things and thoughts I might know—behold, I might know. So of course, I want you back. Gloriously, you bring another handsome man with you, Mr. Joseph Max, extraordinaire."

"I have to tell you again we originally came to talk to your daughter and pick up any other things of Jeffrey's."

"I told you she's off to Hong Kong for the next three weeks, but I can tell you more about Mr. Trainer if you wish."

"That would be helpful."

"First off, he was full-muscled."

"And?" Max prompted.

"The thing was he brought this disturbed person with him, this Gene, who would walk around the house like an alien, lifting lamps to look at their bases and peering under couches. Those books in the cases were his favorites and he'd sit on the floor and leaf through them like they were treasures. Afterward, he always asked for a drink of bourbon politely, but not too often, and Jeffrey would give him the whole bottle, smiling at me and leaving a few dollars on the counter. Jeffrey was so attentive to this guy. What could I do? Then Gene would smile at me too, be so adoring when he was done sniffing around. Besides, what did I care about the booze. They—the three of them: Franklin, Jeffrey and Gene—would go out into the workout room near the garage. They wouldn't let me go in there, but I could hear them laughing for a couple of hours, and then Jeffrey would carry Gene out into Franklin's car, and they would drive off."

"Do you know where they'd go?"

"No, but Jeffrey would come back later and pick up his gear, that's what he called it. When he did come back, he would come in and give me a little salute as well as take another bottle or two. It was usually wine then. He loved his wine, that boy did, even when he stumbled over the names. Do you like alcoholic beverages, Joseph dear?"

"Yes, ma'am, in their place, and what about you?"

Bowed Flower was about to elaborate on all the bottles she had when Laughlin interrupted with, "What about books? Did he have an interest in them?"

"Maybe, but it was that Gene who liked the books and carried a paperback with him all the time, the double helix, no less. You know, Watson and Crick."

"Anything else? Did they mention any other people or places?"

"Let me think for a minute. Imagine those guys didn't even credit Rosalind, or Roselund Franklin, or whomever, the woman who discovered the helix on X-ray. Bastards. Do you want a drink, Sergeant? You, Deputy Max?"

"No, we'd better be going. We've got the bag from the workout room. If you think of anything, let us know," Laughlin said quickly.

"Yeah, anything that you noticed would be helpful, Ms. Flower," Max followed up.

"He used to talk about a 'fair Nora.' Does that mean anything?" she said, desperate to keep them there.

"Any last name?"

"No, merely Nora, fair Nora. Do you think that was Jeffrey's girlfriend?"

"I'm not sure."

"Oh, oh, trouble. I have a pain. Please sit me down in the living room and bring me a big drink,"

Max and Laughlin exchanged questioning looks, and then Laughlin signaled for Max to go ahead and help her, while he went into the kitchen.

Pulling a few drawers open, he found only paper scraps and takeout menus. He poured the distressed woman her favorite and brought the can of Coke to let her dilute her bourbon.

She was sitting on the velvet orange couch with her head on Max's shoulder, crying and moaning.

Max was holding her hand and humming. He looked up shocked at seeing Laughlin and said, "She asked me to sing to her, Sergeant. I thought she might be having a heart attack. I didn't know all the words but I sang Fats Waller's 'Ain't Misbehaving' and she liked it."

"He's good at it too," Ms. Flower added.

"Are you all right now?"

"Better. I get these spells and think the end is coming, but it never does. My doctor says I'm an imbiber. Do you know what that is? Imagine, I'm old, and he thinks I'm treating my own symptoms. It works too. Isn't that a kick?"

"Here's your drink. Ever think you might be taking too much liquor?" Laughlin suggested, righting himself after tripping on the steps. He still didn't get the need for sunken living rooms.

"No. I know about withdrawals. Had them once when I had to go for a colonoscopy, barium enema and upper GI. Weakened me for a few days and, boy, did I start to shake. They said I went out of my mind and saw rats and stuff. No big deal. When I was a kid, we had rats in our house all the time. People are so uptight about rats, aren't they? Hallucination is quite common in us old people." Bowed

Flower smiled, straightened her dress, and downed her drink straight. She filled the empty glass with the Coke and then drank that. "Are you joining me, gentlemen?"

"Do you want us to call somebody to be with you?" Max asked.

"Maybe take you someplace where you can be with someone?" Laughlin wondered.

"No, dear, I'm fine. By the way, I've got one more bit of information for you. This book here on the coffee table, the small one about Edvard Munch, Gene left that for my daughter one day. He said Jeffrey gave it to him. Maybe that will help."

Laughlin lifted open the cover. It had an inscription—"To Emerald, for all of it, Jeffrey loves you"—and a bookmark from the same Santa Monica bookstore Laughlin already knew from Dr. Weber's photo. He showed it to Max.

"Did your daughter have anything to do with Jeffrey or Gene?"

"See, the thing is, I don't know. She could have met them somewhere else. She was never home when they were here with Franklin."

After monitoring Mrs. Flower for a good hour while she put on CDs and discussed Chinese string music, Laughlin and Max made their exit. A housekeeper had come in to clean the rooms, and they explained the situation, got no information about anybody or anything from the newly hired woman, and left.

"Man, sometimes you forget how many old people are left alone," Max commented as they drove off.

"More coming as the population ages. At least your folks are together. My mother is all on her own and she refuses to come out here."

"Why's that, do you suppose?"

"Oh, she gives me this answer that she doesn't want to burden me, wants her independence, too much trouble. I think she likes teaching still. All sorts of stories."

"Do you do anything about it?"

"Nope. I get so caught up in the stupid job, and she merely keeps trucking along. So, no. We're both in denial, as the saying goes."

"Guess I'm lucky. My folks have been together for forty years." Max added, "Once my mom took off after her brothers were killed in the war, but she came back."

They drove in silence to the station and parted with agenda outlined: investigate the bookstore and talk to Gene again as well as Dr. Weber. Max dropped by his parents' house to say hello and stayed for one of his mother's vegetarian dinners, which she was now serving three times a week.

Laughlin pulled the trash cans out and went up the steps, hoping he might find Mr. Winkler and Rosie on the porch. He paused, but there was no one waiting for him. He peered in the refrigerator and the freezer and wound up eating a bowl of frosted mini-wheats. Picking through his mail, he found a letter from his mother, but he couldn't read it. He'd call her tomorrow, if he remembered. Christ, how humiliating. A detective in the great City of Angels, and all he had was a letter from his mother. How come he was the only detective who had a mother and no lover? Damn Maggie.

CHAPTER 11

After finding out from Mr. Lobbler that Gene had been returned to the board and care for only two days and was back in the county hospital, Laughlin decided Gene would keep while he and Max checked out the bookstore and its possible tie with Franklin Mo.

Moving down beaten streets, Laughlin handled the car as it stopped and started forward with each light like an obedient horse carrying the two cowboy sheriffs. The store was on a Westside second-tier street, in the middle of a crowded block, a used CD and record store still struggling for existence on one end, and a job and apartment resource center on the other. Cleaners and shoe repair hemmed in the bookstore, which had a window stacked with cloth-covered books and postcards in file boxes.

Laughlin and Max, wearing civilian suits, entered the narrow doorway, stood on a scruffy wooden floor, and looked at the setup. Bookshelves' blunt ends were the avatars inviting the browser to choose an aisle and go deep into the conglomeration. It was a neat, organized place, a miniature library.

Laughlin went in further and began pulling books from the shelves, holding their spines carefully in his broad hand and checking title pages. Max saw how comfortable his sergeant was and began to check out some of the boxes of postcards at the end of one of the aisles. There were two other customers down the way, and they went over to a desk on the far side of the store together. They bought three books between them, all paperbacks, ninety-five cents each. Laughlin thought that was a good deal, although he didn't know what they were or in what condition.

The woman taking the money was a chunky sort with electric orange hair pulled up and tied with a green scarf. Max decided she looked like a strawberry. She wore a purple cotton sweater over a white blouse and black skirt. Laughlin figured her to be thirty-five to forty-five.

She sat at the dusty desk and moved papers around, then carried a stack of books to a locked glass bookshelf and went back for the key and more books. She took her sweater off and brushed some dust off her blouse from the last volume stacked. Smiling, Laughlin went over to help her with the pile and began looking at the imprisoned collection. There were some old cloth-covered fairy tales embossed with butterflies and flowers and one *Arabian Nights* with gold lettering.

Laughlin smelled the musty airs the books gave off and thought of his grandmother who loved to take him to used bookstores when he was young, but he had hated it, always wanting to skateboard instead.

"These for sale too?" he inquired.

"Well, some is and some isn't. The owner, he keeps some here for himself and then sells them later," the woman answered. "You got one in mind for yourself, do you?"

"Wondering about the fairy tales there?"

"A big guy like you. That's funny. Those Arthur Rackham pictures, we got some torn out from a book over there. People like to frame them. I just don't see what's so great about them, really, but the customers, they eat them up."

"Thank you, I'll look at those in a minute," Laughlin responded and continued to examine the titles lined up in random order. "Who's the owner anyway?" he asked casually.

"Oh, that is private. He don't like to talk about himself so he asks the staff, that's me, to keep it to ourselves, you know." She nodded in satisfaction and smiled slyly, revealing red bulbous gums and unbrushed teeth.

Laughlin moved away to some stacks by the desk and looked at the license permit, but it merely said Eric Manfred, which meant nothing to him.

Then smiling superiorly, the woman approached Max and said quietly, "You looking for a particular era or place? We have some special old California. Tinted really fine like."

"No, I'm just browsing with my sergeant over there," Max said quietly.

"Sergeant? Are you with the police? Did something else happen to Gene?" the woman asked anxiously.

"Gene, Gene who?" Max followed up.

The woman stepped back and looked over at Laughlin. She squinted and pursed her lips like she'd tasted something sour. "Why are you here?"

"I'm Sergeant Laughlin and this is Deputy Max. We're trying to get a lead on a missing person by the name of Franklin Mo. You ever heard of him?" Laughlin asked.

"No. Please don't bother me now. I'd be so relieved if you would leave the store. Now. I don't have to answer any questions for the likes of you, no matter how good-looking you are."

"No, you don't, but cooperation with the sheriff's department would be a good community service. Maybe we could help you with Gene as well," the sergeant added.

"What do you know about Gene? Is he in the hospital again?"

"Tell you what, you talk to us about what you know and we'll reciprocate. Here are some photos. Know any of these people?"

"No, I don't."

"You didn't even look, ma'am," Max observed.

"Elvira Moody to you, and no, I don't know them," she said as she tossed the photos back at Laughlin.

"Gene's in the hospital again," Laughlin offered.

"Oh no, damn that fool."

"How long you known him, Ms. Moody?"

"Nine years now. He and I, we met at a group therapy session at the county outpatient clinic. We're kinda like close and all. Could you take me to see him, Officers?" she requested with a suddenly sweet voice. "I would be ever so grateful to you."

"No can do at this time," Max stated.

"You obstructing justice if you don't. I'll get you back. Maybe I'll tell Franklin Mo, and he can have you eliminated with a snap of his fingers."

"Speaking of fingers, has Gene lost another finger?" Max asked.

"Drop dead, buster."

"Franklin, where is he? I thought you said you didn't know him."

"Don't try to fool me. I know exactly where Mr. Mo is and so do you."

"Look, Ms. Moody, we don't. Please cooperate with us, and we will do what we can to get Gene a message from you," Laughlin offered.

"Say, what's your deal? Franklin Mo is at the jail, you guys know that. He runs the place. Right?"

"Did he tell you that?"

"He was the big shot who advised all the newspapers about what went on in the jail. I know that for a fact."

"Aren't you aware that he's missing?"

"Now you're saying Mo is not back at the jail and Gene's in the hospital. I don't know. Are you guys on the level?"

Slipping out of a back door at the same time as the question was asked, a large Siamese cat and a corduroy-jacketed figure with a striped vest attached to a short trim man appeared. Between a large domed forehead and a squashed chin, the man wore green glasses on his deep-set eyes. He clutched a small frayed notebook, stopped suddenly, started to smile, and looked at Elvira and then the sheriffs. He was about to turn around and go back through the door when Laughlin called to him.

"Mr. Manfred? We need to talk to you."

The corduroy-suited man's face suddenly showed alarm as he looked at Laughlin. He didn't say anything and quickly went back through the doorway, shutting the door, clicking the lock, and leaving the cat behind out in the room. Laughlin took three long strides to the door and tried the doorknob. The door held.

"Why's he avoiding us?" Laughlin asked Ms. Moody.

The shots muffled her answer, and Laughlin broke the door down. Mr. Manfred lay on an old blanket-covered couch while the back door slammed open and shut with the stirring wind. There was no one in the alley. Max called for an ambulance and assistance. Ms. Moody had disappeared.

"Can you tell us who shot you? Manfred, Manfred, talk if you can," Laughlin coaxed as he pushed hard against the little man's chest to stop the blood. Red continued soaking into shirt, pants, and stripped blanket.

The man looked at Laughlin. His glasses were askew over his large brown eyes, and he smiled when the sergeant replaced them gently. "Ach, I die without raging 'against the dying of the light.'"

"Who did it? Who was it?"

"Find Dylan, ask Dylan."

"Who is Dylan? Where is Franklin Mo?"

"I am only fifty-eight. Tell my sister the store is hers."

"Who shot you? Manfred, tell us. Manfred!"

The paramedics were fast and efficient, and there was no more stopping to talk. Their report quoted the shot man as saying, "Nora Weber's books have to be sent out still. Ralph Steward's are mailed. All the rest are done. I tried, even if I die without raging. Find Dylan. Isabel Manfred Porter, call her, call her."

Laughlin and Max stood still as the stretcher slid past, and they were alone in the now quiet bookstore. Dust particles drifted about seeking surfaces. The men looked idly around.

Afterward, they surveyed the alley again and the back exits to the stores next to the bookstore. There was one parking lot shed built along a flaking fence across the store. The murderer had to have slid into one of the exits or into the shed to disappear so quickly. No one knew anything when asked, except there were customers going in and out. There were no security cameras.

"Nobody seemed to care what the hell happened here," Max observed.

"You would think somebody would show something for the guy. Maybe they're afraid," Laughlin mused.

They returned to the back office. By then, forensics was puttering around in ghostlike jumpsuits. The detectives stood aside and took the scene in with regret. They had been on the wrong side of the door by a few seconds. That was all and that was enough.

Beside the alley exit was a coat rack with a bunch of jackets and a beret. The wall opposite the couch had a glass bookcase pushed between two open ones with shredded leather and cloth-covered books shoved and stacked randomly.

The books said nothing. There was a periodic table next to Da Vinci's stretched-out man on the wall facing the books and a mirror hanging on a chain above the bloody couch. Those, too, told nothing. Laughlin surveyed the murder scene, studying the stacked *Life* magazines crowding the stained couch and the old desk by the door Manfred had backed into. The notebook Manfred had been carrying lay on the floor near the couch.

The whole room held dust like it was a first edition in itself.

Laughlin put on gloves and thumbed through Manfred's book. It was a journal and had daily comments about customers and books they wanted. Some days it was a diary with dashes before each entry as though they were hurried thoughts. He read the last entry, which was two days ago, *"It's difficult to know how to approach this last seller. His estate contains many old books but I'm not sure how to tell him that old doesn't necessarily mean valuable. I can see his struggle to please his wife, wanting to move to a retirement community with more services and yet his distress agreeing to leave his home of so many years. I'll meet with him again and offer some recompense. This year was good for me. I'd been lucky finding the Edgar Allan Poe and that nice first edition of Zane Grey with the dust cover.*

"I still feel some danger and must keep a lookout. He is saying I owe him money now. What if he sends some men to hurt me? I called the Asian Crime Unit but they hadn't heard of him. The agent said something about he wasn't triad, and he wasn't a problem but I wasn't sure what that meant. Still I'm afraid."

Four days before, he wrote, *"I finally mailed the modern library edition of The Brothers Karamazov along with The Poems and Fairy Tales of Oscar Wilde to Mrs. Abrams. She was so insistent that I search for them even though*

I told her they weren't worth much. She wanted them for her collection and said cost was not the issue. Money means nothing and everything. I wish I could be so cavalier.

"*Today I brought a big box of paperbacks to the hospital candy stripers collection. They really appreciate the donation. I figure it's better than leaving them on the back shelves for twenty-five cents. I've got to clean out some of these beaten books anyway.*

"*My Siamese is always with me. He enjoys following me and inspecting.*

"*I organized a set of books to warn the investigator, but he'll never see it. It was pleasant to do for my own sake. I refused to give him more money.*

"*That homeless man was here again. I'm not sure why he picks my store to loiter near. I wonder if I should give him a book instead of a donut?*

"*I should sell some of my first editions too, even though they are dear to me. Oh, if only I had found my child. There doesn't seem to be any hope for that. I should have someone who loves books because Isabel doesn't care much about them. Maybe I could send out a letter to my best customers and ask them if they want the Huckleberry Finn or the hand-painted Botanical Gardens collection. Begin to give it all away.*"

Laughlin flipped pages to entries from over a year ago. "*It's been enjoyable to reread Dickens. I'm not into these new writers. I must be getting old or too discriminating. I wonder what my child would like to read. The detective got nowhere in the search, and now there's this possible lead. For ten thousand dollars, this county guy will follow through.*

"*Anyway, I do like the Kurt Wallander character. He appreciates a diverse society. For his daughter's sake, I hope he doesn't commit suicide.*"

Max stood by restlessly, and Laughlin leafed through the rest of the journal quickly, deciding he would read it fully after it was processed. In the back was a series of names and request for books and Nora Weber's name was there with a request for an early edition of *The Magic Pudding* from April 1977. It was the only one along with Ralph Steward that had not been checked off as sent. He closed the small book, aware it was like stopping Manfred from talking anymore and regretfully handed it to one of the technicians who put it in a bag.

After the photos were taken, one crime team investigator found some keys in the desk's side drawer and invoices in the center drawer but, again, nothing stood out as relevant. Pulling the desk out from its corner, he also found an envelope with a hundred dollar bill taped behind the back of a drawer.

"Not too original," Max noted as the envelope was slipped into an evidence manila cover.

One technician pulled the couch away from the wall and found the gun down among the dust. The team finished photos of the forlorn weapon, after which it was dropped into a bag.

The store studied and sealed, the team left. When Laughlin and Max were alone, all was quiet and only the rush of the outside traffic intruded.

"Was this a suicide or a murder? Let's hope we can find out," Laughlin wondered, and Max suggested they lock up around the yellow crime tape. Moody, telephone and credit card records, Manfred's sister and also owner of the bookstore lease were the immediate investigation pursuits. The sergeant said he'd follow up on Weber and Gene's interview. Max was fine with that and said he'll talk to the other storeowners and the parking lot manager again, see if there had been any threats, find out about the gun, and turn in the report. They shut the peeling front door and then stood on the mottled sidewalk as bunches of cars plowed past. It was dark. A warm wind was blowing. No one knew why the detectives were there anymore.

When they split up, Max went to Kim's, and Laughlin went for a beer near his house. The bar was dark except where his eyes were hit with tubes of neon. He drank his beer at a table gouged with initials, tipping his chair back and forth to some distant Johnny Cash music.

About midnight after five beers and a deep breath, Laughlin drove carefully to the morgue. The attendant was miffed at the inconvenience but escorted him for a look at the body of the bookman. The refrigerated storage was opened and six or so bodies stacked in bunks lined the locker. Manfred was pulled out and the detective looked at his craggy but peaceful face with its slack jaw hanging in awed response to dying. Manfred wouldn't be able to open and close that jaw and speak anymore. He couldn't tell anyone about his intentions.

Even as a sheriff, he still was disturbed by the slack jaw of a dead person. There was no need for closure. The mouth was gaping and hollow.

The autopsy was scheduled later in the week. Walking away, Laughlin thought he had not timed that interview well, and he was sorry for Manfred, the serious bookstore owner.

CHAPTER 12

After Manfred's shocking death, many worthless interviews and fatigue followed Laughlin. He decided to try a new approach. He went to check out the much talked about Dr. Weber.

Her home was on Pacific Coast Highway. He got there in the late afternoon, after finishing another detailed report on the bookstore incident. There was a small brick planter border abutting the garage. He squeezed his car in between a blue garbage can like a forgotten sentinel and a silver Mercedes. The house, surrounded by a formidable fence, was made of wood painted a dusky blue. Surprisingly, Dr. Weber answered the door herself. They crossed a lushly planted courtyard and went in the house.

"Come on, come out on the deck, Sergeant. See there!"

"I'm here about Franklin Mo," Laughlin began.

"The sky has a line of purple goblin-like clouds on the horizon. That's the sign the rain has finished. A late rain. Isn't the wind marvelous?" she emphasized and, nodding yes to herself, went on. "Those clouds are natural chaos, and I desire my own order for the moment. I can tolerate rustling and banging of the waves on the beach, the dusk as the sun settles in a nest of spent colors, and dark as it comes slowly straining my sight. Any more unpredictability will have to abate as tonight comes for this poor poet."

Dr. Weber seemed to have little reserve and went on as if she were talking to an old friend. Laughlin wondered when she had seen anyone else.

She turned to him suddenly and asked, "Are you comfortable in this humidity? It takes me a while. The hot air hangs around in spite of the breeze, but for me, it is like a smooth covering to pain. Still, memories crop up inside my mind's horizon and insist on my conscious shinning on them. Relax, don't get too impatient."

Laughlin didn't know what to make of this monologue. He tried again with "I'm here to asked you about Franklin Mo."

She ignored him. "I usually distracted myself with novels, Turner Classic Movies, baths, apple chips. Nothing really works, and so I tell you. Understand me. Do something to signal you understand. That's a reasonable nod. That will do.

"It all began with a desire to do good. Not well, but good. I'm talking about contributing to the world. Does it end with your accusations about Franklin Mo?

"Who cares if he's missing? I became unable to put up with the shit, the incompetence, the charade of his superiority. Is he missing that too?"

Trying to respond in a straightforward manner, he said, "Nobody is accusing you at this time. We just want to get more information about his interactions, okay?"

"Okay, okay, Nora. Be quiet. No more wine-induced loose associations, true as they are. God, I talk a lot." She stopped and took a big swallow.

Laughlin sat on the edge of what he knew was a Brown Jordan lounge chair on the long gray-painted Nantucket deck and listened patiently to the outburst. The woman downed red wine from a thick-rimmed green glass like you could get in Mexico. She quickly poured more liquid from one of the darkened bottles standing on a wood table. She swayed slightly while pouring out another glass full, righted herself, and shimmied her body into the lounge chair again.

Competing for his ear were the irregular falling waves rushing the beach, and the soft wind scattering typical sounds of seagulls and barking dogs. He could have lain down on the beach and fallen asleep way below the long decks of the many tiered beach houses, and easily slept to the caresses of those sounds. Pulling his thoughts back to problems, he looked at her. Her face didn't fit the serenity of the scene. Scraped by worries, which had settled in wrinkles pointing to her eyes and framing her full mouth, she was still attractive, maybe late thirties, and, he thought, very poetic for a psychiatrist, even if she didn't make sense the whole time.

"Larry, my husband was diagnosed six months ago. I took a leave from the endless job at mental health sometime after that and weaned off my private practice. Then I hoped we could travel. Instead, I sit here drinking. Sure you can't have one, Mr. Laughlin, Detective, Sheriff, whatever?"

"I'm sorry."

"For what? His death sentence or that you can't have a drink?" she countered and then went on, answering her own question. "He's dying of goddamn lung cancer, like any good addicted person, even though he wasn't a smoker. He had three surgeries, chemotherapy, radiation, and morphine pumps endlessly. He lay in the room behind that wall until he wanted to go to a hospice, didn't want me to have to sell the house having to say someone died in it. He moved in August and I quit thinking then and there." She grabbed a Kleenex box and pulled a handful of tissues to wipe her eyes and blow her nose.

"Well, the man went missing just about that time," Laughlin reiterated.

"What?" she asked and looked at him questioningly. "Missing? I just went missing too, and nobody's sent the sheriff out to find me," she shot back and gulped more wine.

"The thing is, when they found his car recently, there was blood inside it, and so the case was turned over to homicide. That's me," he said almost apologetically.

"I'm on the list of suspects after all this time. This is September or October already, I mean, months since I worked there."

"There were staff who said you and he didn't get along, and that caused you to leave after you made threats to get him transferred."

"Rightfully so. He was a ghost, dead or alive. A hologram, you could never get a hold of any opinion from him, never get him to commit to anything. Always covering his ass, I resented him. Surviving, getting paid and not contributing anything but discomfort.

My husband was coughing up his lungs, only forty-three- years old. Do you think I remember particulars about someone so amorphous?"

"When did you see Mr. Mo last? He had a photo of you in his apartment."

"Are you kidding? A photo of me. That's frightening. Why did you tell me that? Should I be scared? I told you he was a hologram. He appears but you can't hold on to him. I was ticked at his undeserved power. Do I have to worry about this now?"

"We want to find him, and his wife is concerned."

"Ah, a concerned wife. Took her long enough, but we have that in common. My husband is a fine man who created bioengineering inventions. He brought life, not death, to my world of medicine. Always helped before the fact rather than after. He was happy and he let me do my thing. He helped me when I became sick with disillusionment from incompetence, HMOs and greed."

"I'm sorry, Dr. Weber," Laughlin interjected again.

"Thank you, thank you. You can call me Nora. We're drinking buddies even if you don't drink. I always wanted to taste 'pruno' after the inmates concocted it. Now I have wine."

She raised her glass to him and then drank the red liquid down in one masterful gulp. He watched her wipe her mouth on her forearm, and then stare out at the span of white foam from the waves coming right up under the deck.

"Oh, look, the goblin clouds, those dark purple ones are . . .," she paused, sobbed, and said, "Sometimes the house shakes from the force of the waves falling down and rolling under us. Real power."

"Yes, I feel it."

"My husband, he would try to go surfing with friends when he had time. He is not as tall as you but he was built well. Over the falls and dumped down from the crest of the wave." She poured herself another drink, stood up suddenly, and wove her way into the house and around the overstuffed chairs. She tripped on a throw rug and fell against him. He held her, and then she righted herself and gave him a smile in thanks. She gave off a subtle fragrance as well as the wine on her breath. He stopped and watched her and then followed behind her. She went into the kitchen. "I need to eat, or I'll throw up. Do you want anything?"

"No, thank you, Doctor. I just need to ask you a few routine questions." He watched her fumble in a cupboard above some Mexican flowered tiles on the counter and behind the stove. She took a broad chef's knife and forcefully cut chunks of cheese. She stuffed some in her mouth.

"Okay, okay, what can I say about him?" she answered, swallowing quickly. "I have to stop eating dairy so my someday grandchildren can have a habitable earth, but now I won't even have grandchildren with my husband to enjoy. Shit. Sorry. Okay, now, how did I know that man? I worked at the county hospital and had a private practice when I met the vanishing ghost. He interviewed me for a job and lied about leaving me free to do what was necessary to make improvements. They were all so desperate., They figured a woman would be the one to try to 'duck dive,' as they say, any Department of Justice investigation, and if they failed, so what? What are women's careers anyway? Anyway, I joined the staff. Dr. Brandt was very encouraging and he approved of my plans for more consistent mental status exams."

"What were you supposed to avoid?"

"I was supposed to help stop the place closing down. I was supposed to do good and do it well," she said and stuffed a mound of brown bread smeared with soft cheese into her mouth. She stood there, chewing slowly, and looking at him. She was thin and tall. Her dark hair, a mixture of black and brown, framed her face like a curtain. A crumpled T-shirt hung all the way to her hips, she had a flowered bra underneath, and a strip of black shorts cut across her white thighs. She was barefoot and kept curling and uncurling her toes.

"Well, we're trying to interview people from work as well as his friends and family. We've got a couple psychiatrists, program heads, two social workers, his administrative assistant, and the people downtown in mental health. Since you worked directly with him, your name also came up. Do you know of anything regarding his whereabouts?"

"Oh please, let's go out on the deck and watch the clouds again. We've been at this house for thirteen years, planning it since we first got married. It cost a $170,000. Can't beat that, and the clouds are as spectacular as the waves. Really."

"They are for sure, but I need to get this information."

"My husband wouldn't listen to me about staying at home, and I couldn't overrule him, that last bit of autonomy he has now. Such a delicate balance. I did consulting to medical and surgical patients— that is, before I took the job with naive hope at LA's own Bellevue Bastille. I loved teaching medical and surgical residents as well as the psychiatry residents. The lay public doesn't know about how often the mind and the brain are affected by any illness, and they, in turn, affect the illness."

"It has to be fascinating to talk to people about all this," the detective offered lamely.

"Whole life experiences, mind fears, brain status are interwoven, interplay with all diseases and recovery. It was an amazing time in my career except that the busy queen bees in charge of the psych department didn't care one piss cup worth about medicine, yet they were in charge of policy and money. I chose to take the jail job."

"I can believe how interesting the medicine and the politics must have been," Laughlin placated, "but could you tell me more about the Mr. Mo and his interactions with the staff at the jail mental health?"

"You don't have to be patronizing, I get it. All you care about is your own case. Well, Franklin Mo was a discredit to his Asian ancestors. Capitalizing on physiognomy, he was a slime bag, and I got totally taken in. He wanted to chum around with me like a leech hanging on to competency. I couldn't stand him. He offended me. I'd always tried to be tolerant and compassionate. I guess the strain of my husband's treatments made me a bitch, but he deserved my disdain. I have no idea why he had a photo of me. He must have hated me. I'll get a gun if I have to.

"Oh, there are the dolphins. They come almost every day. See them over there? They're just lallygagging around, at least six or seven of them right over there."

"Were there any people close to Mo?" Laughlin interrupted, but looked out to the blue expanse.

"Of course, there were the program heads he threatened with all sort of made-up power."

"Program heads, the ones we're talking to, right?"

"The mental health treatment used to be overseen by psychologists who stayed with county jobs and got the security of the county benefits. The areas they take administrative care of are MOP, HOP, WOP, and inpatient services. Those acronyms stand for men's outpatient, homosexual outpatient, and women's outpatient.

"Remember, though, outpatient only means the inmates are not in the jail hospital or medical hospital, but they're all in jail, mental health side."

She poured another glass, gestured at an empty one for him, and lay back on the lounge.

"Didn't you have to rotate through the jail as a beginning deputy?" she asked.

"Yes, but then mental health was up on the central jail's top floor in these individual cells. There were slots in the door, and food and talk went through them."

"Oh, I know, I was there, worse than dungeons, but the patients thought they were safer locked up there than with the criminals, gangs, and deputies who all hated them. That was before the move to Twin Towers."

"Are things better now?"

"Well, maybe, things were changing just as I left, but the housing isn't only on the basis of mental illness. The quote Blacks unquote have certain mental health floors, and the Hispanics have the old jail cells, and Whites are scattered in between. If you're sick, you die unless you get sent to mental health and hope someone gives a damn. Of course, kind as they may be, the social workers and Psych Ds don't know a tumor from a hangnail and couldn't care less.

"As I was finally told, Franklin Mo was an administrator who had once done some counseling under the supervision of a so-called therapist but never was able to get a full license. Everybody thought he was Black because of his reputation and his name. He wasn't though. He was Asian, born in America, and never spoke anything but Bay area English. He came down to Los Angeles after he wasn't promoted in his job in Stockton, supposedly because of budget restrictions. Who knows the real reasons?"

The wind began to move more of her hair across her face. She pushed it around behind her neck and took another big swallow of her wine. Laughlin watched her trying to dissolve herself in the alcohol and wanted to take the bottle away. He did nothing but listen and question his impotence.

"Personnel, or excuse me, human resources—what a name—like water and minerals and such, human resources, scored him on his years of experience, his recommendations, and the like, and he was hired as a deputy director without any formal degree or experience. He was in charge of handling the program heads, the payroll, the hiring and most egregiously evaluating the care that inmates received.

"Of course, the jail general medicine staff was just as bad. Anybody that had sickness unto death was punted over to mental health to get them out of the way, to let them languish labeled mentally ill. Ask Chase Conner. He had to deal with it too.

"If a sucker got sick after screening and died, it was always, after an extensive review by the medical staff, who had also treated or not treated the guy, passed to the baton of fate as the leading cause, and they themselves were exonerated. With every death, there was a need for the inmate's physiology to be blamed or the incompetency of mental health.

"Franklin was always pointing the finger back at the sheriff's department, which oversaw medical care but had to trust doctors, believing them, not their cover-ups, and so they were always returning the insult by asking mental health to get its act together. Those medical staff doctors would like to get rid of him too. That's how it was, and the stupid, careless, and seasoned inmates mainly in the jail for drugs, went with the flotsam and jetsam of the bickering between services. Do you like the sordid details, which some would say are only a bitter woman's view, not the truth? I'm not sure why I should apologize to you for my views or chastise myself. Actually, it feels good to be nasty and truthful."

"I'm trying to get an idea of what went on that might have contributed to Mr. Mo's disappearance," Laughlin answered with a weariness as well as concern for the woman venting. She was in such distress, but what could he do? He had to get some firsthand information somewhere. He waited and looked out at the sky again until she continued.

"The jail became a drug user and withdrawal hotel. Maybe he was involved. I don't know. Drugs and more drugs for good guys to hunt and bad guys to sell. A hundred years ago, drugs weren't illegal at all.

"Then in the twenties, there was all this political intrigue about racial prejudice, fear the Blacks and their meth, the Chinese and their heroin, the Mexicans and their marijuana. Make sure they didn't get too much of the money, politics cloaked in morality. I mean has anything changed? Why people cared if anyone used drugs was beyond me. No one gave a damn about booze after prohibition failed. Now over half the kids in jail are there on nonviolent drug charges."

"Did Franklin Mo deal with these offenders?"

"Oh, Franklin Mo? He didn't really care about these kids. I'll tell you who did. It's like the ex-druggies found a new industry on drugs. 'Like, man, we been there' is the treatment of choice, once they were out. We could do so little prevention once they served their sentence. The world is crazy. There must be a cuckoo virus churning around in the air, believe me."

Curled up on her side and looking out to the waves, she took a sip of wine and closed her eyes and whispered, "Great swimmers, the dolphins." Her face relaxed and puffs of warm wind stirred loose hair over her neck.

"Dr. Weber? Dr. Weber, can you talk?" Laughlin questioned.

"What about? It all comes down to questions about an administrator who believed in blaming others and keeping the status quo as long as he was on top.

"I was always trying to be aware, trying to learn. I went through all those milestones and memorized and memorized what was known of electrolyte balance, acid and base tissue stains, varied cancer cells with dark, twisted nuclei, the amazing bones of the wrist, red and blue vessels, pink lungs.

"I remembered patients with drum-tight ascites filled bellies, eroded stumps of teeth, bruised and scaled skin, tumors of head, neck, throat, breasts, chests, balls, uteruses, necrotic and smelling of time release decay. I saw the open body with gushy brains, stringy nerve tendrils, leftover raw red limbs from amputations, hearts pumping right in front of me, swarming guts tumbling out on blue cotton, and babies slipping out greased for protection. I sewed up heart, guts, skin.

"I heard hearts thump, some dancing, some plodding along, some racing inside chests of owners who submitted to me in my white coat. I felt scalp, tongue, armpit, breast, belly, cervix and rectum, penis and prostate, fingers and toes, pulses.

"I witnessed the long paralyzed body of the boy with jackrabbit front teeth whose parents wouldn't visit him, the man whose cinder death dusted but handsome face presented with an open rounded mouth holding small dark teeth in his final sleep on the white pillow, the plump hydrocephalic baby who needed an IV, the stingy-haired woman who was afraid to let anyone see her rotting breast, the cut-up mother who sat for chemotherapy with her baby in her lap, the young gangbanger who had his arm cut off and saluted with the other."

"Dr. Weber, please, could you get back to Franklin Mo?" Laughlin asked gently, not wanting to jar the fragile woman and yet not sure where she was going. He felt himself confused by her and concerned she was going crazy.

She answered, "Most amazing was the endurance, fortitude, and saintly acceptance of what had to be done. The first patient I examined on my own was a young black guy. He and I both timid.

We did all right. Yet, there were the other patients as well. Silent, secret, under cover of normalcy, or too loud, too erratic, irritable, not examined by touch, X-ray, blood. 'Mental' is the word used. They needed help too." She paused and sipped some wine. Then went on.

"Genes were already revealed, and Thorazine, Haldol, and all the antipsychotics, as well as antidepressants, increasingly prescribed. Then there was the lithium craze and Valium along with its derivatives, big commotions about multiple personality disorder, attention deficit disorder, and now autism.

"How do I get you down the right road to understanding? What signposts will help point the way? Most has been torn down by insurance companies, administrative expediency, and ignorance, but, like some others, I loved trying to discover and delineate the problem and help solve it."

Without opening her eyes, she finished with "Goddamn, everything has changed, and all everyone wants is glory and money. I'd cry and complain more if I could but I've talked enough for now, haven't I, Detective Laughlin? My husband is having his line changed and so I can't see him right now. I had the afternoon off from watching death and don't need to waste it on Franklin Mo.

"Please show yourself out and come again soon. I am very sorry if you got bombarded by my thoughts. I hope you forgive me. Maybe another day when I am not so under the influence of death and alcohol. I apologize, but then again why should I? Take what I said and leave it at that, a woman's point of view without being sweetness and light."

The dismissed detective sat quietly watching the sad woman breathing evenly, the respirations of sleep. It was past six o'clock. With all her knowledge, she could not stop her husband from dying. This was a grief he could understand got some relief by obliterating consciousness. He removed her wine glass, put it on the table next to him, and looked out over the dimming expanse of sky and water.

A few lumpy clouds could be distinguished in the dark, those "goblin clouds," she'd called them. There was a real name for them but he didn't know it. Clouds now had names, so you could talk to someone about what you saw without merely saying big and fluffy, streaky, gray, and threatening.

Laughlin took a deep breath and stretched his arms above his head, catching wind in his hands. She had revealed the politics of the jail, but her information certainly wasn't narrowing a list of possible enemies, and Franklin Mo was still gone.

Most missing people show up after all their money is spent or they've worried people enough to satisfy any vindictiveness. This guy wasn't going to be one of them, not with blood in his car and no trace of used credit cards, telephone calls and such.

The detective leaned back and closed his eyes. A wave rushed in on the shore and then dropped back quietly, then there was another, a pause, then another. With a start, he shook his head to stay awake. Dr. Weber was snoring. He rose quickly, went inside, and got a red throw, soft like cashmere, and draped it over the forlorn sleeper. She looked lovely even with tears or drool on her cheek. Too bad he wasn't a prince who could kiss her and wake her to happiness.

Gripping the railing and looking down to the frothy water, he wished he lived on the beach just like this. *Just like this*, he repeated and left, closing the door and making sure it was locked. None of the jail staff he interviewed seemed okay. They were frightened, angry, depressed, tired. Were they any different from the inmates?

His car was hot from the autumn afternoon sun, and he let the windows down adding cool evening air tumbling in along with the car air conditioner. The coast highway was crowded with rush-hour traffic, but he got a break when the traffic light changed, and swung around going north west. The sun glared in defiance of its setting. He had to shield his eyes until it slid behind a bluff. He made his way to Malibu Seafood. He ate fried clams in his car.

CHAPTER 13

Gene was Eugene Biskoff; this time he cut off his penis and right foot. Laughlin parked in the multi-floored public garage and walked over to the graceful tiered hospital. He went up the broad shallow steps and into the lobby. There were gilded paintings of famous physicians in blue skies on the ceiling. It had been impressive the first time he had seen all that art in this dismal place built in the 1930s and designated to help the poor. He wondered if anyone even knew who Vesalius, Galen, or Harvey or any of them were. The dimly lit art deco lobby now had cages in front of the walls, and you needed a badge to get in past the guards. Some guy had brought a duffel bag of guns in a few years back and shot up the emergency room, wounding doctors and nurses. Since then, there were these supposed safeguards.

Finding the elevator bank jutting off from the always crowded wide beige halls, he walked the long passageways, got to a surgical wing and to the desk clerk. It was the usually set up of a central desk where every staff member congregated to talk and write. The preoccupied clerk, sitting in the center of the half circle of Formica, quickly gestured to a man in scrubs, and then she fell back into wads of papers.

The surgical resident, sleepy-eyed and eating a candy bar, told Laughlin that he knew of about a dozen penises that were cut off every year; 50 percent got anastomosed, sewed back on with decent results. Gene was somewhat special because he'd done multiple self-amputations. The foot took some "major sawing" on his part, but he was going to survive to try again. The penis was recovered, but the foot was too mangled. The surgeon excused himself when a nurse came over to the desk with an order sheet.

Also rounding, the psychiatric resident spoke heavily accented English, said he himself was from Russia. The patient was schizophrenic but not dangerous. The doctor told Laughlin it was okay to talk to Mr. Biskoff, although he might be a little sedated. He accompanied the sergeant to the bedside.

The square ward room contained six men in narrow beds with light brown tightly gathered curtains. There was no privacy. Gene, one of all the sedated sick men, lay in restraints with an IV running into his vein and a bag of urine with a tube full of yellow liquid coming from under the covers. Laughlin figured it had to be threaded up whatever was left of the man's sorry penis now. Gene no longer had a beard. He had closed eyes and a long nose that ended with full lips. He looked peaceful.

"Hey, Gene, man here to talk to you. Gene, you to vake up."

"Mr. Biskoff, remember me? I'm Sergeant Laughlin. I need you to answer a few questions. Are you up to it?"

"Up to it. Up to it. There, they're up all over the place. You can hear that over there, making fun. I can't get it up," the patient said and pointed to the wall with his thumbless hand.

Laughlin grimaced at his tactless question and looked at the psychiatrist but the man merely shrugged, obviously not getting the inadvertent pun.

"Mr. Biskoff, where's Jeffrey Trainer Faulk and Franklin Mo?"

"Jeffrey, is he here? We go around together. We go around. It gets dizzy. Spinning. Alanine and cytosine. Jeffrey, he didn't do this. His genes come from the good Gene." The man tried to sit up, but the restraints, light brown leather cuffs with something like wool linings, and a belt around his chest held him down.

"I think you got to vait until he more stable."

"If we had a stable, then eugenics would be held there. Not run free. I need to find the little Vietnam girl who was running naked with her mouth open. Can you find her? She needs to stop screaming and running. I'll stop if she stops. She's got to be tired of the bombs. The bad Gene dropped all the bombs, right? Her chromosomes will be damaged. Find her," Biskoff pleaded and grabbed the resident's arm.

"Quiet down, Gene. This is hospital," the resident offered.

"Is she too? Here, I mean. I need to talk with her."

Gene Biskoff started crying and mumbling about needing the little Vietnam girl.

Shaking his head in bewilderment over Gene's train of thoughts and remembering that news photo, Laughlin interjected, "Mr. Biskoff, you can help. Do you know the whereabouts of Jeffrey Faulk and Franklin Mo?"

"Cut out the damaged arm of chromosome 18."

Laughlin turned to the resident, "How long will he be here?"

"Couple more days, maybe more. Then rehab."

"How come he's in restraints? He's not arrested."

"No. We have to use something to stop him from doing more harm. He's on a fourteen-day hold as danger to self. Straitjackets not used in the United States. In olden days, people got drugs and then hydrotherapy, wrapped in sheets, and put in water. Sometimes days. Not so long ago, 1920s and '30s. Not so many years from us. Then induced insulin coma and bromides, not good."

"Don't you sedate them instead?"

"Yeah, there were some good drugs in the '50s—you know, Thorazine and antidepressants but drugs have side effects still. Anxiolytics best, but patients can get dependent on them. Have to be careful so patients don't get too much. Now we go back to posey belt around chest, restraints around arms for agitation, along with touches of Valium and Haldol."

"What about this stuff about genes?"

"Delusions."

Gene picked up the word and ran with it. "Franklin, he's deluded. God mutated me but Franklin is radiation. He is the sinner. Delusions of grandeur, grand master, Grand Pre. Drive away. Gregor Mendel, the good monk, is going to save me." With that, Gene escaped by pulling the blanket with his teeth and lifting it over his head with one hand. His wrist restraints were loose enough, but Laughlin figured the medical team decided he was too far gone to do any more serious cutting.

"What's with this poor guy anyway? Does he really believe all this stuff?"

"We got many patients; Maybe he too respond to medications. We see."

It was clear to Laughlin the resident didn't much care about the genetics of Gene, and Eugene was in no condition to help find Franklin Mo. Maybe Mendel could help the patient but right now, he wasn't about to clarify the sheriff's case. He gained about as much information from the resident as he did from Gene. Both were foreigners and there was no translator. He sure wasn't up to the interpretations required.

Laughlin walked slowly back to the cavernous elevators and waited. He could picture the little Vietnamese girl screaming and running. He was distracted when a patient, gown parted to show his hairy legs with a catheter bag swinging carefree, wheeled and steered an IV pole, and entered the same elevator going down. The patient melded into the large hall of wandering people, like another shepherd tending his flock.

He purposely walked as straight a line as he could through the crowded twenty-foot hallways full of gowned patients with exposed rears, brown-shirted guards, white-coated orderlies, and dark-haired women holding kids. He was relieved getting back to the lobby and then out on the plaza steps. The pallor of his futile line of questioning blocked the sun's warmth. He coughed from the smog.

That was his day. He felt the smog in his brain. He returned to the station, and Max strolled in about an hour later.

"Got anything?" Laughlin asked.

"Nope. Here are the phone and credit card records from Manfred. Store people still silent, and Elvira Moody hasn't shown up at her apartment in a very trendy part of Culver City, by the way. I'm going to see Manfred's sister tomorrow. She said she was too busy today for much background info. Apparently, there was no will and no other kin, so the whole store is going to be sealed up for probate, but the brother and sister own the building." Max sat down and loosened his tie.

"So what do we have?" Laughlin summarized, "Nothing. Ballistics not in yet, and the gun is still being traced. A mental health administrator guy goes missing and nobody reports it until his car shows up with the blood of another guy all over the seats and in the mouth of a bird with a finger stuck in its throat. The other guy is missing too but he used to live in a board and care with good old Gene. Both these guys used to come over to Mo's home in San Marino and hang out. Doing what we don't know except for some boozing.

"The first missing guy, Franklin Mo, has a Pasadena apartment with elaborate furnishings in the bedroom and kitchen for someone or something yet unknown.

"There, we find the picture of Dr. Weber, one of the suspects, or main one, in a possible murder of Mo. Along with a book in the Mo's house, that photo leads us to a bookstore owner who immediately is shot." Laughlin scratched his head and screwed his face up in frustration.

"From what you've said before, no one gives a rat's ass about Mr. Franklin Mo at home or at work. They certainly didn't know him in Mr. Manfred's neighborhood," Max added.

"The FBI's got nothing either, and it looks like they're putting pressure on us because of the bookstore shooting and the blood."

"Okay, so who else is a suspect?"

"For what? Mo's murder? Jeffrey Faulk's murder? The only real murder we have is Manfred's, right under our noses in a matter of speaking," Max complained.

"Let assume they're all dead. Who are we looking at? I opt for Mo's wife and maybe the son but he's out of the country. Some of the staff at the jail. Maybe that program head Poplar or Mason. She was so defensive and didn't want to talk about Mo as being gone."

"You gotta include Weber, even if you like her."

"True. Everybody at the jail mentioned her as his nemesis. Her name in Manfred's journal was about a book and nothing else. How does she tie in with Faulk and Manfred?"

"Let's not forget that Moody woman. She was one prize and knew all three, Mo, Manfred, and Gene. And probably even Jeffrey."

"But she was with us, Max, when Manfred got shot." Laughlin sighed.

"Yeah, yeah but she was a piece of work I don't trust," Max concluded. "Hey, man, I'm splitting. Long day. See you in the morning, okay?"

Laughlin watched his partner move rapidly out of the station because he obviously had somewhere to go. After putting all the scattered notes together, the detective looked around and saw only stragglers in the large room with barren desks; finishing his report, he pushed himself off his chair and decided to go home.

His car had a big bird shit splat on the windshield; it resisted the wipers' attempts to wash it away. When he pulled into his driveway, he was intent on cleaning the damn thing off, so he took a throw-away newspaper and started rubbing.

"Shit, shit, shit," he muttered and saw the image of Manfred bleeding to death. "Shit," he said again and tensed his shoulders, waiting for a blow from his dead father. Both his parents had insisted he talk like a well-educated person and not some hick from Detroit. He thought about the times in the alley behind his house when he and Tommy Foley looked at dirty flip pictures and used the word "caca" and "fuck" like they were grenades to toss over parents' fences. Now he tried to live up to his sergeant status and only succumb to swearing at specific times.

"But shit," he said loudly and wondered why Manfred had not come in to talk to him rather than return so quickly to the back room only to be shot. If he had come forward, maybe he would still be alive. Maybe he thought Max and he were the danger.

Laughlin wadded up the dirty paper, tossed it into a garbage can, and sat back in the car to turn the windshield wipers on again. He watched them smooth the glass clean and then slouched, resting his head way back. Intruding on his musing, he could hear Biskoff's babbling and wondered if he was adopting the same derailed train of thoughtlessness, not able to decide what to do next, go in the house, go to Denny's, or down to the little Italian restaurant for meatballs. He visualized menus from these possibilities. His refrigerator was a blank, and he felt too tired to go in and open the door to find the stacked Chinese food cartons, beer and dried-out clams in Styrofoam. Denny's had these glossy menus with perfectly arrayed dinners. He could almost taste the salads and the fried patties, but Gino's had stained placards with good old spaghetti. He shook his head, impatient with himself over such a simple, stupid question.

He got out of the car, slammed the door, clicked the lock, stood for a moment, looked down the street, and then started to walk. At least he could make a decision about eating.

CHAPTER 14

He walked to Denny's, used the john to scour his hands, and quickly sat down in a booth. Before he could look at the menu, the wizened body of Mr. Winkler slid in the opposite side and then a still tinier person with a cane sat down next to him.

"Good evening, Sergeant. May we join you?" Mr. Winkler said and continued with "This is my wife Rosie, Rose Rankin Winkler. We come here often, and seeing you is a delightful surprise."

Laughlin's face went from irritation to a slight smile at recognition and then a greeting. "Well, Mr. Winkler and Mrs. Winkler, please do join me. How is the cat?" After his uninspired walk to the restaurant, it pleased him to have his old nighttime comrade face to face in the light.

"The cat is at home tonight, but we had chicken, so the leftovers are for her." He gestured to the takeout container he had put on the table.

Mrs. Winkler offered, "She's a little spoiled but then why not?"

"Why not, indeed. We love her and she is so good to us," Winkler added.

"So you've already eaten, I take it?"

"Not dessert, not dessert. Rosie wasn't feeling well a while ago." He turned and looked her up and down. "Now I see that color coming back in her face and her hand is steady again."

"Oh, that was last week," she countered.

"I mean tonight, before, remember?"

"Well, Sergeant, I'm three years older than my husband who just retired, and I have some arthritis, but I'll make it a little longer, especially for dessert. I love the cobbler."

"Not as good as mine, Rosie."

"True, but less commotion in the kitchen, Jacob."

A tall, hefty young woman with a blouse of bright balloons prints came over with a pencil and pad in her hands and asked for orders. She gave her full attention to Laughlin, and so he ordered the cobblers for the Winklers and a hot turkey sandwich for himself. He made sure his company knew they could leave before he finished if they liked.

The couple ate with such delicacy that Laughlin was finished before they were, and ordered the cobbler as well. What was it that made him feel so comfortable with these older people? He knew he should be out at the bars, finding a woman and slow dancing with her pushed up against him, and here he was, eating dinner with the geriatric set. He looked at their crinkled faces and questioned away about their lives and places they'd traveled to. It was nice. What a corny conclusion, it was nice, but he felt it just that way.

Then they all had some tea, and Mrs. Winkler brought up her purse. She took out at least ten tan bottles of labeled medicine and began sorting through the collection. The vials were a whole family of varying fat and tall labeled containers, and while she sorted through them, Mr. Winkler looked elsewhere and fingered the sugar packets. Finally, she took three different pills and continued with her tea. "I'm trying out these new pills, so excuse me, but they have to be taken every eight hours."

The three of them took some more tea, and the Winklers were appreciative when Laughlin paid for their cobblers along with his dinner. They insisted he must come to their house for dinner one night and he demurred.

"Let's have cobbler now, Jacob."

"We've had it already, Rosie."

"I like to have pudding, and then there was Ma, always making noodles. Let's have pudding now." Mrs. Winkler began tapping all the bottles and scratching her right arm. There were already purple blotches on her small hands, and her gnarled fingers worked vigorously on the reddening skin.

"Rosie, are you all right?"

Rosie didn't answer but looked up startled at seeing Laughlin. "Who are you again, young man? You look like Robert. Are you Robert? I'm so glad you came to see me finally. They said you were dead. Vietnam and fire, then Grenada grenadine and Gulf or golf. Anyway dead. They said you were dead." She began scratching again and picking at her sweater, making gestures to take something off the front of it.

"Rosie, Rosie," Winkler said and took her hand in his.

"Mrs. Winkler, Rosie," Laughlin echoed.

She withdrew her hand from Winkler, stood up and took her cane to hit something she saw coming at her and then sat down again to pick at her sweater. She wouldn't answer her husband. Her head fell into all the bottles, which scattered on the table and floor. Other people stared or yelled, and Winkler cried out and grabbed her.

Laughlin took the slumped figure from Winkler and laid her on the floor with his coat under her head and raised her legs. Then he called 911. While he gave directions, he felt her carotid and told Winkler to gather up all the medicine. "She's alive, Winkler, she alive. Get her things together. Has this ever happened before?"

"No, no. She's healthy. Rosie, Rosie can you hear me?"

The paramedics were in and out in their usual time, and her husband was helped into the ambulance. They were gone in less than ten minutes. Laughlin picked up his lonely coat off the floor and sat back down in the booth. He finished the last of his tea, drank the rest of his water, and got up to leave. The cashier came up to him and said, "You were so great, I mean, really, so great. It was cool the way you helped her. She's not your mother or anything, right? Otherwise, you would have gone with them, right? I'm off work now. Wanna go get a drink?"

"Right, I just met her," Laughlin answered and looked at the woman with more interest than he had had when he came past her on entering the place. She was tall, dark-haired and her eyes danced with invitation. She grabbed his arm and escorted him out the door.

"I have my car right here and I'll take my hero to the little bar three blocks away and toast him. Okay, huh?" she offered.

There was a lilt to her voice and a soapy scent coming from her hair.

He needed a drink. The pink-faced, pleasantly ripe and eager woman in her best years tried valiantly to supplant the image of the old woman falling on her face and lying there on the floor like another dead body. He said yes and got into her Nissan to be taken away. Always questioning his moves, he wondered why he went along with her and what he would do with her.

They sat in a red plastic booth and had plain beers with peanuts. It was a dusky dark in the bar and the TV blared in a far corner. There was no music; she still smelled good. Her warm thigh was right up against his, and he put his arm around her shoulders.

He didn't hear much about her life story, although she told it and ended with the caveat that she was going back to Chicago in two days.

"I've been here three almost four years and got only one part as an extra in a historical movie about Romans, and that was it. Too many girls and not enough roles. I'm going to try Second City and see my old boyfriend again. He'd been writing me, sending me a little money, and he's doing really well in his cleaning business."

"Well, that sounds like a good plan for such a pretty girl. Stand out in Chicago rather than get lost in the crowd here."

"I'd like to take a memory or two back with me, hero. You understand? What is it you do anyway?"

"I work for the county,"

"Like at inspecting or something?"

"Yeah, or something. Hey, I'd rather listen to your dreams."

"Well, come on home with me, and I'll give you somethin' to dream about, okay, huh?"

Her apartment was in the back of an old yellow stucco, stillborn Spanish-type complex. She led him up a couple of chipped red painted cement steps and into a one-room studio. The bed stood out in the center of the carpeted area and had a big puffy comforter of red cherries covering it. There was a two-chair dinette; a big TV with table, and a space heater to complete the area. In one corner were a sink, half a refrigerator and half a stove. A narrow door led to what he supposed was the bathroom. Except for a framed photo of a double-chinned man with a big wrench in his hand, there were no pictures anywhere and only a few magazines on the floor near the bed.

"Sit down, sit down. I'll get us a drink from the fridge." She pulled out a bottle of vodka, some strange colored juice and packaged donuts, carefully putting them down on the dinette. "I gotta go to the little girl's room for a sec, will you pour us?"

He nodded and took up the bottle but left the juice for her. She came out with her blouse and shoes off. Her bra was a bright yellow, and she began unzipping her skirt with one hand and pulling him to the bed with the other.

"Don't you want the juice and donuts, honey?" she asked as she slid toward a propped pillow.

He juggled the two glasses, held her hand, and answered, "No, thanks, anyway. You? Should I bring them over for you?"

"Oh, that's so sweet. I'll take mine on the rocks. Oops, I forgot the ice." She popped up again and emptied a metal ice tray into a bowl and brought it back to the bed with the bottle, downed her vodka, dumped some ice in the glass and added a couple inches more of the vodka. "Refill for you, hon?" She took a sip and then downed the drink again. "My radio's busted, so we'll have to do without music, is that okay?"

"Sure, I'll have another. Let's talk a little," Laughlin reached for her hand and began rubbing it gently between his hands. He turned hers over to kiss the palm and saw all the slash marks crisscrossing her pale wrist. He touched her scars and asked, "What's this all about?"

"Ah, nothin', just need to sometimes to feel, you know, alive. I haven't got much out here, and that helps."

Laughlin looked at her eyes, innocent and unperturbed by her admission. He took a swallow of his drink and lay back against a pillow. What was he doing here? He closed his eyes and saw Winkler's wife again and Manfred, who had been shot, and amputated Gene with his fucked-up genes. Her hand began stroking him. He knew about women who cut themselves but was somewhat shocked at how cavalier she was about her actions. She poured herself more vodka and started to kiss his neck. Her breast was slipping out of her bra and he felt its soft contour. She took his hand and pushed it up along her leg, and he observed how easily he was aroused by this strange encounter. His fingers had encircled her thigh, but when he slid toward her center, he felt the raised scars. Struggling to clear his thoughts, he pulled away and looked at her leg now that her skirt was all the way off. It was covered with red scabs in straight and jagged ridges.

"Jesus, what have you been doing to yourself?"

"I told you. Just the same thing. When I get all bummed out, it helps."

"Are you getting help? This isn't right?"

"Oh, it's no big deal. No other guys give me trouble over it. Come on and kiss me and forget about it all."

"How do you forget about hurting yourself?" Laughlin sat up in the disheveled bed and ran his hands very lightly over the cuts.

"Don't worry about me, mister. I'm going to be just fine. Do you want me or not, big hero? Are you scared of some old cuts?"

"Jesus, you need help."

"Fuck you. What do you know about anything? I invite you to my home and you start carping on me. Fuck you, you shithead bastard." She downed another drink and leaned against the pillow.

"You're lucky I don't swat you for that talk," he said and took her shoulders in his hands and shook them. Her jaw flapped with the shaking and she laughed in his face.

"Go ahead, tough guy, beat me, I dare you. You're a big nothing coward!" she yelled.

"Shut up! Stop doing this to yourself, and don't ever bring unknown guys over to your place. How'd you know you could trust me?"

"Who the hell are you to tell me what to do? Drop dead," she said and downed another drink.

"I'm sorry, but it's wrong what you're doing," he said and realized he didn't know her name as he turned to again say, "I'm sorry, miss, don't do it to yourself."

"That's great. I told you my name in the car, and you were ready to fuck me, and now you can't even remember my name. Well, it's Flora to you, Flora Johnson, and you can get the hell out now. I mean it."

Putting his feet on the rug, he slipped his loafers on and hunched over, leaning his elbows on his legs. He rubbed his mustache and combed his hair with his hands. Still sitting on the bed, he said nothing. Minutes went by and he couldn't move.

"Flora. That means flower. Why hurt yourself? You're young and attractive." What more could he say? The alcohol had seeped into any thoughts he had, and yet he knew he had to get up and out.

Finally, he turned to say he was sorry again. She was breathing softly and regularly, the breathing of sleep. A cut flower in the cherries. He grimaced and then left quietly. Stumbled on the two red stairs and jogged home. His cellphone was quiet. His house was quiet. He closed the door, locked it, switched off the lights and felt like he had escaped some unknown specter.

CHAPTER 15

A dead man, a missing man, a crazy man were what facts the detective woke up with. Multiple days had passed and he was nowhere nearer to an answer. With an annoying hangover, but also with resolve, Laughlin returned Dr. Weber's call. Her message machine said she was at the hospice.

He drove over to West Los Angeles, where there was a cluster of convalescent buildings on Centinela, and parked at the three-story totally white hospice facility with its floor-length shaded windows and generous parking lot. Inside, the top floor was devoted to the dying. Dr. Weber was in the room with her husband. The attendant said she wanted the sergeant to come there so she didn't have to leave the patient.

The wide hallway had bright leaves of primary colors on the rug and a wainscoting painted yellow. A sunny dying was implied. Laughlin didn't buy it and felt like an intruder into the light blue room where Dr. Weber sat in a vinyl chair while her husband lay propped up on multiple pillows.

"Couldn't let this all wait. Thank you for coming here," she said quietly.

"It's all right, Nora. From what I heard, you had to apologize. It will break up my day. Come in, Sergeant, I'm Larry Weber," the prone man said quite loudly. Laughlin waited for him to cough but he didn't. His nasal catheter only moved slightly as he talked.

"I don't know for sure how much I told you when you came to interview me, but I felt it was important to clarify anything I said in my, shall we call it, toxic state.

"Look, I'm really sorry to have intruded, but I still need to know about Eric Manfred and his connection to you and Mr. Mo."

"What's there to tell? Isn't Manfred the bookstore owner, the one in Santa Monica? I go in there sometimes for, of all things, books. I have no idea that Franklin went in there."

"As I told you, we found a picture of you in a folder from the bookstore. It was in an apartment of Mo's. There's some connection. Manfred was shot and mentioned your name."

"Oh damn, damn. Oh, Nora, it's . . . it's coming I can't control it. Oh God," her husband moaned. The smell permeated the room immediately, and he bowed in defeat. "I lost . . .," he began and then pulled the nasal catheter out and deep spasms of coughing took over. He turned to his side. His body heaved up and down, and she went over to him and stroked his back.

Laughlin stood absolutely still. The coughing lasted a horrific five minutes, and then the man lay back again and sighed. "This is utter humiliation. Forgive me, Sergeant. There's no dignity in this death. Nora, please take him out while I get cleaned up. I rang. The attendants, they come in quickly. Don't want me to get bedsores. Ironic, isn't it?"

A stout young woman wearing with an apron knocked and entered the room.

"We'll have it all taken care of in a few minutes, Mrs. Weber. I'll call you from the waiting room, if you like."

"Yes. Thank you, Linda." She turned and whispered, "I'll be back, sweetheart."

"Okay, now, let's get you cleaned up in a jiffy, Mr. Weber," Dr. Weber and Laughlin heard her say as they slipped out the door. They walked down the hall quietly and then sat in a little alcove lined with pastel couches and tables full of magazines and pamphlets.

"To be coughing is one thing, and to be incontinent of urine is one thing but of feces, he can't stand the idea."

"I'm very sorry. Forgive me for intruding. Sometimes murder seems so important I forget, you know, about other life and death issues."

"Yes, that's for sure. I don't want to leave my husband during this time, you can understand that," she said, as she took a pillow from a chair, placed it behind her head and leaned back on the couch. Her dark hair pulled back revealed high cheek bones surrounding a straight nose and full lips.

"Look, I guess I wasn't too logical when I talked to you before. A bad day and good wine. Let me say it more clearly now. Franklin Mo is nothing to me other than a lost opportunity. Let me put it this way," she continued slowly, "I remember the last time we met. Civilized, we all sat in the one side of a long table in the employees' lunch room and, settling down from little exchanges, began to listen to announcements. He spoke first. His voice sliding along the words of well-being, ignoring complaints, but soliciting smug satisfaction in the group. A group groping for guidance. There was no truth, fact or objectives, only status quo in bureaucratic ennui and bungling.

"I knew instantaneously the irritation, the annoyance, the competition I felt and still the ever-present weak trill of my own voice, never booming forth, calling out, exposing him and his sacrosanct, slimy confidence. I was the coward, silent, soft, a muted monkey to his great aping.

"The meeting ended, we all trailed away into the thicket of our jobs. Acquiescence of this display and my husband's illness led me to walk away all told. Now I'm going for a real walk, goddamn it. Out in the courtyard. It will take them a good half hour before he's cleaned up. You'll have to come along or not. I need some air."

They went down the small shiny elevator and into a beige lobby of veined vinyl tile. In an alcove stood two vending machines, one for drinks and one for brightly covered treats of potato chips and candy bars.

"Out here," she motioned and went down a back corridor. The door outside opened to a small area with built-up flowerbeds and a couple of olive trees surrounded by benches. She sat down and looked up at what must have been her husband's window and then down again to her hands, which she rubbed back and forth.

Laughlin sat beside her and said nothing. The area was another little dedicated oasis from pain like those he'd seen in hospitals. Simple remembrance plaques set out by good and naive sufferers trying to do something.

"Look, it's okay if you leave. I liked Eric Manfred. We had good discussions about books and he was a kind and decent man. I have no idea why he knew Franklin Mo, and I'm sorry. If I think of anything, I'll let you know. I do know he had a sister in LA."

"Yes, he said he wanted her to have the bookstore and something about not dying raging. Does that mean anything?"

"Well, his sister is not god's gift to the book world according to him, but who knows." She paused, smiled, and then recited "'Do not go gentle into that good night. Old age should burn and rage at close of day. Rage, rage against the dying of the light.'"

"It's from that poem? Is that what he said?"

"I'm sure you must know it. Dylan Thomas. It's a good ending. Mr. Manfred knew it. Yet you said he didn't die raging."

"That's right."

"Oh well, he at least died quoting a great poem. That's a rage in itself in this day and age, right?"

Laughlin was silent until she suddenly stood up to return to her dying husband. Dylan Thomas wrote another poem. "A fine one, 'Though lovers be lost love shall not, and death shall have no dominion.'" She took his hand and held it. "Thank you for accepting my apology." Taken off guard by her gesture, he stifled the impulse to hug her.

He mumbled goodbye, watched her return through the glistening door, and then walked around the building to the parking lot. He was going to go to the station now. He thought of Mr. Weber. How does a man shit in his pants in front of his wife and face her again? That takes courage. What did she say? "And death shall have no dominion."

Dylan Thomas, was that a clue? That guy had been a raging alcoholic.

How did the whole line go, "Though lovers be lost, love shall not"—or something like that—"and death shall have no dominion"?

Nonsense and yet profound,. How does anyone keep any hope, much less mental health, in this world, which was really a mess?

Chapter 16

While Laughlin had tried talking to Eugene and ended his day trying to rescue women in distress, that morning Max had found the sister's house off Westwood Boulevard and Pico, a small trim house with the ubiquitous four-by-four pillars on the 1950s built porch. Isabel Manfred Porter was shorter than her name suggested, and Max bent at his knees to help equalize their heights. She looked him over quickly, checked the badge, and invited him into her home. The room they sat in had large front windows, two green wingback chairs, a rocking chair, and a settee of gnarled gargoyle-looking carved wood all standing on a geometric-patterned rug.

"Now what can I do for you, Officer?" she asked while gesturing for him to take a wingback chair next to a roaring fire. She sat on patterned rocker and covered herself with a crocheted blanket of green and yellow zigzags.

Max began sweating in the dense heat of the room and longed for the outside again, but answered politely, "We need some background on your brother and any ideas you might have on why he would be shot."

In the elevated temperature, the woman's white face, when she swept away straight black bangs, looked like a hard-boiled egg with eyes, nose, and pursed mouth drawn on the surface. On her lap she repositioned two striped yellow stuffed cats. She wore a white long-sleeve blouse and a plaid pleated skirt with brown plastic boots up to her knees.

"Well, foremost, he didn't have a will that I can find anyway. He basically lived in the old store, and his condo was a stark storage place for old books and not for him. He made me so angry, never visiting, never caring about anything but his books, and now he wants me to have it all. I don't want it."

"Did you see your brother often, Mrs. Porter?" Max asked while studying the ivory complexion of the straightforward woman, who looked nothing like her brother.

"Not too often. He and I were different from the beginning. You know how sisters and brothers are. Neither of us married, but we both had causes. Mother was a social worker, and Father was an accountant, and my brother went into books, and I went into running a cleaning business."

"Do you know any of his friends? Do you know a Franklin Mo? Do you have the address of your brother's apartment?" Max felt he had to be more direct or get nowhere fast.

"Hold on a minute, one question at a time. I'm not a machine, you know. Let me see," Mrs. Porter fired back. She put on round black framed glasses, quickly got up, pushing the toys cats off gently, opened a door near the only side window in the hot room, and waved her hand for Max to follow. The room was full of file cabinets and two large-screen desktop computers. Alongside these were intricate old cabinet built-ins with paintings of seascapes on them.

"I can leave the cats in the living room. They're fake, in case you didn't know, since I'm allergic. Now start again with the questions," she instructed and highlighted a file with Manfred's name and entered friends of Eric Manfred. No names came up.

"That's not too promising," Max noted out loud.

"Isn't that the truth, you astute young man," Mrs. Porter agreed, pushing her bangs back quickly.

"He must at least have had some business acquaintances, you know, for the bookstore." While Max looked around, he enjoyed an air conditioner going full blast.

"You'd think so, but after he hired that maniac Moody, I never had anything more to do with the store."

That declaration startled the sheriff's deputy and he began to reevaluate this supposedly starchy woman. She went on, not missing a swallow or a breath.

"He used to have some special customers when I helped him out, and he bought good books from some of them when they wanted to trade up or down. He never did anything illegal and always ran a respectable place until she came in and made eyes at him and unbuttoned his"—she paused, typed in a few words and then finished with—"his prudence and pants."

Max stood still and looked over her shoulder. Up came a list of people's names and he spotted among them the name Franklin Mo.

"Ma'am, maybe you could clarify a couple things for me, please," Max began slowly. "Did you know this man?"

"As far as I know, Franklin Mo was only around because of that Moody moll at the psych hospital. If he bought a book much less read one, I wouldn't know."

"I thought you said that you had a cleaning business and your brother ran the store, but then you said you had worked at the store."

"True on both accounts. When I started out, I wasn't doing well, and Eric asked me to help him out. That was about twenty-odd years ago, something like 1976, something like that. It wasn't my thing, but I did it anyway."

"Were you married then? You said you and your brother never married, but you call yourself Mrs. Porter."

"Oh please, what do you know about women in business? I had to show some credibility and act respectable. I took to the image of Bette Davis in *Now Voyager*. You're probably too young to remember that old movie but I liked to watch her make the transition to glamorous. I, however, adopted the retiring brown thick-hose, brainy-girl look, and it did wonderfully for me because none of the millionaire matrons were intimidated or threatened by me and my Chicano crews. I would go into the interview and give them a fairy tale about being without my dead husband, having to take care of my poor cats and promising to mind their homes like they were my own—me, the poor, struggling, humble waif of forty-two years. Damn if I didn't score big and raise my prices for the great job I did caring for their possessions and not their husbands. That launched me, and Manfred's bookstore did all right too, until big book chains became the trendy place to be seen, and the Moody thing asked for a job." She poked another computer key, took a breath and said, "Oh, goodness gracious, sit down. I won't bite."

Max shook his head and took the seat she offered. She certainly didn't need the hot stuffy room. Her demeanor had melted into a tough and straightforward ice pick.

"So tell me about yourself. You picked up quickly on any of my apparent discrepancies. Are you going to get the fool who killed my innocent brother? Maybe they were after Moody, not Manfred. That's a big possibility in my mind."

"Why is that, Mrs. Porter?"

"Did you get the pun about Porter? Husband carried bags and wife cleaned houses. It was a blast. I thought of Butler as a name but decided that was too obvious. Also, I decided I couldn't completely lie about the cats, so I got stuffed animals. Furry things get me sick for real. What was it you asked?"

"Why someone might want to kill the Moody girl?"

"Deputy Max, you'd be a good bookkeeper. You follow up on statements."

"Need to follow up as a detective too, Mrs. Porter."

"Oh, that's probably true. Gets you farther as a black man too, doesn't it?"

Max nodded, but he didn't like the comments too centered on him and redirected, "The Moody girl, what about her?"

"She is a second-class tart when she's on drugs, pretending to be alone in the world, and sucking up to old men who need their itchy egos stroked, if you get what I mean. She suckered my brother for all he was worth. He said he was merely helping a distressed widow. Huh? It'll be the same with that Franklin Lo guy as well."

"Franklin Mo," Max offered.

"Franklin Mo, Lo, Ho, so and so. Who cares?"

"He's missing, and your brother has been killed."

"Look, ask me what you want and I'll try to cooperate."

"Why did you think the Moody woman might have been the target?"

"I told you. She was a bad girl, who bit off, so to speak, more than she could chew."

Eric Manfred's sister extolled on her dear brother now that he was dead, added some more bitterness but not informative answers to Max's questions, and the conversation tapered off to childhood memories.

Max left after getting the condominium address of Manfred and not much else. The list of contacts to the store, which include Mo, was extensive and had to be run down, at least by phone. He'd take a look at the apartment first and then meet Laughlin at the station.

But the plan changed when Ms. Moody finally was spotted coming into her apartment building. Max beat it over to Culver City to make sure she didn't disappear again. Laughlin arrived late after his escape from the hospice to back him up.

"There's no back exit. We'll go up together."

Laughlin knocked quietly and waited. He knocked again.

"I'm coming. Who the hell is it?" a man's voice said.

"Sheriff's detectives. We need to talk to Ms. Moody." Laughlin wondered where a man come from, considering the apartment had been staked out without that information.

Max shook his head and pulled his gun.

A tall thin man with a full beard and no hair opened the door. "What? What did you say?" He rubbed his eyes with his knuckles and farted. "Gees, I was asleep. It's late. What didja want?"

"Ms. Moody."

"She don't live here. She lives down the way, uses this damn address, and it ticks me off."

Of course, by the time they got to the right apartment, there was no answer. The super opened the door, but there was nothing but a few open drawers and limp clothes in an apartment full of bunched up pillows and not much else.

"What a bust," Max stated flatly.

Laughlin peered out the window, looking at the street below where headlights were glaring. He turned suddenly and bolted out the door. Talking five stairs at a time and jumping over the railings, he pulled his gun and pointed it at a small yellow car that was squealing out of the covered parking. It stopped in front of the crouched sheriff with his gun clutched in both hands. When Laughlin stood up, it appeared that he could have picked up the car by the bumper and towed it himself. Elvira Moody was behind the wheel, stunned and stopped.

Max sauntered over and opened the car door. Ms. Moody got out shaking. She was wearing a bright blue feather boa and an orange dress.

"Listen, you assholes, nothing I can say. I have to get away, and you can't stop me. I didn't do anything and you can't stop me. I was on my way and you can't stop me. I don't know about all this, and Mr. Manfred was a smart man and he adored me and I don't know about all this and there is nothing I can say. I've got to get out of here and you can't stop me," she squealed and fluffed her hair with a hand full of giant rings. Her whole body jingled with bracelets and big beaded necklaces.

"Hold on a minute. We need to talk to you."

"No, no, no. You can't stop me like this. I need to get going. I need to go to the bank and the store and the cleaners and get the bus to San Diego. I need to get some lipstick and—"

"Calm down and tell us what you know about Franklin and Gene. How did they figure in the bookstore?" Laughlin insisted as he slipped his gun back in the holster.

"Shove it. I don't know a thing. I do not know a fucking thing. Why the big need to connect these guys? Jesus Christ, leave them and me along!" the agitated woman screamed and took a swipe at Max with her buckled purse. "I'll call the police if you keep trying to capture me."

Laughlin stepped up and held her. She squirmed and yelled, "Help, help! Police!" She started to bite his arms and kick.

They took her to the county psychiatric emergency room. She could be heard all over the hall yelling "help" and "get me my lipstick." It was quiet in the actual area except for Ms. Moody fuming. The room had a few curtains around gurneys waiting for the night influx. The detectives milled around the nurse's desk. A psychiatrist came over and said she was a well-known "manic" usually drug-induced, and she would be there on a seventy-two-hour hold. She met the criteria. Talking with her would have to wait. They heard her reciting the words "Lover come back to me. I'm waiting here for you. Lover come back to me" as they walked out.

Laughlin and Max returned to Elvira's apartment but found nothing relevant to Franklin Mo's disappearance. They sat down and considered their search for a connection.

"We're looking for this tie in between the missing man and the dead one because of Nora Weber. Because of Eugene and Jeffrey. Because of the bookstore label at Mo's house."

"All of them, right?"

Max related his interview with Mrs. Porter, and they decided to go look at Eric Manfred's condo to start the next day.

CHAPTER 17

Morning gusts of warm winds cantered from the desert covering the basin. The Manfred's home was silent and stifling, absorbing the heat in a town house complex in Santa Monica, one of a string of eight. His was an end unit with a fenced-in patio and a balcony overlooking an alley. Max had a key from Manfred's sister. The place was still off-limits to an anxious condo manager and owner. She was watering the lawn, questioned who the detectives were, and said Manfred had been up-to-date with his condo fees and gave no one any trouble. He'd lived there since it was built in 1973. His death was a real shock to everyone. The detective assured the woman their's was an official visit, and with that, she trundled back to her unit at the head of the houses.

Inside they found books piled like small skyscrapers. The downstairs consisted of one dining room table made of what appeared to be walnut, three matching wooden chairs, along with an overstuffed blue and green flowered chair and a bronze floor lamp. The walls were covered with bookshelves filled with books in perfect alignment. The jackets and fronts gave the impression of one enormous scroll of colored bar codes. The kitchen was spare and orderly with a shelf of cookbooks along one wall. The refrigerator had milk, butter, and eggs, plus a book on finances with seven twenty-dollar bills lying in the vegetable drawer.

A small upstairs bedroom contained a single made-up bed with a solid blue cover, an overstuffed chair exactly twin to the one downstairs, and a duplicate bronze floor lamp and floor covered with stacks of books. The closets had built-in shelves with more books. A few suits and stretched-out sweaters hung in the occasional empty spaces, and built-in drawers held shirts, modest jockey shorts and dark blue socks.

The larger bedroom was also lined with bookshelves filled with leather-bound books and one small reading table next to a padded chair. It held an old cube Macintosh computer and scratch pads. Both bathrooms had open books Manfred apparently had placed on little footstools for reading. The garage down below had stacks of books still to be shelved but piled in precise towers.

"Now I know what obsessive-compulsive disorder is!" Max exclaimed. He sat down on one of the dining room chairs.

Laughlin laughed and began studying the books. "I think they're grouped according to the author, but it's hard to figure it all out. Look here, this series is all by Melville, but it's next to Saul Bellow's books."

"How the hell do you sort through all these books and maintain your sanity? Are there some mental health books to tie him to Franklin Mo? Maybe that could explain his knowing Franklin."

"Good questions, Max. Let's go back upstairs and take a more thorough look. Come on, we owe it to the bookman."

In the heavily grained reading table there was a file box with a myriad of index cards like a library. The square old computer opened up, but the only document was a list of books to match the index cards and addresses of other bookstores. No personal correspondence was in the files.

"So where are his accounting books and bills and stuff?" Max asked.

"Maybe he kept those at the store. All I found at the store was that journal. I don't remember, but we didn't go through the desks here yet," Laughlin answered. He opened drawers but found nothing.

"I tell you I've seen enough of apartments. We've had a real tour. Has it gotten us any information? Nope," Max expounded.

"Well, you can say these apartments reflect their owners. Franklin's was like a hidden but raging narcissist, and I use the word in its strictest sense. Of course, his San Marino house was a gem. I didn't get to see Manfred's sister, but from what you described, maybe a split personality or at least hot and cold. Of course, Moody's orange pillows certainly have an over-the-top quality just like her mood."

"What about our bookstore man, at his home at least?"

"Safe to say, he loved books, that's for sure."

"Brilliant. I think I liked the tile in the Pasadena place the best, you know, the fountain and the stairs going up to the second floor. Of course, Mo messed up the apartment itself."

Laughlin took a deep breath and nodded. "All these places have only one thing in common. These people had enough money to pay for them, not like Gene and the mysterious Jeffrey, who lives at the board and care."

"Yeah. Money, money is the answer. I tell you I remember my first apartment here. A little place off Adams. Great big house with an enormous banister and built-ins in every room. Mine had a fireplace, but the john was down the hall. I got out when I could put a deposit down for first and last months' rent on a real pad with my own shower."

"Me"—Laughlin rubbed his chin—"I had this apartment in Venice. Third floor in an old yellow brick building where the rats had better accommodations than I ever saw in Detroit. I wish I owned that place now. It's near the beach and all spruced up to its original glory."

"Who's to know what fortune favors?" Max speculated, laughed, and nodded wisely.

"Well, I've got my house now. It's a pain in the ass to keep up, but it does give me privacy."

"What do you need that for, old man?"

Laughlin ignored the teasing and pondered, "How did Manfred maintain this place with what income must have come out of the bookstore? I wonder if there're any great books here—collector or auction quality stuff? You said Manfred's sister didn't care about the bookstore. I wonder if she's seen this place."

"I say we eat," Max suggested.

"No dinner with Kim?"

"Nope, she went to see her grandmother, and you?"

"Nope," Laughlin offered no more about his Denny's dinner but concurred with, "Good thinking. The pier has some reasonable places, and we can cool off at the beach with a beer. Just hold on one sec. I want to see if I can find Dylan Thomas. You know the guy Manfred asked us to talk to. Look for a book with his name on it."

They found nothing but more editions of his poetry in the humid closet of the small bedroom. It was past five in the afternoon when they shut the apartment door and walked into the evening; the air still thick with heat and humidity.

"I don't see any smoke smudging the sky, but fire season is coming for sure," Max observed.

"Yup, maybe we'll get some rain before the winds really take over," Laughlin added. "It's weird to get ashes of burnt trees like snowflakes floating down on cars. Hope for rain."

Chapter 18

And rain it did—all that night. Laughlin listened to the pounding water but didn't worry about his roof. He'd patched it the year before. A sultry dawn followed.

He awoke rested and peered out at the backyard. There were a few branches down, but mainly everything looked clean. In the front, there were dark curled palm tree fronds littering the street, but again, everything looked cleaner. That very morning, one week since they started the case, Laughlin and Max finally were to meet with the director of mental health. He'd been away on vacation. The medical director and the mental health chief legal counsel had been testifying at the Board of Supervisors about big plans for the mentally ill in Los Angeles, which took priority over dead or missing people.

The office building in the Wilshire district looked like a department store white oblong gift box or a poorly constructed faux marble tower. It was in stark relief to the one or two-story businesses wrapped in red and black Asian calligraphies. Within walking distance of the metro station, nevertheless, cars piled up all over it in the mini malls up and down the street.

The detectives stopped at the squeezed-in ground floor snack shop and got ice coffees and relief offered by the air-conditioning.

"Should be in Rosarito with margaritas now," Max lamented.

"Or in the ocean, body surfing, not sweating like pigs," Laughlin added.

A narrow elevator of marred sides and stained floor carried them to the top, and they stepped out into a wide pasty hall. The blond walls were peeling like eucalyptus bark. To the left, they found a large room of desks, files, cardboard boxes and papers distributed on most of the available floor space.

"This looks more like a movie set for a newspaper than the offices of the Department of Mental Health," Max mumbled.

Laughlin stood and took it all in. There were spokes of side offices every few feet and suit types busy deciding the fates of their ill minions. No one approached and no one even looked at them.

Laughlin took the lead and approached a streaked blond, full-bodied woman of indeterminate age in a light green dress. She was carrying an armful of charts toward an empty desk tucked in a corner when he intercepted her with "Excuse me, miss, er, ms, I'm here to talk to the director. We have an appointment. Where do I find him?"

The woman had red plastic-framed glasses embedded in a thickly powdered face with just a touch of wrinkles around her eyes, which transformed into crevices when she set her bright eyes and smile on him.

"Oh, yes. You must be Sergeant Laughlin. I'm Gloria Cross, Dr. Pinkley's administrative assistant. He's on his way," she said, putting the charts on the clean surface, and gestured for the detectives to sit down. "You are?" she asked Max.

"Senior Deputy Joseph Max."

"Would you like some coffee or a donut?"

"No, we're fine."

"You're here about Franklin, right?"

The detectives nodded, and Laughlin asked what she knew about Mr. Mo.

"It's been difficult with the reorganization and so many staff shuffles. We lost track, I'm afraid, of some of our managers, especially those at the jail. It used to be that a psychiatrist was the head of mental health but the county supervisors didn't understand much about the differences in degrees and training. They began giving the position to the psychologists and social workers and finally to business administrators. Things got a little confusing administratively. That was years ago, but it set up power struggles, and I think that Franklin wasn't popular with people who'd had years more of training than he did."

"Whom exactly were these power struggles with?" Laughlin asked and leaned forward to signal his interest in Ms. Cross's opinions. She leaned forward too and began to talk more softly.

"I guess he didn't think training in mental health was that necessary to being an administrator, although he had some sort of social work degree. He said it was more important to run the organization no matter what the organization was. I think that was Dr. Pinkley's philosophy and Franklin shared it. He felt justified in ordering psychiatrists and psychologists around even though he hadn't the long tenure at the state mental hospital that Dr. Pinkley had."

"What's Dr. Pinkley's degree?" Max asked quietly.

"Dr. Pinkley is a business administrator with a bachelor's in accounting. I don't know his other degree. He was the chief administrator of the biggest state hospital in California before it closed. He knows a lot about running things, advanced from a general accountant to chief. I guess that's why they chose him. Of course, there weren't too many applicants at the time he came. Pay and problems made the job awfully undesirable, but things are getting better."

"Franklin Mo, who did he have run-ins with?"

"Let me think," she answered and shuffled some papers.

"Anybody come to mind?"

"Well, he didn't seem to care about what the patients might have as far as mental illness goes, just so they behaved, and that went double as far as caring for the staff. Did you ask Fred Poplar? I mean, he knows."

Ms. Cross sat up suddenly and said, "Well, I hope you get what you need for the case. Here's Dr. Pinkley. I'm sure he can answer all your questions."

Coming into the room was a trim man clothed in a speckled brown tweed suit and light brown shoes. A delicate mustache centered his face, which was framed in gray sideburns and topped with a reddish-brown head of hair. His pants made a scuffing sound as he hurried across to shake hands with the detectives. He had been delayed because of traffic but quickly ushered them into a conference room where they could sit and talk in private.

"What can I do for you? Honestly, Franklin Mo and the jail were not our main priority. The Department of Justice may make us focus more on that area than we have previously. Those suicides and deaths and all. You see, our mental health department, separate from the county health department, has many divisions including child adolescent services, adult outpatient clinics, hospitals, conservatorships, and the jails. It's lot to juggle.

"I have to say that this man's disappearance is a complete mystery to me. Anything you can tell me about it?"

Laughlin took a sip of his coffee in the hopes of overcoming the distinct smell of mothballs emanating from the director's clothes. He looked again at this guy and saw corroded teeth in the ingratiating smile and a striped tie embossed with what looked like ketchup.

"We're here to get your thoughts. It seems no one even knew there was a problem until he had been gone for a couple of months. Why is that? Didn't he have to report to someone?"

"Well, Franklin Mo was hired before I became director. He was reporting to us about once a month. As I said, he seemed to do his job. We didn't hear any particulars about him. No problems. Oh, here is out chief counsel and our medical director. I need to talk to them about the supervisors' meeting after they finish with you."

Entering the office were two small, neatly dressed men. One clothed with a three-piece beige suit, a tie that matched his pocket-handkerchief, and a smile of condescension. He was the attorney according to his name tag. The other, red hair combed into a parted mat, a herringbone jacket and khaki pants, wore a tired, bored look and sat down immediately. He was, by elimination, the medical director.

"I'm sorry but I am going to have to leave you. I think these gentlemen can help you with any questions you might have," the director explained, stood up, and started out the door without further facilitation.

Laughlin stopped him, introduced Max and himself again, and queried all three about their knowledge of Manfred and their thoughts about the murder. Each of them denied knowing him well and each had unasked for alibis.

The director looked at his watch and this time asked to leave. Laughlin nodded okay.

"I've got to talk to you for a minute, Peter," the lawyer said as he slipped out of the room with Dr. Pinkley.

"I'm Adam Berryman. What can I do for you?" the baggy-eyed medical director offered.

"Has anyone got further information on Franklin Mo?" Max answered.

"I don't know what you have already, but Franklin was mainly at the jail after he moved from a clinic up north in the early '90s or thereabouts. Most of the jail staff are under his separate administration, and he reports to us," Dr. Berryman responded while opening his laptop and tapping away. "I'm merely recording our conversation with the supervisors while it's fresh in my mind. Please ask any questions."

"Who did he report to when he did report?" Laughlin asked impatiently.

"The administrators had their monthly meeting and usually Peter Pinkley, the director, Curtis Dash, the attorney, the chiefs of the main divisions, and me. A secretary sat in. I'm sorry I can't give you more information."

"Aren't you the medical director?"

"Yes," replied Berryman absentmindedly as he continued to type a little on the computer, and then looked up. "If you really want to know, let me clarify some things for you. About twenty-five years ago, the supervisors decided that anyone could run mental health. You didn't need to be a physician.

"Used to be historically that physicians ran the state hospitals where the mentally ill patients were separated away from society. The doctors were called superintendents, and there weren't many other types of mental health personnel except nurses and attendants to manage the patients.

"Two things happened after World War II. Many more doctors— that is psychiatrists who had medical degrees—moved out into public arenas with the novelty of psychoanalysis and medication discoveries like antidepressants that were associated with the needs of non-psychotic patients."

"You talking about treatment for mental illness spreading its wings?" Laughlin interjected.

"Yes, that's a reasonable image. Why should psychiatrists limit their professional expertise? The economy was booming. Neurosis was fascinating and treatable in offices. People complained and struggled and needed help.

"Others got interested in mental health big time, the army, psychologists, social workers, psych-techs, psych nurses, and all sorts of degrees were given out from all sorts of places, some legit like universities, some dubious, some mail-order diplomas. Everybody got to be called a so-called therapist and even titled as doctor. The public was okay with it all and assumed some sort of homogeneous training, but that's not so," Berryman expounded.

"Licenses from the state are still needed, right?" Max added.

"True, if the therapist cares to label himself. However, the second big thing that happened was Kennedy wanted outpatient mental health clinics instead of state hospitals so that made it even easier to distribute undesirables. It was to be a bonanza for the field.

"The clinics never really happened, and the mentally ill began their migration to the streets along with the bums. The department got inundated with needy patients, but no one was sure who would lead the rescues," the medical director looked up from his computer, stared at Laughlin for a moment to see if he understood and then returned to his laptop.

"Are you saying you have limited authority?" Laughlin asked.

"Damn right. That's the way it is, yet physicians retain all the responsibilities of what happens to the patients in the county system. We have many other types of trained chefs in the kitchen, but we get to be responsible for the soup if it sickens and when big trouble happens to patients."

"Mental health seems as dysfunctional as any big organization. Why the split from the health department? Did it help?" Laughlin asked.

"Oh, you heard about that. Well, that happened a little later as a political move to get more money. The split is really ironic, goddamn it, especially now when it is strikingly obvious more than ever that mental illness and brain malfunction are evidently intimately connected." Berryman turned his head, bit his lip, and sought the computer again. His frown slid the plastered hair along the scalp.

"Jail services were not a big focus, and Franklin Mo could do what he wanted, considering he was an unobserved player in this whole setup. Does that sum it up, Dr. Berryman?" Laughlin asked.

The medical director nodded in a slow rhythm similar to his typing.

Max checked his cell phone, which rang with Sting's "Every Breath You Take, I'll be watching you" and his face went sour. He stared as he listened, and Laughlin asked Dr. Berryman one more question, "Do you know of anyone who Franklin Mo considered an enemy?"

The doctor pursed his lips together, swallowed and said, "You'd have to ask Mr. Dash. They were friends of a sort."

"Excuse us a minute, Doctor," Max said softly and tilted his head to Laughlin to follow him.

"What's up? I need something good to happen."

"Sorry, that was Daniels. Eugene split, and Dr. Poplar from the jail called."

"Max, are ever going to get rid of that song? What the hell, how did Eugene get away? He was in restraints when I saw him."

"Staff apparently let him out to hop around and pee. He threw a match in a wastebasket and, while everyone was distracted, rolled out with a wheelchair down the hill and off into the crowds. Security said they looked around but couldn't really stop him when his hold expired."

Mr. Dash came back in to the conference room. Berryman picked up his computer and left, and Laughlin asked the attorney why Eugene hadn't been held longer.

The little man had a gravelly, deep voice, a George C. Scott sound, which he definitely liked to use, and he sat down to expound on the ins and outs of the Lanterman-Petris-Short Act, which had been enacted about fifty years ago to prevent people from being held without due process.

"You see, gentleman, you can only hold a person against his or her will who is a danger to self, others, or gravely disabled. If you hold them, you have to justify it after seventy-two hours, that's three days, for another fourteen days. Of course, there are more ways you can hold people longer but we won't go into that here. Now, what can I do for you?" he inquired politely.

"Like a conservatorship or a ninety-day hold, for example," Laughlin added to indicate knowledge of the law.

"True, true," the lawyer agreed and blinked hard a few times as if something were in both his eyes. "I don't know about this patient because he was at the county hospital, part of the department of health, so I can't comment further. Anything else you would like to know?"

The gist of Dash's observations consisted of his "deep respect for Franklin Mo" but his "very limited acquaintance" with him while he was overseeing the jail. With further questioning, he said he had been to Mo's house for dinner a couple of times, but now his wife was sick, and so he didn't see him much anymore. His eyes blinked repeatedly, and his handshake was like holding a cooked spaghetti. He strolled out of the conference room before them.

Max offered a side comment, "What's with the eyes? Is he trying to focus or avoid any relevant information?"

"I think it's a tic. Word has it, he was a former litigator who couldn't earn a decent living and took this position as a graceful way out of his financial dilemmas. What did Poplar want?"

"He said he needs to talk with us and could we please meet him at the head psychiatrist's office in the jail. I guess your cell phone was off."

Laughlin checked his pocket and flipped his cell phone. It had a blank screen. "Damn it. I must be going senile."

"There, there, man, you've no real excuse," Max admonished.

"Well, I'll tell you this, senile or crazy, I wouldn't want to consult with these mental health guys. They're an evasive, punting bureaucratic clan and depressed as hell, maybe that's the side effect of dealing with mental illness."

"Yeah, and these are our mental health leaders. One with mothballs, one with doormat hair and one with a blinking disorder, and that's not a substitute for a swear word."

"Oh, you're a mean critic, Max. I'm not sure whether they really know any more or are trying to cover up what they do know. 'Underwhelming' would be a good word for the whole department," Laughlin concluded. "It's troublesome when you think of all that can go on in the jail and no one has time to look at it. One big mentally ill problem and lots of sick people roaming around on their own. I wonder if they're better off sleeping with drugs on third street rather than being rounded up and taken to jail. Those department guys are brainy enough, but they got lost in the morass of too disorganized an organization."

"Exactly! Disorganized organization. Now for lunch and then jail."

CHAPTER 19

The chief psychiatrist's office was buried in the Twin Towers, down the corridor from the medical ward for mentally ill patients. It was furnished all in steel. Burnished expanses, cabinets, and rails of five cold chairs surrounded him as he sat with his arms propped up on the six-foot desk surface. He had been scrutinizing Freddy Poplar until the sheriff's men pulled open the steel door and entered. Then he stood up and smiled. His light brown eyes and sandy eyebrows matched his hair, a broad smile finishing his face, which was long and symmetrical like his body. His silver wire-rimmed glasses reflected the overhead fluorescent light but could not detract entirely from sharp eyes.

"Sergeant Laughlin? Come in, come in."

"This is Deputy Max, Dr. Brandt."

"Yes, we've already met. Please sit down. I think you will find Fred's statement interesting," Brandt added and then sat down to face the still sweating Freddy Poplar.

Laughlin noted the room decorated with large woodcuts on the walls, a beer stein filled with pens and pencils sat on a desk stacked with paper piles. This guy went right to the point of the meeting.

"I tell you, Dr. Brandt, this is too hard to tell. My whole life I've been a decent man and this—"

"You still are a decent man, Fred. This is merely a stumble off the right path, and you'll get on again right now," Brandt offered.

Poplar sighed and took a shredded Kleenex out of his pocket to pat his forehead. Brandt pulled some fresh tissues from a box nearby and offered them as well. The sweating man took them and wadded them up.

Poplar took another deep sigh and began, "A couple of months, no, three months ago, Franklin Mo asked me to do something unethical. He said it was vital to him, and he would make sure I got a very good evaluation. I need it. I was hoping for a grade increase. My family and all. I needed the good eval, and he wouldn't give it to me otherwise. He even said so."

Brandt sat quietly with his hands intertwined. The elaborate explanation didn't bother him, but Laughlin was impatient for the finale and Max was looking over his notebook, a sign of his boredom.

"I knew it was wrong, but Mr. Mo kept telling me it was for the good of a patient and would have a happy ending. That was all before he disappeared—Franklin, that is—and I don't know what happened then. I only just read about Eric Manfred's death and got really upset. I didn't have anything to do with it, believe me."

Laughlin finally broke in. "What did you do that was so ethically wrong? Tell us, please, if it will help with this case."

"See, that's what I'm not sure about."

"Well, maybe the sergeant here could make that determination for you, Fred," Brandt suggested.

"Yes, give us a try, Dr. Poplar, give us a try," Laughlin urged.

"Well, he asked me . . . he asked me to look up the personnel records of Dr. Weber."

"Dr. Nora Weber, the psychiatrist?"

"Yes, yes. It's true. I was going to be down at the mental health offices filing an application for a new psychologist, and he wanted me to pull the file and copy it. I did it."

"What did he want it for? Do you know?"

"It was easy. I got her social, her age, and address, even her husband's car license plate, all that stuff."

"For what?"

"I don't know. It was strange because he never cared about her before. He just said he was doing a favor for a friend, and she might not understand, so it was best he knew as much about her as necessary, and there would be this happy ending. The only other thing I did, which wasn't really my job, was later he had me deliver a letter to Mr. Manfred at his bookstore. I was just to drop it on the desk while looking around. It was easy and I got my good evaluation that next day."

"Did you talk to Manfred or watch him open the letter?"

"No, no. That purple woman was there. Elvira. She told me her name and said she was running the store. She took the letter and tried to sell me some books on outer space. I left in a hurry."

"Did you ever go there again or get any clue about the letter?"

"No, no," Poplar whined and wiped his forehead with his ever present rumpled tissue.

"How was the letter addressed?"

"It was typewritten and sealed. I didn't try to open it."

"And did you see Franklin Mo again after you gave him the information and delivered the letter?"

"Yes, when he gave me my evaluation. He was very pleased and told me that I could go home early that day. I did. I didn't see him after that. He was always off at conferences and trips. I didn't think anything of it. Is it related to Mr. Manfred's death?"

"Are you sure you don't remember anything else?"

"I am, I am. Oh, this is so terrible. Do you think Franklin is okay?"

"Well, we don't know at this point, but your information helps us tie Mr. Manfred directly with Franklin Mo. Thank you. If you think of anything else, here's my card and number."

Fred Poplar stood up, looked down to the floor like a beaten Saint Bernard, bowed three times, said he was "so sorry," and left the room.

Dr. Brandt pushed his chair away from the desk and asked the detectives if they wanted any coffee, left the room for a moment, and came back with three full Styrofoam cups.

"You can believe Fred. I think that's all he knows." Brandt took a sip from his cup and then took his glasses off to clean them with his tie. The silver wires that held the lenses looked like they could be bent easily and Brandt handled them carefully. His eyes were deep set and looked exposed surrounded by indention marks from the glasses.

"Was Franklin Mo that powerful?" Laughlin asked while watching intently as the psychiatrist wiped his glasses.

"Way unethical to go snooping in someone else's records," Max added.

"Off the record, gentleman, he intimidated many staff, insecure staff. Nora Weber clashed with Franklin about his use or abuse of authority. There was an aura about Mo, or maybe everything about him, that irritated Dr. Weber and when she had her own family problems, she left. My philosophy was to bide my time and get him out eventually. The county works slowly but in the long run, it usually gets things right," Dr. Brandt offered and then sipped his coffee again.

"What is it about him that so many people are intimidated?"

"Good question, Deputy Max. People with his kind of confidence can corral others with fear. Remember, the staff is often no more sophisticated than the inmates. The jail milieu of control and strict hierarchy can breed intimidation even in supposedly free people as well as inmates."

"How do you protect against taking advantage of innocents or ignorance or power?" Laughlin asked.

"Someone like Franklin Mo is an unfathomable person. No one knew where he stood on any particular issue. He wavered with the wind. Yet as time went on, his need for deference became apparent. He would destroy uncooperative underlings with unsubstantiated gossip. Uncoiling his arrogance, he revealed himself. You understand this is all off the record, but I am angry about it nevertheless.

"Of course, he hasn't been around since I've made some further changes in procedures. That will irritate him I assume, but I'm not sure he would give up what authority he has with the staff members he claims he supervises. That's going to have to be solved soon at the director's level."

"I'm not sure what you mean by the term 'unfathomable?' Is it the Asian 'inscrutable' thing?" Laughlin challenged.

"I'm not prejudice against Asians if that was what you thought the implication was. Anyone could have those traits regardless of race, creed, gender, and the like. 'Unfathomable' was my poor way of defining someone whose values were too noncommittal, too amorphous, too removed, too flexible, and, in all likelihood, loaded with antisocial personality traits. No matter how deep you dug, you couldn't find out what he stood for," Brandt answered smiling.

Laughlin smiled back, nodded and offered, "I've known many an inmate who meets that description, but why was an administrator allowed to bully the likes of Dr. Poplar. Isn't your job to oversee?"

"Yeah, when the person is supposedly caring for the mentally ill," Max added.

"With the constant problem of trying to hire at a jail, not a job as desirable as others in the outside world, you attract leftovers and many agendas besides the need to help."

"What about you? Are you a left over too?"

"Why did I come here, Sergeant Laughlin? In these last years, a lot of us came on here to do some good, believe it or not. Before we came, much of the jail system was calcifying. Leftovers or not, I have boards in neurology and psychiatry and wanted to look at all the brain-damaged kids who end up in jail. I thought with the right staff, we could do some rehabilitation and stop the revolving door. Too many mentally ill are shuffled off to jail because of limited psychiatric facilities and minor infractions like pot smoking and possession."

"So if he was on the staff, wouldn't Franklin Mo have to comply with those goals?" Laughlin asked.

"Don't give up on me, Laughlin. We're on the same side. To me, Franklin Mo cared about himself above all else and collected county money as a complacent status quo kinda guy. I have encounters with him periodically. Changing the goals of the jail mental health and cooperating with the sheriffs didn't give him the leverage he seemed to want. I haven't gotten all that I want either," Brandt offered.

"Sounds like you want big-time leverage too," Laughlin countered.

Max interrupted the parrying with "Well, thanks, Doc, for getting Mr. Poplar to admit his misdeeds."

"He's an example of the fear Franklin was able to instill in many of the staff. I hope Fred will protect himself better from now on."

"Maybe some other authorities like you should have stepped in to protect him if they knew this was going on." Laughlin added, "Anyway, thank you for the information, Dr. Brandt."

"Bill, Sergeant Laughlin, Deputy Max, call me anytime. I won't argue with you on the need for more intervention but the county setup doesn't give me all the authority I would like," Brandt replied.

Max stood up and Laughlin followed.

"I'm Joe and he's James, but there are so many of those names we go by our last names. No insult meant," Max said and offered his hand.

"Say, would you like to come with me to the staff meeting. About two hundred people. It might give you an idea of what we're dealing with."

Laughlin agreed. He and Max walked with the psychiatrist to a large meeting room with a string of tables around the periphery. One sheriff deputy with a thick dark mustache in full uniform sat alone at the end near the door.

Causally dressed individuals of all races and ages trickled in, scraped chairs, and fussed with papers. Dr. Poplar came in with the fifth-floor entourage. There was Dr. Mason clutching her files and Dr. Banting exchanging laughs with two of the psychiatrists, both with silver gray hair. During the meeting, someone complained about coverage and someone else complained about not enough overtime. Someone else complained about the new forms that had to be filled out on patients. Only one staffer asked whether Franklin was coming back or if they could use his office and no one had the answer. There were no other questions or protest about the missing man. He was gone as always.

Dr. Brandt explained the need for further hiring and justification for the forms to document mental status changes. Everyone looked bored and wanted to talk about Halloween.

After it was over, Dr. Brandt commented that it was like all other meetings, except these people were caring for the severely compromised.

"Good luck with that. I wonder if there isn't another Franklin Mo growing in this group to replace the one missing," Laughlin said pointedly. "I hope there's better screening soon."

Max added, "Thanks very much for your time, Doctor. I'm sure you understand our concerns."

"I do. Good luck."

The detectives left the conference room and stood for a moment in the hall until they got their bearing and then followed the lines to freedom.

CHAPTER 20

"What's with you, Sergeant Laughlin? You got a bug up your ass?" Max asked the minute they were out on the street.

"What are you talking about?"

"I mean the way you went at Brandt. The guy gave us a break in the case, so why the shit? What's with you and him?"

"Nothing, Jesus Christ, let's get out of here," Laughlin shot back abruptly.

They drove in silence, and when they got to the station, Laughlin said he'd see Max at report and they'd look into Elvira Moody again and her apartment, try to find Eugene, and recheck the bookstore for the letter or any connection with the dead and the missing men.

Max agreed and told Laughlin to get a good night's sleep. He again broached the attitude Laughlin had with Brandt but it went nowhere.

Laughlin shook his head, twisted his mouth in impatience and went to his car. The day was waning with stagnating heat. October should be less hot, he predicted, and turned on the air-conditioning, or at least it should have the Santa Ana winds. His cell phone disturbed his thoughts. The station had received a call from Dr. Poplar, who needed to talk with Laughlin immediately.

Poplar answered in a hushed voice, saying his teenage kids wanted to talk on the phone, but he wanted Laughlin to know that he, Freddy Poplar, was a good person and very sorry about the theft of materials. He was sick with worry over what had happened to his moral compass and that it caused a death.

"Hold on a minute, Dr. Poplar, take a breath. You didn't cause the death of Mr. Manfred. Take it easy."

"Yes, yes, you're right. I just wanted you to know I'll never do that ever again. I'm so sorry."

"I know, I know. You take it easy now. I'll keep you informed. You didn't kill him, okay?" Laughlin explained.

"Yes, yes. Thank you. I'm sorry."

"Take it easy. We'll get to the bottom of this. It's not your fault. Take it easy," Laughlin consoled. It was stupid to keep saying "take it easy," and he wanted to find better words to help the guy. He was going to say more but the phone went dead. Laughlin tried to call back three times but the line was busy. He thought he'd try a call back when he got home. What would be the better words to use, "Calm down, it'll be all right. We'll find out what happened. It's okay." Aware that he was upset about this remorseful man and wondering why he took these extra attempts to get him on the line again. He drove slowly home. He decided he should call his mother.

His house was dark. He dragged himself out of the car, stood silently looking at nothing and finally mounted the steps. Winkler was there against the windowsill, humming his own tune.

"Ah, the Lone Ranger returns," the old man sang out.

"So you're back, you old devil. Looking for more beer?" Laughlin laughed.

"Sounds good to me."

"Well, come in and sit. I don't want to drag chairs out on the porch this late in the night."

"I can come in, but leave the door open for Rosie."

"Which Rosie, cat or wife?" Laughlin asked as he pointed to a stuffed chair and went to get two beers. He liked the old man, and his visit was a good diversion from all that was eating him.

"Rosie the wife is still in the hospital due to her mind. It's a delirium. When she gets all confused, the doctors call it that, but she's way better since they adjusted her medication, and Rosie the cat is out with the hair ball heaves, so I walk alone tonight until the cat comes looking for me here."

"Sorry to hear about Mrs. Winkler. Delirium caused by too many pills from doctors, right?"

"Don't be too hasty to judge," Mr. Winkler responded and took a long delicate sip from his beer.

"Oh, I guess I've had my fill of doctors today."

"Now that's an interesting statement. Transference problems, huh?"

"I'm sorry I didn't drop by your place to ask about your wife, but I'm glad she's better," Laughlin answered, ignoring the transference comment.

"Yes. Here's the thing, she didn't give up medicines. She had been told to stop when the new ones were started. She's one smart cookie, she thought, and decided two meds were better than one. I got to scold her major, and she took it this time."

"Self-medicated, huh? Want another beer?"

"One's enough for me, but prescribe for yourself as you like and tell me why are you so down on doctors, physicians, and the like?"

Laughlin flung his leg over the big arm of the stuffed chair he filled easily and smiled at the inquiry. Not many people other than his partner asked him about himself and expected an answer. He'd been cooped up in cases and caught between women since Maggie dumped him. Now the audacious Mr. Winkler forged ahead with ease.

Laughlin took a long draw on the beer, wiped his lips with the back of his broad hand, and answered, "I guess I thought these educated guys were devoted to helping and would rescue abused people."

"Oh, now I get it. What did you need? Rescuing? When? When you were a kid or what?"

"Look, there are tons of abused people out there, and they seek help and get egomaniacs and the like instead," Laughlin shot back and got up for another beer.

"Compassion for abused people coming from a sheriff. That's wonderful, but why are you mad at the doctors?"

"I told you they didn't help people from being bullied."

"What do you know about being bullied?"

"What do I know about being bullied? I'll tell you, Mr. Winkler, sir, I had a tried and true bully of a father. A policeman, no less, who beat the hell out of my mother and me when he felt up to it. I wasn't big then but I tried to defend my mother and me. I threatened to tell my grandmother when she was alive. He said if I told anyone, he'd kill her and my mom," Laughlin paused for a drink and then went on. "Eventually, I was able to get out of the house before I killed my so-called father. He did stop hitting her when I grew bigger than him. Still, she wouldn't leave him. Someone could have seen what was going on and helped us before I could get out. No one did."

"The doctors?"

"Today I saw these guys and they sat in their little citadels making policy but letting abuse go on anyway."

"Transference, boy, transference, you transferred your resentment to the doctors who represented the rescuer you didn't get when you were young, right?"

Laughlin took a swig of beer and a quizzical look overtook his angular face. Then a bright flash crossed his thoughts. He had been mad at Dr. Brandt, ticked that the psychiatrist hadn't protected Freddie Poplar like he had wanted someone to protect him. When he was a kid sealed in his room, staring out the window and figuring how to shimmy down a rope, he'd see the man named Robertson, a neighbor, out trimming trees and singing stupid songs. His wire-rimmed glasses flashed with the sun on his oblivious face. He could have heard the yelling but it didn't dawn on him that this boy was caught, was panicked in a barricaded room his father would easily break into and come at him with that distorted, gnarled face of anger. The neighbor had silver glasses just like Brandt's.

Winkler went on talking, "We all used to think physicians could rescue us, but now they're painted as avaricious and non-caring specialists. Psychiatrist are physicians who eat people. Talk about images and *Silence of the Lambs*." The old man started to stand, pushing his body up with his hands and extending his kindle wood arms to raise himself. "Rosie's come. Thanks for the drink. I have transferences too. I have great faith in most professionals, especially physicians with their white coats, even if I've only talked to them a few minutes at a time. And you, I trust you. Have you earned that trust? I don't know for sure but I remember others in uniform and put you with them. Thank you again for the drink and helping my wife. Come see me sometime. We old people like interesting company—occasionally, that is."

Laughlin came to the moment, smiled, stood quickly to accompanied the provocative figure to the door. He then stooped and picked up the warm, fat cat, took Winkler's arm and walked him home. He wouldn't forget the Winkler's home address again. There were lights on upstairs, but the old man didn't make any more comments about his Rosies and lumbered up the stairs quietly.

Winkler called back to Laughlin. "Come in, have a cordial. I'm alone tonight."

The detective hesitated, not wanting to offend, and went up the steps to an open door and a smiling Winkler. "This way please."

He led the way past a living room of inviting stuffed couches, sloping easy chairs and sleek glass side tables to a big kitchen with painted wooden chairs and a carved round table. All rooms were bordered in dark moldings. The house was like its own wood carving. Everything was immaculate and cool. Laughlin had expected a musty smell and decay, neglect, disregard. The home was the opposite and radiated settled taste. Another assumption shot to hell. He realized he wanted to ask more about this Rosie man.

Winkler began talking immediately as a good host after fussing over drinks. "I grew up in Chicago slums with a single mother, made it through the University of Chicago on a scholarship and became a commodities broker. Everything was about 'getting and spending' as I and Wordsworth observed. Then we had our boy, and then he was killed, and now we enjoy being a sponsor to a boys' club. That kinda summarizes me as I wait for Rosie to come home from the hospital."

Blue painted mugs of tea and small crystal shot glasses were set before him and they drank a toast with amaretto to the Rosies. Winkler yawned and rubbed his eyes.

Laughlin felt the comfort of this home but knew he had to leave it to Winkler. He thanked his tired host and left.

He meandered slowly through the warm night, searching for perspective. On returning to his empty house, putting aside his own taunting memories, he called Poplar again. The distraught man answered and pleaded he was deeply sorry and needed to repent somehow. It was hard to convince him it was going to be okay. Finally, he promised the detective he'd try to get a good night's sleep. When Poplar ended the call, Laughlin still held the phone to his ear as if to get a reassuring signal. Finally, he reluctantly hung up.

Later, as he splayed out of his big living room chair, he asked himself how many of the persecuted really got rescued? Then he climbed the stairs, threw off his clothes, felt childish as he brushed his teeth like a good scout, peed, and fell on his back into the bed. The eyeglasses image came before him. He understood the wire-rimmed glasses were his insight. As an adult, it was up to him to make the little boy safe and secure.

CHAPTER 21

"We got a hit on one of Moody's credit cards," Max informed Laughlin and pointed to the paper that showed the address of a drugstore in Torrance. "Too bad, she got released before we could talk to her. Some coordinated efforts, huh?" Max had called the pharmacist and gotten the details of a prescription for some "psychotropic medicine." It was Valium, and the guy remembered her in a flaming velvet coat and purple streaks with blue hair. She talked about meeting him in her room or even in the back of the store, but he demurred, saying he had to stay at the cash register. She was so loud and was undoing her blouse buttons. He'd been afraid merely to say, "No way."

The address was a Howard Johnson's on Hawthorne. She was registered under her own name, but the room was empty. Inside there were feather boas and fuzzy scarves hung on all the lamps. The TV was going and so was the shower; the room reeked of some gardenia perfume, but there was no Elvira. The manager turned off the TV and shower, and a deputy was posted down the hall.

"What a bust," Max lamented. "You'd think with such a flamboyant character, we could find her quickly. I guess she's not that much of a standout in LA."

"We've had our share of weird in this case, but it goes nowhere. She's the one that can help tie it together if she hasn't gone off on another speed bender. No luck with the fancy tailor, no luck with Mo's apartment refrigerator, all paid with cash, no luck with Manfred's sister, no luck with Jeffrey the trainer, Gene or Mrs. Mo herself." Laughlin took a deep breath and decided they would go back to Manfred's apartment and the bookstore.

The apartment had the hum of silence and still dark furniture. It was already disturbed with packing, but whoever was doing the job had left it for another day. Max and Laughlin brought meatball sandwiches and cans of Coke into the musty air and sat on the wooden chairs lined up together by the window near a big leafy sycamore.

"This is like my grandparents' place in Detroit," Max observed.

"How's that?"

"Well, they didn't have all the books, but they had dark wooden furniture, which was damn uncomfortable. They sat ridged backed at their one table and laughed whenever I said anything. They sure did love me, but I sure would rather sit on the floor than in their chairs."

"Well, better that way than the other."

"What's that mean?"

"I dunno, Max. It just means they were fine people, not hard."

"Yup. They had a big iron bed with quilts piled on it. I used to love to jump on the bed and hide under the soft covers with my toys. They would pretend they couldn't find me, and I'd fall asleep until my ma came to get me. When they'd gone to a Lion's football game, I got laid there when I was fifteen."

"A great way to show respect, huh?"

"I thought so."

"In my house, there were no quilts, just one knitted blanket my grandmother made for me, but my father, he burned a hole in it one night. He fell asleep, all boozed up, smoking an awful cigar. He didn't even get singed."

"Was he sorry?" Max asked quietly.

Laughlin snorted. "My dad? Are you kidding? Anyway, I don't want to go down memory lane anymore. Somehow this case gets me thinking too much."

"Yeah, you've been uptight. At least you haven't chewed my ass out."

"Getting laid in your grandparents' bed—a little bizarre, I'd say. Excuse me, maybe I should start yelling at you now."

"Don't be so holier than thou. No judgments from you, buddy. Save it for the psychiatrist you need."

"Well, thanks for your recommendation, you well-adjusted expert. Anyway, let's just start looking around here again and see if we can find the Dylan Thomas answer. Lunch is over for us."

They crumpled their wrapping and began another search, but the closets were full of boxed books and a load of real stock certificates.

"This man was loaded but didn't leave us any clues here. Let's move it."

After a short silent drive, Laughlin and Max stepped in the bookstore; it was still a crime scene and lay dormant. They began looking for something; some trigger that would shoot straight to an answer. Where was Franklin Mo? What was the connection with Weber and Manfred? Had Elvira Moody intercepted the letter from Mo? What was Gene Biskoff's role in all this? Laughlin insisted that he cared about those answers. He had to care, or what was the point of his job?

They started at the stubby desk, again searching the drawers and shelves enclosing the proprietor's small space. There was the debris of business, canceled checks, credit card receipts, telephone numbers, order sheets, invoices, and little business cards stacked in rubber-banded piles not boxed yet. The wall behind this array was covered with quotes and forms. Laughlin stood silently, looking at a saying from Buddha, "All created things must pass. Strive on, diligently." Next to that was a page from a book with a picture labeled "Macbeth, the warrior," and the text "Tis a tale told by an idiot, full of sound and fury, signifying nothing."

"Damn, this guy really was a downer. I wonder if there were any upsides to having all these books," Max said as he flipped through some books collected on the edge of the desk. "These are all books about death and dying—creepy."

"I guess book lovers think about what we deal with every day. In his journal, Manfred sounded like he thought about life too. Maybe it's easier to read someone else's ideas than conclude about your own in real life," Laughlin philosophized.

"Oh, great, no-escape fiction. Historical novels are for me," Max replied.

Laughlin's phone rang, and he answered quickly. He was silent as Max ambled around, flipping books open. "It's okay, it's okay. Listen, Poplar. You didn't have anything to do with Manfred's death. I know, I know you would let us know if you knew where Franklin was. Tell you what, I'll call you when we turn up something. Sure, sure. I know. Take it easy."

"What's up?"

"Poplar . . . he's, quote, sick at heart, unquote, he says. The guy blames himself," Laughlin related and shook his head. "The guy has got to give me a break. He needs to listen. Hey, let's look around a little more, and then you go on home, Max."

The stacks were labeled in broad subjects, and the poetry section was small, and the books alphabetically arranged. There was no Dylan Thomas book. Max thought about the biography shelves, but again, Thomas was absent. It was getting dark, and the narrow spaces hovered over the tired men. There were no answers.

"Too bad we couldn't just help ourselves to some books and go home to read." Max sighed.

"Go on, Max. I'll just take a look in the back again and then close it all up."

"You sure?"

"Absolutely. Think of some answers while you're with Kim, okay?"

"I know what I think of when I'm with Kim, but I'll try."

"Yeah, yeah. See you at report tomorrow. Hope we don't get hell from the brass."

Max shut the door firmly, the glass rattled, and then Laughlin was alone. He wondered about the stacks and then opened the back office door. The lights were still working, and he turned on an overhead ceiling fixture hanging like a full moon, full of pocked marks from dead bugs. He didn't want to sit on the dead man's couch, but there was a wooden stool near the glassed-in bookcase and the paltry desk. He sat and looked at the elements listed on the wall. Hydrogen was on top. He remembered it was the lightest element and the commonest. School chemistry had been something he liked.

He figured Manfred was more interested in books, and he swiveled to the glass case; it was full of the histories of Germany. Dylan Thomas was English or Welsh or something, but not German, he knew.

His eye scanned the open bookcases, and of course, he grumbled. There was a Dylan Thomas book; the cover said *Thomas* in gold letters. He felt a modicum of hope, opened the green gilded volume, but there was nothing in it but the poetry. He threw the book on the desk and sat again, staring at the bookcase. The next book was Orwell. That book and the Thomas book were on the top shelf and were relatively new, compared to the burned brown leather and ragged cloth-covered books on most of the other shelves.

Maybe these were the English writers Manfred admired, but the book after that was Sigmund Freud. Laughlin tried to decipher Manfred's words: "Find Dylan." Was it the beginning of something rather than the book itself?

He took his pen and notebook out and wrote the names of the rest of the authors on the top shelf: Rousseau, Aesop, Nabokov, Franz Kafka, Lucretius, Ibsen, Pablo Neruda, Herman Melville, Ovid, Pepys, Dr. Seuss, Friedrich Nietzsche, Wilfred Owen, Marianne Moore, John Osborne, Rilke, and Johannes Eckhart. There was Goethe down below. That was it. Some of the books had full names, others merely the last name. There was no message he understood in any of them but penciled prices on the inside first pages—no letter, no other clue. Behind the books, he found an envelope, but there was nothing in it.

This was all he had for the day's efforts. He wanted some discovery that would lead him to the rest of the case. He wanted a beer. He was angry, sputtering about like an amateur and getting nowhere fast. Damn, he wanted a cold tall beer.

The cat jumped down from a shelf and landed on the desk. Startled, Laughlin yelled, and the cat scurried away. Damn, he'd forgotten about the cat. He looked around but couldn't find him. Trudging down to the drugstore across the street, he bought a couple of cans of cat food, a plastic dish, and a big water bottle. He set the cat up with these and wondered where Manfred had fed him before.

Satisfied he'd done enough, he bagged all the books and the envelope, took them to the lab, and went home. Trash had blown around and settled in the bushes clustering near the house. Winds carried the contents of dumped garbage cans through the neighborhood like scavengers looking for shelter. He got himself a beer and walked around, picking up the odds and ends of paper, cellophane, waxy wrappers, and deflated balloons. He hadn't taken his garbage cans out in the morning, so he didn't have to hunt for them in the night. At least he had been smart about something. Every autumn, Southern Californians ignored the desert winds galloping through the passes and figured their garbage was never gonna blow away and cared even less if it did. What was lost garbage anyway? He felt uneasy. The whispering, warm winds finally arrived and were calling out.

He should ask Brandt or Nora Weber what the books meant. He wanted to go down to Denny's only after until the girl was gone to her boyfriend, coward that he was, so he drove to McDonald's and then the beach.

Along the coast, he smelled the pungent skunk-scent that permeated the air occasionally, even with civilization spreading. It seemed less often now, and yet he didn't mind it. He hoped the skunk got away.

At Zuma, all was quiet, and he admired the bare breast of the beach while the tide was out. The sand's smooth complacency felt fine. The waves, the wind, the stray sandpiper birds still busy finding morsels to peck amused him with their similarities to his searches. He resolved to get out of his funk. He headed home and settled in bed, asleep in moments.

Chapter 22

Morning report was slow and dull, but Laughlin and Max were not hassled about the case, and both of them felt relief. Max looked at the list of books and suggested the code guys take a look. Laughlin agreed.

Although it should have been easy, the one-thumb, one-legged Gene was not found among the street people downtown, and he didn't return to the board and care. Elvira was still gone even though she too should have been just as easy to spot. Jeffrey was an unknown, and, of course, Franklin Mo was nowhere to be found, as they say.

Max and Laughlin sat at the sergeant's desk and made lists and calls and decided to start all over again. Then Laughlin saw the message that Nora Weber had called and would be at the hospice. Max went in pursuit of what poor leads they had regarding Elvira Moody. Laughlin went to see Dr. Weber.

When he got to the stark building with opaque cataract like windows, he couldn't decide whether the bright orange and yellow inside was better or worse on his mood than the gray, moldy Rosewood Board and Care where Gene had consoled himself. The desk clerk told him Mrs. Weber authorized him to go into her husband's room. He walked down the hall tentatively. Why had she called? Was her husband dead, and now she was going to confess to something?

He knocked gently on the closed door, and she opened it and stepped out, gesturing to come with her to the lounge. Her hair bundled up in a bun; she wore a bright blue dress with red shoes and belt. She dropped into a chair and remained silent. He sat beside her, and had the urge to hold her hand but didn't. Minutes toiled by. He waited. A nurse peeked in the open doorway and left again.

Nora Weber took a deep breath and said, "My husband is slipping into a coma. He's going to start Cheyne Stoking soon enough and then the end."

"Cheyne Stoking?" Laughlin asked softly.

"It's breathing driven by carbon dioxide building up after not breathing for a while. It's not a bad end, merely going into an irretrievable state. I want to be there with him while he still knows us, but his parents may come too late. I will be with him." She began to cry. "We were planning a family last year."

He waited.

"Let's go in the kitchen for a minute and get something to drink."

They returned to the lounge, sat down and he waited again. She took a deep breath and began, "I got a call from Fred Poplar's wife. She wanted me to know that Freddy had committed suicide. He'd left a note, and you'd been mentioned as someone he wanted to know he regretted his wrongs. She thought it best if I talk to you because she had many other things to deal with. We were sort of friends before all this." She took another deep breath, sighed, and finished, "I didn't think you should hear about this over the phone."

Laughlin's jaw fell. His mouth stayed open as he tried to comprehend. The words were a punch to his gut. He looked at her questioningly. She nodded. Both of them looked down to their forlorn fingers.

Each word made him wince. She went on, "He shot himself in the mouth. They found him in some bushes down at the park near their house. He'd covered himself with leaves."

"Covered himself with leaves? Covered himself with leaves before he shot himself?" he repeated.

"Yes."

"I'd told him he wasn't to blame," Laughlin pleaded.

"Yes, you did. I'm sure," she answered.

"What the hell . . . I don't get it." He thought to himself, *I've got to calm down and fathom this. Take it easy.* Suddenly aware he was consoling himself with the same words he had offered to Poplar, Laughlin shook his head in disbelief.

"Look, he went over the edge. He was such a conscientious guy. Whatever it was that tipped him didn't fit with his view of himself. He got depressed, delusional about how big a deal it was. It would be hard to figure that out from the outside. He put on a good front even with his wife and kids. His note spelled it out, said he couldn't be trusted anymore, wasn't a good human being. His wife's not sure why he couldn't be trusted. He was always good to her. Your words or anyone else's weren't going to convince him. His mind was made up."

Laughlin looked up into her eyes, watery and sunken. He saw kindness and patience. He felt exposed and righted himself by standing.

"Suicide is always terribly difficult. It's like a robbery and murder of the person by the person. We can talk later if you like. It's a great shock."

He nodded and put out his hand. "Thank you, Dr. Weber. I would like to talk with you later about all this because of the case, but now I understand you must get back. I appreciate your taking time for me." As he said goodbye, he had made a decision not to mention what Poplar's concern was. It would be too much on her already painful agenda. She had been kind.

He got out of the hospice and resolved he was through for the day. He called Max and thankfully got voice mail. He left the message he was taking off and please cover for him. "Fuck," he repeated a few times. He'd been swearing way more than usual. What was it about "fuck" that decompressed him but felt so inadequate? "Damn, Poplar. You didn't need to do that."

He went to his house, sought solace, and stretched out on the bed. He tried to imagine what more he could have said to the guy. He wasn't to blame—he told him that. Why didn't Poplar listen? Should he have been more persuasive or gone over to the jail and told him? Now all this questioning was self-torture after the fact. He wasn't going to go bananas. He closed his eyes and took some deep breaths.

As the sun settled down, Laughlin got up, ashamed he had fallen asleep and startled again by the image of the man covering himself with leaves. He decided to go to Harvell's and drink.

The bar was half full; the music was light jazz. It all suited him fine. He had beers and stuffed himself with junk. He felt better. There was a starched black-haired woman on a stool, and he went over to her. Her long hair belied her age but she was still in the running and he offered to buy her a drink. She looked at him suspiciously and then smiled.

"You made some mistake, handsome. I'm not hustling."

"Hey, neither am I, merely wanted some decent company."

They bantered and got to the city's life story not hers until she kissed him goodbye about the time the bar closed and sent him home. If he came again the next night, they could go to dinner, she suggested, and she'd give him her name and talk about what she did.

After taking her to her blue Honda, he embraced her, and she complied, but she turned her face away when he tried another kiss. Dismissed, he stood on the ramp and tried to figure out which parking structured he'd pulled into; he wandered about. After circling around the second parking structure levels and setting off his car alarm, he finally found the car on the third floor and made it home. "What a total bust, a failed day," he lamented, and that was it. When he got home, he avoided stepping on leaves and left the covers off when he fell into his bed.

CHAPTER 23

The doorbell rang. Mrs. Porter started to get up.

Jeffrey Faulk sat in the big wingback chair and took a shiny blue jacket off, pulling his T-shirt down over his khakis. Like a flexible monkey, he bent his right arm to scratch his right armpit. He looked sideways at Mrs. Porter who was wrapped in her throw by the fire with her two ersatz cats and a black cloth purse. Then the big man rubbed his fat nose and then put both hands on his knees. He clicked his tongue. He held his hand up to stop her.

"Don't answer that yet, okay? Sit down a minute. I figured you know where he stowed the money for the information. Manfred was a careful guy but always true to his word. Franklin never did contact me after the shooting, but I betcha the enveylope is still in the store somewheres."

"Now tell me again what in damnation happened to your little finger?" Mrs. Porter said in a wavering but loud voice.

"A little accident, that's all. Lost the finger and a ring."

"My brother never mentioned you or that Franklin Mo was doing business with him. No. You are totally mistaken, and after you finish your drink of water, I suggest you get out of here immediately." She pulled her blanket up further and pressed the cats and her black clothed purse close to her heart.

"Ah, Mrs. Porter, I've come like a friend-like. I was out of town but need money. You'd know where it is. Come on be a friend-like."

"I don't have friends with mutilated fingers."

"Look now, lady, be good about this. I'm pinched right now, and you knowed it would really help me out. I'll move some furniture around for you if you like. I got major muscle from workouts. I could even instruct you. Old people need exercise too." His biceps popped up and down while he talked.

"Are you out of your mind? I never heard such blather," Mrs. Porter retorted.

"Yur'd be shocked at what I can lift, honest, even you, about one hundred pounds, maybe," Jeffrey explained.

"Don't threaten me, you fool," she retorted and stared at the worms of veins on his arms.

A loud knock on the door made them both jump. Mrs. Porter shouted, "Come in!"

Jeffrey put his finger to his mouth to signal quiet, but she yelled again. He quickly got up, put a wooden chair against the doorknob, then smacked the big-mouthed woman even as she raised one of her cats as a shield against him. He took her purse. It rattled with pill bottles.

A man's voice outside called, "It's locked, Mrs. Porter. Please open it. It's Deputy Max. Are you all right? I heard voices."

Biting his lower lip, the trainer smacked his fist into his damaged hand and made for the kitchen and back door. This time Mrs. Porter shrieked, "Come in! Break the door down, but get in."

Max slammed his shoulder against the fragile door, and its hinges tore from the frame. The chair flung aside.

"In there, in the kitchen, get him! He was trying to extort money from me. He's got my favorite purse," Mrs. Porter yelled but continued to sit with her throw on her lap, consoling both cats.

Max nodded to the seated woman, swiveled his head, and headed into the kitchen. The bulky man was going out the door.

Both men leaped down the small set of stairs. Max grabbed Faulk, but his shirt ripped away and threw the deputy off balance. Faulk swung the purse in an arc, banged the deputy on his ear, and started over the old wooden fence. Max stumbled forward and lunged again. This time Max had him. He spun the man around and punched him in the stomach. They both paused for breath, and then Max pulled his gun and said quietly, "I'm not going to hit you again. I'll spare my knuckles. Next time, I'll take you down with a bullet. Got it?"

The backup men arrived quickly. Faulk only said, "I have the right to a lawyer. Get me a lawyer. What did I do? Get me a lawyer."

Then there was quiet while Max tried to wedge the front door shut and sat down across Mrs. Porter.

"He'll be held for attempted robbery and assault. How are you doing? Are you all right? Did you know him, Mrs. Porter? What's his name?"

"I tell you, Deputy Max, you still ask too many questions at once, but I am very glad to see you and to answer them," she replied with a smile while patting the red imprint on her cheek.

"I'll get you some ice. Hold on," Max answered with a smile.

"Ice and tea, some tea, please, in the silver set. I want to celebrate my survival."

After multiple instructions pertaining to the ice, a plastic bag with a particular kitchen towel, the cupboard with the tea set and the tea, Max poured the hot water and brought the laden engraved tea tray to the calmed woman.

"Thank you so much. I can sit here and give orders, but I think if I tried to stand up, I would crumble," she explained and sighed. "I love that purse, it was my first from my own earned money. Of course, I would never buy such a big bag again. It was so extravagant. Now I buy nothing but the littlest Le Sport Sac." She petted the cats and readjusted her cover.

Max listened to her ramble on as he negotiated, pouring the tea into the cups. He felt like a child at a new task and held a vague suspicion she was demeaning him.

She asked for more tea, paused, and then admitted she was able to distract herself with mindless trivia about life when she suffered stress. It seemed like a natural tranquilizer, talking about unimportant things.

"Hey, it's okay. That purse meant a lot to you, and he tried to take it away."

"So true," she agreed while petting the cats. "I only have possessions now that I have no family." Then she sighed and continued, "You did a really excellent job with the tea. I didn't see you spill a drop. Precise touch for a young man like a Sidney Poitier. Where did you learn to handle things so delicately?"

"Oh, it just comes naturally, being a southern gentleman," Max answered mockingly.

"I get it. You're putting me on. That's mean after I suffered such a fright. Very naughty."

"Yup. In reality, I came from the south side of Detroit, Michigan. My mom and dad were hoping I was going to be a fireman."

"Well, I excuse you since you rescued me like a real firemen. Do you have a real bad chip on your shoulders because of your skin pigmentation? It didn't appear that way when we first met."

"I'm not too prejudiced," Max said, smiling while his defensive thoughts dissipated toward the candid woman enveloped in her protective blanket. He liked her. She was just a plain straight talker. A rarity, he concluded.

"Well, that's good. You can be my son then or maybe nephew if your mother is still alive."

"Then it's tea every Sunday, right, Aunt?"

"Yes, a great idea. Now tell me, my boy. Why did you come on this special day to see your aunt? I am extremely grateful, but let's not delay any further until we finished our cookies and business."

Jarred back to the murder case by her question, Max chewed a raisin oatmeal cookie quickly. He swallowed his warm tea and looked up.

"I came here to ask you about some books we found at your brother's store. I didn't realize you knew that man. I believe this Jeffrey Faulk, the name he told you, is a suspect in Franklin Mo's disappearance and maybe in your brother's murder."

"He came here for money not books. He said something about Eric giving money to Franklin Mo, and I don't remember exactly, but something about it not being there, wherever that was. He was smarmy at first, and then he began to show his muscles literally and figuratively. I don't understand what he was talking about, but I understood his threats. He had all those terrible muscles exploding in his arms. Thank goodness for your pursuit of good old fashion books."

She knew nothing more about Faulk. Max called Laughlin and filled him in. The sergeant told him to go on with the book questions. He'd take care of interviewing Faulk now that he was in custody.

Mrs. Porter and Max spent two hours going through the list, discussing stocks, celebrating her wealth and the cookies. There was no pattern they could discern. She pointed out there were Asian, European, and South and North American authors; there were women and men; modern and ancient writers. There were philosophers, historians, and poets and a whole hodgepodge of types.

"My brother is clever. This puzzle is too much for me and certainly way over the head of that Jeffrey," Mrs. Porter opined.

"I guess I'll have to read them all. But listen, right now, do you have a hammer so I can repair your door till someone can replace the frame?" Max asked at the end of their meeting.

"Why how kind of you, thanks. You're the best relative I have now. In the kitchen, to the left of the refrigerator, lower cupboard."

Taking a shiny hammer from a well-organized tool kit with an incongruous pink pad and paper in it, Max put the hinges back as best he could in spite of the broken frame. The door opened and closed, but he cautioned she should use the back entrance until the real repair job could be done. He turned the lock. Then he took the tea set and washed it and asked if Mrs. Porter wanted any more. She thanked him but said she would nap now after she read a little more of a detective story she liked written by Parker. The apparently unfazed woman adjusted her covers and thanked him again. Max went on his way only satisfied by the memory of having tea with a dignified lady and punching Faulk in the guts.

Chapter 24

At the jail, Laughlin sat patiently that morning and continued Faulk's interrogation again. No need to shake him sober. Laughlin repeated his questions about Eric Manfred and Franklin Mo. Faulk answered that he wanted a deal before he would answer. A public defender sat quietly next to him, told Faulk to be quiet, and looked in his briefcase for no apparent reason. The unrepentant thief persisted that charges be dropped on the purse purloin until Faulk's public defender finally suggested dropping the potential theft charge in return for cooperation.

Jeffrey Faulk flexed his muscles, stared at his biceps, squirmed his butt around in the steel chair, and finally looked up at Laughlin. His eyes were a dull gray with shoots of red vessels radiating form the pupils.

"You work out, Sergeant?"

"What does that have to do with the time of day?" Laughlin said, shaking his head in disgust.

"Me? I do it in the morning, but they say it's more better in the afternoon. I just can't get the energy then. I do curls and stuff at least around four. I could have been a child progeny in body building."

Laughlin tilted his head in response to the strange claim, computed the misnomer or malaprop—or whatever he should call it—sighed, and then straightened up and went on. "Look, Faulk, let's not get off on your lineage. It's too confusing. Do you want me to help you or not? I'll see what I can do about the charge. That's all. This is a murder case, and you are a suspect."

The attorney nodded. The big jock relented. He caressed his biceps with his eyes and stated in a slow pensive manner, "I didn't kill nobody. I pick up the yellow enveylopes at the store. That suspect is true, but they was empty this last time, plain empty. Franklin was mad at that, and I got a little spooked and thought I better visit with my brother in Fresno till Franklin cooled off again."

"When did you hear from him last?"

"While I was with my brother. He called and said to stay away. He wouldn't tell me where the money was."

"He called how long ago?"

"Let me see," the detainee answered and began counting with his thumb, the fingers on his intact hand. "Wednesday, Tuesday, Thursday . . . No. Wednesday, Thursday, Saturday. Ahh. Umm. About a week before I read about the bookman getting his."

"A week? Are you sure? Where was he?"

"I dunno. In the bookstore?"

"Franklin Mo, where was he?" Laughlin exclaimed.

"Wasn't he at the jail?"

"When was the last time you saw him?"

"I had a key and goes in at night. I never saw the book guy except in the newspaper. There was an aurora about the place, eerie-like."

"Yeah, I'll bet. Franklin Mo? When did you see him last?"

"Umm. At his house?"

"You tell me."

"Yeah, at Franklin's house, we'd had some beer. He gave me classy clothes and shirts and a new gear bag."

"Why?"

"I guess it was easier for him than to drive some other place."

"Why were you picking up money from the bookstore?"

"That's where Mr. Manfred left it."

"Damn, give me a real answer."

"It's true. Elvira said it was okay."

"So Elvira knew about the money. Did she know why Manfred gave it to you and Mo?"

"You'll have to ask her. She knew about messages, more than money. All's I know is he been leaving money for about . . . I don't know . . . maybe about"—Faulk looked at his fingers again—"for about four months or something. Hey, you know, I'll only be able to count to nine for the rest of my life. Wow. That happened before my birthday. I had some ecstasy. It weren't that good. Of course, if I take my clothes off, I can count my toes and, hey, my pecker—it counts as one too."

"Why'd he give you clothes?"

"I see now, 'cause I was prompted at getting the yellow enveylopes full of money."

Laughlin sighed and asked the guy if he wanted some coffee. He said he'd like a Dr. Pepper. Laughlin walked out of the room, rubbed his eyes, and brought back two paper cups with coffee.

"I don't drink black," the suspect said, adding, "I likes red and white wines like 'cabin nay' and 'pina noah.'"

Laughlin refrained from telling him tough shit.

"That's all there is, mister."

They went over the whole thing again, and nothing significant dropped out of the suspect's pitiful brain. As Laughlin called it quits, he tossed out his last question: "What's with the finger?"

"Oh, I did that for Franklin. I made Gene feel we was brothers. Damn that there knife! A chief's knife they call it. It was sharp, man, really sharp. I didn't need the pinky, but I miss the ring. Threw the whole thing out the car window. I had to do it twice 'cause the first time, I only took the little nail, and he wanted me to take it down to the knuckle. Fucking blood made me sick, but it healed real fast-like. Had some Dilaudid to sleep it off. Love the Vicodin best. Once I had a bad trip on some angel dust, pain, man."

"For Gene? Eugene Biskoff?"

"I guess. You know Gene. Franklin's helping the guy. Nice sediment, huh?"

"Yeah, it sunk right to the bottom of my heart."

"Yeah, you know, being sweet and such. Gene lapped it up because he wanted to be saved."

"Sentiment, Faulk, sentiment."

"You too? Yurse trying to help Gene too?"

Laughlin went on with questions about how Franklin was helping Gene. He got no coherent answers other than he was "being nice" and called it a day with the former addict and presently brain-impaired man.

At the station, Max filed his report and shared his tea making abilities with his partner. Laughlin filled him in on the tenuous connections among all the players in the case. Alibis were checked: Jeffrey Trainer Faulk's brother confirmed that he was with the suspect the day of the murder. Elvira was with Laughlin and Max during the shooting. That left Franklin Mo and Gene Biskoff or some unknown.

"I don't know, Sergeant, but from this senior deputy's experience, it didn't seem plausible that one-legged Gene could fire the gun and run out of the back of the store with that much speed. Besides, why would he want to kill Manfred?" Max offered.

"Gene Biskoff was sedated and in restraints at the County Hospital that day. No way he got away. When he escaped, poor Manfred was already dead," Laughlin mused.

"Franklin Mo was apparently sucking money from the bookman, but why?"

"My question is where's Franklin Mo? Is he dead or maybe a missing murderer?" Laughlin stated emphatically. "Remember, Faulk said he talked with him by telephone only a week before Manfred was murdered. The guy may still be alive."

Max stretched his arms above his head, stood up and sat down again.

"Let me get this straight. Mrs. Mo is going out of town. She's the only other suspect that could have done this. Yet she'd already was in Hong Kong when Manfred was killed, and now you're saying it may just be the missing husband she offed instead."

"There's the sister as well," Laughlin offered.

"Nah, she's not the type, and she talked about her brother as though he were still alive," Max replied immediately.

"Oh, well, then that's all the testimony Mrs. Manfred Porter needs," Laughlin added sarcastically.

"Honest, Sergeant, she's concerned, and she was afraid of Faulk."

"So of all the known players, that leaves Mo as missing and Mo as the possibly murdered and the possible murderer. He was taking money from the bookman. We need to know why."

"Maybe Manfred killed Mo and someone else retaliated, like Dr. Weber or one of the mental health jail people," Max tossed in.

"Shit, that reminds me of poor Poplar. He killed himself over this case. How do you get over that? He just didn't believe me when I told him it was okay and we'd find the killer."

"Unbelievable. Wow. Damn. That's a bummer. Why would the sweaty guy kill himself? Now we have two deaths from this case. We better get the killer."

"It just eats at me. What should I have done? How do you get a closed-minded person to believe you?" Laughlin reflected.

"I guess you don't if you look at what happened to Poplar."

The two men sat quietly, each scanning over recollections of the dead psychologist. Laughlin finally picked up a pencil and started making lists. Max watched, nodding approval.

"Look, Max, let's follow up on what we know are leads. The books mean something, and Weber's connection has to be explored more. If none of that pans out, we'll go back to the jail staff, okay? Right now, my brain feels as fried as Faulk's, but we have to get some answers."

"Damn," Max said and stretched his arms out, "I concur on both points. Tomorrow then."

Laughlin nodded and headed for his car. Instead of things clearing up, things were worse, and he didn't know what to do. In this case, people's emotional states, like lead sinkers, were dragging him down with them. He didn't want to drown.

CHAPTER 25

That night Laughlin headed back to the dark-haired woman at the bar. Chagrinned, he realized he didn't even know her name. What was the matter with him? The case was a bust so far. A mental health administrator or his murderer was making an ass of a sheriff, and there was no one to set it straight but his good old stumbling self. Yet all James Laughlin wanted now was a stiff drink and a woman.

Of course, his cell rang. A call had come in to the station from a woman named Dr. Mason. She needed to see him right away. It was nine twenty in the evening. The number she left was from the valley, and he called it with all the self-control he could manage. He remembered his last call from Dr. Weber, and he remembered Dr. Mason. She was the psychologist at the jail, the one who didn't like having phlegm all over her arm. He frowned and waited impatiently for her to answer.

Demanding he meet with her, she said she could not stay at her home and would meet him anywhere but in the valley. She didn't want her husband to see them. Laughlin suggested the Santa Monica Pier. It would be near enough to the bar where he still might meet up with his black-haired woman. Dr. Mason refused to talk over the phone and agreed to meeting him at the merry-go-round. She liked it there, and she could talk more freely.

Did he have time to see the woman at the bar? He decided to chance it. She was there, but a man on each side of her had captured her attention.

"I'm back again, sweetheart," he murmured in his fake seductive voice as he put his hand on her shoulder. "Such dubious company, you've got. Let's take a walk and go over to Ocean Avenue. There are some reasonably good restaurants all along there. The Blue Plate Oysterette has a great selection. I've just to meet someone for a few minutes. Will you wait?"

She turned, looked him over, admonished him for not having reservations anywhere, and wondered what his game was. "I'll wait here, darling dear, and you come on when you're done. I don't go with just anyone." Her mood was lighthearted, and he floated in her accepting banter, even while her new companions eyed him with distain. The one on her right was a bald guy with dark-rimmed glasses in a brown suit who could have done every bar patrons' taxes, and the other was a younger short-sleeved Levi's lout who slid off the stool and stood tall in challenge to Laughlin.

"Listen, macho man, we'll let the lady choose. Sit down and enjoy your drink until I come back for her."

Laughlin didn't want to think he was just "anyone," so he accepted her terms while he debated the odds he finally got her alone. He'd bet he could go home with her or maybe she'd come with him. Motels were another option, and they were nearby.

He nodded and took off for the unwanted meeting. Ocean and car sounds rolled up the Palisades bluffs, and he could see the Ferris wheel spinning in lights of merriment. He caught sight of Mason coming across the street. Her hair was in long curls and bounced as she scurried. She had a bulky sweater on with fat glass beads hanging down her front and a full skirt with black boots. He couldn't tell much about her body in that getup. In the time he'd been on this case, he'd observed as a rule that the psychologist women wore dramatic adorned clothes while psychiatrists wore uninspired, tailored outfits.

"Let's go to the pier for a walk over the ocean," she suggested quietly.

He tried to hold her arm to guide her across the streets, but she pulled away. They walked a foot away from each other, she clutching her arms to herself, onto the arched bridge and into the wandering crowds and rushing waves, going forward and then returning to the darkening water.

"What's going on?" he asked.

Suddenly, she took his arm and leaned on him, stumbling on the planks. She talked in short spurts, panting and sighing, and told him she had seen Franklin Mo and was worried he was going to hurt her. Laughlin started to speak, but she said, "Be quiet till I finish. I haven't got much time or energy. I feel faint."

Before they even passed the merry-go-round, she consented to sitting down at a brown cedar board restaurant with a tawdry Hawaiian theme. He offered her something to eat and ordered. She sat, gazing at her hands neatly folded in her lap or held them up against her cheeks with her eyes closed.

When the orange juice, veggie burger and fries, and his chicken burger with fries came, she still sat there with opened palms flaccid in her skirt. He pointed to the juice and offered her a fry. She said she couldn't eat. She'd had a "bad food day." Her stomach was too acidic. Wiggling her sweater off because she felt stuffy, she revealed a camisole with pink straps hanging over her bones—bones so pronounced that her shoulders looked like little full moons stuck on sticks. He looked at her face and could tell her hollowed cheeks had no padding and her eyes were drawn in sadness with bags holding them in place.

"Are you sick?"

"No, no. And I am not anorexic," she insisted.

"So please eat. You may feel less faint then," he offered.

She looked at him with scorn and ate everything on her plate with periodic mounds of ketchup added to her carefully arranged fries. She daintily wiped her mouth, folded the napkin like it were an origami, and took her pulse at the wrist and at the neck.

"My neck arteries are strong, but I am always worried that my blood pressure varies too much," she observed to no one in particular. Then she rubbed her left leg at the shin and stretched her left arm up above her head. "I've always been thin, but I try to stay healthy, although I have my father's fat ankles," she lamented and bit her lip.

He watched her and waited for some sort of elaboration.

Dumping her enormous buckle-laden purse on the table, she took out a spiral book of index cards and wrote down her pulse count on the blue pages. "I never get a migraine when my heart rate and pressure are good. That's why I have to tell you about Franklin. I cannot afford any headaches. With stress, I get irritable bowel syndrome. Oh, the gas and cramps are unbearable."

"Okay, okay. Tell me what's going on."

"I told you to shut up. You know shush until I finish. I cannot stand the tension if you press me. Please be respectful."

Laughlin was ready to stress the hell out of her by walking away to his dark lady. Gulping his beer down, he signaled the waitress for the bill.

Mason squeezed her eyebrows in distress, clutched her hands on her cheeks, took a deep, loud breath, and began, "Okay, okay. He came to my house, but I wouldn't let him in. Thank God my husband was inside, and that made Franklin wary just enough. I didn't recognize him at first. He had long hair and a feathery kind of black beard."

"What about his clothes?" Laughlin prompted.

"I can feel my stomach tightening." Mason checked her watch and flipped to a yellow section of her index cards. "Ten minutes after eating should not bring me cramps. My record shows it takes only five minutes so I'm safe for now, but stop pestering me."

Laughlin ate a cold french fry, pursed his mouth, shook his head, and stared her in the eye.

She talked. "He said he'd found my address in a shirt pocket and wanted to talk to me. He acted like he didn't know the place and me. Can you beat that? Bastard. After all I'd been through for him. My pulse went right up to 112, and I hadn't moved a muscle." She took a drink of her orange juice and asked for some more ice water.

Laughlin wanted to grab her neck.

"I was scared. He had this vacant look in his eyes. I wanted to slam the door but—" She stopped and began gasping and then sobbing. The waiter brought the ice water. He looked at Laughlin as though he should do something.

Laughlin reassured him that the lady was upset but all right. Mason kept making honking sounds as she took in air but didn't turn blue.

"Hey, you're safe now. Take it easy."

"Yes, yes. One, two, three . . ." and she went on counting to ten.

The detective took a deep breath, felt moderately guilty about wanting to strangle her, and moved his chair over to talk softly to the heaving woman.

"That's it. Take it easy. You're being a big help. Yes, calm down. You can do this," he cajoled. "Take it easy" was becoming his stupid mantra. How do psychiatrists deal with these people?

She began rocking back and forth and counting to ten over and over. She wasn't quite hyperventilating. Laughlin was relieved. He didn't need this frail woman to slump to the floor, especially before he got some tangible information.

"One of the other staff at the jail said I have something like panic anxiety disorder. She thinks I can talk myself down from my spells. I try so hard. One internist I saw told me I have hypochondriac-like disorder. They all tell me I'm sick, but I take good care of myself."

He finally gave in and offered, "You've been doing a really good job dealing with your anxiety. It must be frightening to experience these episodes. I hope your husband helps you."

She looked at him, her wet brown eyes ready to spill out tears. "He's an engineer. He doesn't understand sensitive people but he makes an effort most of the time. I try to be patient with him."

Laughlin didn't know whether to laugh or frown over her opinion of her husband. He held the impulse and waited.

"Being a psychologist gives me much knowledge about myself, and it helps me gain control. Franklin always asked my advice about patients and things. I don't understand what happened to him."

Laughlin was grateful the talk got around to Franklin Mo again, and he hoped he could get a better description of the missing man.

"He looked like a different person, all in black velvet-like pants and a shiny yellow vest . . . maybe like a magician. Isn't that weird?"

"Sure is," Laughlin agreed, but then he thought the whole case was weird, and he was getting weirded out himself.

Mason took a very deep breath, sighed twice, and went on. "He wanted to borrow my car, can you imagine? I told him absolutely no, and he shrugged. He wanted to know how come he had my address, and I told him he was a bastard and to never come to my home again. He left."

"Had he hurt you? You called him a bastard."

"Oh my god, are you dense or something? He forced me into an affair with him. He said I needed real sex to calm me down and help my heart rate. I believed him until he disappeared and left me with tachycardia—that's a fast heart rate."

"Did he ever mention Jeffrey Faulk or Gene Biskoff?"

"No. He did tell me his wife was a lesbian and he needed me."

"A lesbian?"

"Yes. She had apparently deceived him, and he was lonely."

Laughlin swallowed hard at one of the oldest lines ever played. He studied the anguished face of this messed-up woman and wondered what would happen to the jail inmates who relied on her.

"Did he ever mention Nora Weber, the psychiatrist?"

"Of course. He said she was a bad person, whom he would never work with because she had treated him so awfully. I never did find out why, but I was glad because I could have been jealous. She's so smart." She paused and looked at her hands. She placed her fingers at her neck and counted. She wrote down the rate. She sighed and looked at the sergeant sitting beside her.

"I think I'd like a mai tai now and with vodka," she requested sweetly.

That was the extent of the interview—two more drinks, which she left half full, and a couple of pulse takings, recording the findings, comparing them to an article in *Redbook* magazine and no more. No direct threats from Franklin Mo but a strange meeting, which frightened the guilt-ridden, uptight woman. Of course, her whole story could be bullshit. He insisted she have two cups of coffee before they left the restaurant.

After getting a sudden kiss on the cheek from Dr. Mason as they stood by her car, Laughlin stepped back quickly, and she sat down behind the wheel. Relief flooding him, he was very glad to see her drive off. It was twelve-thirty, and his black-haired woman was long gone.

Swearing all the way to his house, he muddled through a summary of the case, took a productive shower, and fell in his rumpled bed, bemoaning his lack of a loving woman. Maybe he should take a rowboat and go off to nowhere. He sighed and resolved to be up again in a few hours.

CHAPTER 26

So Franklin Mo was alive and wandering around the city. APBs and the like had not spotted him, but maybe he had returned to his hideaway apartment. Max was filled in with the info, and, as if on cue, the stakeout had called in to say there was noise in the place. The three sheriff's men quietly climbed the stairs and listened. There was silence. Opening the door but expecting nothing, they found the purple-haired head of Elvira Moody between the legs of the indolent manager. She looked up, turned, and smiled.

"You want some too?" she asked as she pushed her streaked frizz from her face.

"You ain't to come in here. Get the hell out!" the manager said as he arched his back, raised his enormous belly, and tried to pull his pants to cover it. "This is a restricted area. Sheriff said so."

"You're so right. Too bad you didn't honor that and don't remember us," Max retorted.

"Stay seated, mister. And you, Ms. Moody, sit down now," Laughlin instructed. "*Now* I said."

Finally wiggling into his paint-smeared pants, the disappointed man began swearing.

Ms. Moody wiped her mouth and laughed. "I'm just thanking the gentleman. He was so sweet to let me stay here. Snuck me right in under the deputy's nose, so to speak. Wrapped me and him in his robe, we did a little sashaying, and the guy wasn't even interested 'cause he thought it weren't nothing but Irwin here just checking the place. We've had a fantastic time, right, you big dog, you?"

Max assured the frowning Deputy Torres he had done the correct thing in waiting for backup, and they checked out the rest of the rooms. All was clear. Laughlin put his gun away and sat down in front of the two disheveled, obviously high interlopers.

"We've got some uncut coke. Want some? First class, I know where to get the best. They love me on the street 'cause I'm beautiful and, you know, desirable, you know. I could get anything I want and give what I want to give to you if you like. I really am good at giving. I give all, and that's better than all the other girls," Elvira chanted and stood up, swaying her hips and cupping her breasts.

"Sit down," Laughlin ordered. Max and the round-faced deputy stood by smirking silently.

"Oh, you great big wonderful man, you great big wonderful man, put your arms around me, honey, oh, you beautiful man," she continued and stumbled into the table. "Come and get me. I'm yours, but for fucking sake, don't tell me what to do. That sucks. Who the hell are you anyway? Comin' in here to boss me—forget it, shithead." Max guided her into a corner, but she kept yelling, "You don't scare me, buster! Keep away, I'm just standing here. I've got rights, fucker."

"Hold on now, baby. Let's cooperate, huh?" the stubby manager offered.

"She's not in any condition to cooperate right now, but maybe you could set us straight about her being here," Laughlin countered.

"Sure, sure. She comes here about six this morning or so, and I let her stay. She's the guy's girl, she says. I knowed I swear I musta sees her here in the past, but this time she was alone. She ain't really got drugs. A naturally high is all. Honest. Maybe a little whisky but that's all. Honest."

Elvira was sitting, then standing. Up and down, she went, humming loudly and fondling her blouse. Then she put her hand between her legs. "Oh, I need some help here, honey. Come on, come on, come on!"

"Where's the apartment renter? Where's Dolmer?" Laughlin spoke sharply over Elvira's yelling. "You said you hadn't seen him in months."

"True, Officer. Hey, take it easy, Elvira baby. Not now. She'd wanted to sell some of his stuff, but I said no way. Honest, Officer, I said no way."

Laughlin saw Max and the young deputy transfixed. He decided the manager controlled Elvira better than they did, but Max was finally on the phone, describing the scene and asking for help.

"I have got to pee, and I mean it. I do it here or in the john. Decide, Officer."

"You, Deputy Torres, take her to the bathroom and leave the door open."

"You can come too. It can be a threesome. I can handle it," Elvira insisted as she lifted her skirt and began pulling her pants down. A frost-colored vodka bottle fell out, and some rumpled dollar bills followed. "Goddamn it! I need those." She fell down to the floor and picked everything up and then began jumping up and down on her way to the toilet. "Get my purse. I need my purse."

Max picked up the stuffed satchel, rifled through it, and tossed it to the deputy.

The quiet, while the hyped woman was in the bathroom, gave Laughlin a moment to question the manager, but it didn't last longer than the moment. She was back with lipstick all over her cheeks and on her nails. She bumped Max with her hip and had her arms around Torres, the young deputy who tried to drag her to the couch. "What a bunch of wusses you guys are. I mean fuck it."

Laughlin took the vodka, the money, some air-freshener, and a big green shampoo bottle off her waist tucked in a belt. The purse had three towels and two bars of soap wrapped in with the makeup and a bra. The address to the place was printed on yellow legal paper and also underlined in a newspaper article.

In five minutes, calm was restored when Elvira Moody, for the second time in a week, went away on a seventy-two-hour hold while she was proposing marriage to the mental health team. Irwin, the unsatisfied manager, demanded a lawyer as he was carted off. When all was clear, the three sheriff's men trudged down the stairs. Torres had a few more hours to sit in his unmarked car until the shift change. Laughlin and Max headed for the station.

"Elvira must have gotten the address from the paper's story, not from being here before. Maybe Mo had some extra money in the apartment. Let's go back. Franklin Mo was definitely the renter. His DNA was the same that as from the combed hair in the bedroom."

"I dunno, it's true he didn't get anything from Manfred and he didn't use his credit cards. He had to have a stash somewhere, but I thought we'd done a good job going over the apartment, and forensics didn't find anything either, Sergeant."

"Yeah, I know. But that's his only resource other than his wife, who was gone, and I can't see the little old Mrs. Flower Lady giving him a penny. I guess he's got another source we don't know about. Mason said she didn't give him a dime," he summarized. "Let's forget it and call it a day . . . after we write this up," Laughlin relented.

Max smiled.

CHAPTER 27

Back at the station, they both reviewed all the reports to date and came up blank. Laughlin looked around at the scattering of desks with hunched over officers working cases, typing and scratching away. He glanced at Max who was rubbing his arm while chewing a pencil. "What now?"

"I'm stymied," Max threw out into the stale air and tossed a balled-up piece of paper at Laughlin.

"You said it for me, thanks. I needed a game of one-on-one," Laughlin responded.

"Let's get out of here, okay? We'll sleep on the whole mess, okay?"

"Okay, as if we hadn't been doing that all along."

They shoved off from their desks and strolled out of the station. The night was coming up quickly, and Laughlin's shoulders felt the burden. He had no dramatic incident to rage against, not even a just cause to motivate him. He had dead men and a missing man, and that was it. He drove slowly through streets already half asleep. It always struck him that Los Angeles was not an all-night city to the visible eye, except for Sunset Boulevard kids spilling out of clubs. All the corruption and intrigue was behind some torn screen, a dark alley, a carved door, a hotel room, a luxurious office, not out in the open.

When he got home, Mr. Winkler was waiting for him, this time sitting on the front steps without a Rosie apparently.

"How's it going, young man?" The old man pushed himself up with his arms, wobbled, slowly straightened his legs, and looked up as Laughlin reached him so he would not tumble flat on his face.

"Not much to report," Laughlin said.

"Well, I've got something for you. I bet it helps, honestly. I've struggled with whether to tell you or not. I believe I must now confess."

"Hey, come on in. I picked up some sushi at Ralph's. You like the stuff, don't you?"

"I wish I had Rosie with me, but she's at home with my wife to keep her company right now. That woman goes in and out of the hospital. I have to keep her at home though she loves the sushi."

"Come on in, and eat it for her."

Laughlin found his feelings mixed with impatience and fondness for the old wanderer. Damn, this case had old people all over. The house was quiet, and only dust motes swirled around the paths of light when the two men disturbed the living room to sit down.

"Did you tell me about Elvira, or did I tell you before you told me?" entreated Winkler.

"What do you mean?" the detective said as he shoved a roll in his month. "I'm not sure what you're talking about." He concentrated removing the lid from the second little tray of sushi.

"Elvira, Elvira. You know whom I mean. Elvira." Winkler took the food and set in his lap. His eyes were fixed on Laughlin.

"Who's Elvira?"

"Oh, why make this so profoundly difficult?"

"I don't know what you mean, Mr. Winkler," Laughlin answered firmly.

"She's very fond of you."

"Who are you talking about? What are you saying? It's late." He chewed a kappa roll and said, "Here's another tray of sushi. Eat."

"She had me meet you at your house when she found out you were investigating the whereabouts of Franklin. Then when she saw you, she fell in love with you at the bookstore. She acted tough, but she told me it was all over for her when she saw you. Of course, shooting poor Manfred was too much for her, and she ran. You understand, don't you?"

"Please wait a moment, slow down. What are you talking about?"

"I'm talking about my daughter-in-law, Elvira Winkler, although she uses Elvira Moody most of the time. Says it fits her ever since my son Robert died in Vietnam just as everyone was leaving, shot, and killed. Bam. Blown to bloody pieces. I knew that because his buddies told me, not the government, which says everyone dies cleanly. He was twenty, and she was eighteen. That was it. He died, and every war from then on—including Grenada and the Gulf—caused Elvira to go crazy again. Twenty-five years of crazy, and she's still so young just in her forties. She's been crazy multiple times since then—that is, till you."

"Elvira Moody?" Laughlin repeated the name and took a drink of beer.

"Yes, she called me. So you put her in the hospital again and underneath it, she's grateful. Sometimes she can't get a hold of herself and needs help before she does a major bad. There is some insight there, but it gets lost in grief gone manic, you know."

"Elvira Moody. Elvira Moody, the bookstore clerk?" Laughlin murmured.

"That's it, my boy. Now I'm going to help you with the case. Elvira said I should."

"You're going to help me?" Laughlin repeated incredulously.

"Yup. By the way, this sushi is fresh enough, but you should try this great place in little Tokyo." Winkler munched while talking eagerly.

"Wait a second, how did you find out I was investigating the missing Franklin Mo? How did you find out where I live? And that—"

"All right, one thing at a time. You working on the case, that's easy. Besides records at the station, the scuttlebutt at the jail after your first interviews came right down the pike, as they say or used to say in Seattle when lumbering was respectable. Anyway, Elvira knows many an inmate. They come to groups at the outpatient clinic after they get out of jail. Too many kids arrested for drug use, damn shame."

Laughlin's face squeezed into a fixed frown. He took another piece of shrimp with rice, smeared it with a big gob of wasabi, and pushed it in his mouth. He waited.

"Now, you don't really believe because you're a sheriff and the DMV hides the address on your car registration and license, someone can't find out where you live? I mean, all you have to do is ask around and maybe have someone follow you. Elvira knew where you lived right after you were assigned the case, and she had me check out what you were like. Then Manfred was killed, and she met you right at the store. I told her you were an upright guy, honest." Winkler stopped talking and pinched some ginger up with his thumb and finger to place gently on his tongue. "Especially after your beer offering and then helping Rosie at Denny's. That was really gallant."

Laughlin downed the rest of his beer and stared at the old man. According to Winkler's observations, the suspects in the case could get any information they wanted, probably his social security number as well as what was in his saving account. His privacy was really an illusion. He wondered how much they knew and if someone was watching them right now.

"Um, that is good," Winkler muffled as he chewed.

Straightening his back, Laughlin glanced out the living-room window to shrouded streetlights, shadows, and blackness. Inside the overhead light beamed bright exposure, and he immediately got up and switched it off. After he stepped closer to the window and saw nothing else, he turned a small table light near Winkler, not himself.

"Oh, don't get too paranoid, Sergeant. No one's watching you now. At least I don't think so."

The detective grimaced and sat down again. He took a deep breath and asked, "So what did you want to tell me? Have you been sizing me up for one of the suspects in this case?"

"I still want to be your Meyer. Don't be angry. People have to protect themselves, you know."

"I figured the law and the sheriff were there to protect people, not be spied on."

"Well, maybe you made the wrong assumptions. How are the so-called people to know merely because a guy wears a uniform that he's a good guy, or gal, for that matter? Haven't you learned anything about the twentieth century and deception? I mean, honestly, you've got to check the person out, and so we did."

Instinctually, the sergeant kept his guard even though he realized he was faced only with this fragile, sushi eating munchkin. He was ticked and tired at the wacky character of this case. "How dare they" was his reaction. Finally, he attempted the upper hand again and decided to pursue Winkler's opening gambit.

"So what is the information you have besides what you know about me?"

"Now that's the spirit. You have to understand the mentally ill. As John Dryden wrote, 'Of all the tyrannies of human kind, the worst is that which persecutes the mind.' It's terrible for Elvira. She can't trust easily, and dear Manfred had been so open-minded to give her a job. Now he is gone. How can she be sure of anyone? So she merely goes off on pleasure to escape. Understand?"

"Hell, it's fine to give me your theories on your daughter-in-law, but get to the point. You said you had some information to give me. I already know how sick Elvira Moody Winkler is."

"Oh my. You're angry, irritated that others don't trust you right off. Why should they? Elvira is not dumb. She's manic at times, not dumb."

"Look, it's late. Give me your information, and let's call it a night."

"Manfred was being blackmailed."

"We knew that," Laughlin shot back.

"Oh, really? Well, maybe the word is wrong. Extortion might be better. Eric Manfred was an honorable man who was willing to pay for information."

"An honorable man. Okay. Let's say he was a sweetheart. What was he paying for?"

"He wanted some information from Franklin Mo."

"Are you withholding for some payoff because I won't give it to you?"

"Oh, Sergeant, that hurt. I'm trying to do the best for my Elvira. She's hurting. She used to go to Pasadena to try to get information about what was going on and what distressed Manfred. She'd search that apartment where you found her tonight, but all she wound up with was a disgusting manager in love with her."

"Did she meet with Franklin Mo or with that guy Jeffrey Faulk?"

"Maybe. I don't know for sure. She did handle some of the envelopes and put them in the books. She told me that." Winkler stuffed the last of his sushi in his mouth, wiped his lips with a quick swipe across a handkerchief his held in this hand, and continued, "I'd begged her to come and live with the Rosies and me to escape from the pressure. We would have gladly supported her but she felt she had to live on her SSI all by herself."

"What do you know about the envelopes?"

"You know, the ones where Manfred left money when he had to go out of town for books."

"What was that about Dylan?"

"Dylan Thomas, everybody knows the poet. Apparently, Manfred liked that poet. The signal was behind the books he had some more money for Mo."

Laughlin took a deep breath, raised his arms above him, and stretched.

The beer calmed his suspicions, and he scrutinized the old man. He certainly had misjudged him. He'd been played by him, but merely a little bit, he decided.

"So is that it?"

"I think so. Elvira said she'd tell you more if she thought of anything. She'll be crashing from the meth or coke or whatever, but she said she'd call you. You know, an unlisted phone number is not a big deal."

Laughlin turned immediately to check the phone, turned quickly back, and stood up. "Come on, let's go."

"I am not going to jail," Winkler declared vehemently.

"Who said you were?"

"I did nothing wrong in informing you, and you should be grateful," asserted the crouched figure as he tried to get up.

"Come on, come on. Look who's paranoid now," Laughlin mused.

Winkler shoved away Laughlin's helping hand and rose in jerks to his small height. They walked out the door and down the steps separately. The air was balmy and calling out to wanderers. Nothing else was said until they reached Winkler's porch steps, and then they both offered, "Good night."

Laughlin jogged back past his house and through the alley and back again, aware that he was looking for someone watching his house. Finally, he went in, turned all the lights off, and climbed the stairs in darkness. "A little touch of paranoia," he concluded, "shouldn't hurt too much. Might as well add that to all the other disorders." While looking out the window, he accepted the inoculation via another beer. He'd carried some neglected mail upstairs, turned the table light on, and sat on the bed, opening his mail. A water bill showed how much water he used, an electric bill showed how much electricity, and the gas and the telephone and so on. Everybody was watching him. He threw the bills on the floor, turned off the light, finished his beer, and closed his eyes.

CHAPTER 28

Max was sitting at his desk, folding a piece of paper into an airplane. He looked up at Laughlin as he lumbered in the office and laughed.

"Wait until you read this. You'll really feel hung over."

Laughlin took the lab report and read the following out loud:

> *The only find for the box of books, other than their literary value, which far surpasses their monetary value of about fifteen hundred to two thousand dollars for these particular editions, is that the order you gave them to us, using only the last name of the authors, reads "TO FRANKLIN MO PS NO MORE."*

> *The envelope, as well as the books, had smudged figure prints with one partial of Manfred and a Jeffrey Faulk.*

> *I'm not sure if that helps but this is all we could find.*

> *B. Singh, M.D.*

Laughlin nodded and swore quietly. He hunched down, elbows on his desk, and clenched his jaw. He smoothed the paper out and stuck it in the manila folder, pensively adding, "Well, that only confirms that Manfred was giving money to Mo and decided to stop. That, of course, could be the motive for killing the man."

"Which man?"

Ignoring the comment, Laughlin stated, "I think we have to go back to the bookstore and look for more messages."

Max grimaced but followed.

They drove in silence after Laughlin filled Max in on his encounter with Winkler. The bookstore still looked forlorn, and sadness settled over Laughlin as he thought about how helpless they had been in preventing Manfred's death. They shut the door behind them gently, but as they entered, Manfred's big cat came up to them in a hurry. It rubbed up against Laughlin's leg, meowed piteously, and let Max give it a hardy rubdown to a loud purring.

"Oh great. No one took care of the cat after I fed him that once. The thing must be starving by now."

"I don't know. This boy seems rather well endowed," Max observed.

The cat followed them around the rooms, but no more messages were revealed from the stacks of books, even from those in the glassed-in cases. Laughlin sat at the counter and flipped through some order sheets. The cat was immediately up and on the papers, asking for his share of attention. Persistent in getting petted, he spilled papers all over and pushed his face into Laughlin's, sniffing, examining, and purring.

"You're gonna have to take this guy with you, Sarge. We've got too many cats and dogs now, and Kim is gone for the next two weeks."

"Wait a minute, how about Manfred's sister? She has first right of refusal," Laughlin retorted.

"Well, I'll call her, but, if I remember correctly, she has a bad allergy to fur and had two fake cats, so she may already have all she needs," Max replied. "You can't let the big guy go to the pound, Sarge. I'll call the poor guy's sister, but I'll bet she'll be relieved if you take the cat."

With the cat lying across Laughlin's neck and equally distributed on his shoulders, the detectives drove up to the sergeant's house. Laughlin wanted to deposit the cat inside, but the animal protested and clung on to the man.

Max suggested he go alone to the store for litter and food while Laughlin decided where the cat could be kept. Walking around with the cat in his arms, they both decided on the basement. "Hey, buddy, you stay here until I figure out what to do with you." The sergeant released the animal on the stairs to the basement and shut the door. Retreating to his chair to wait for Max, he was startled to find the cat up on him shortly afterward; it had merely pushed the door open and took over the house.

The two detectives did their best with a litter set up, and Laughlin picked up the cat and dumped it in the tray brimming with litter. While the litter stayed in the basement, the cat followed Laughlin and ate two cans of food. He again found Laughlin in his big chair and settled down as the two men had beers. After a vigorous amount of another spell of eating and a small drink of water, the cat returned to the chair, and that was that.

"He already thinks he's the king of the castle," Max said, laughing.

"Well, it's just until we get in contact with Manfred's sister. Don't forget."

"I won't, but I think he will," Max said and gestured toward the cat.

"I hope it—or he—has the right food until then."

They shut the door and were on their way to eat when Dr. Banting's call was put through.

"Yes, this is Sergeant Laughlin."

"Sergeant, I don't know if you remember me. I'm a psychiatrist at the County's mental health jail."

"Sure. What can I do for you?"

"It's Dr. Mason. She called me and told me that Franklin Mo has been tormenting her and wants her to meet him at the shopping center at Topanga. She asked me to go instead. She is not willing and said her heart rate was up too high. I didn't think it was appropriate to go without talking to you first."

"Correct. Where does he want to meet her?"

"In the appliance part of Sears on the first level."

"Does he know you've been called?"

"He knows I'll bring him money."

"I don't think you should go. Give me the information, please."

The mental health psychiatrist told him the details and insisted, since Mason said that Mo looked weird the last time she saw him, it would be best if, this time, she went to the meeting to identify him. "I'd know him whatever his getup. Remember, Mary and I met with him daily at conferences—when he was at the jail, that is," she declared. "That will help, right? Besides, he said something strange about being Freeman Molloy."

No one knew where this third name came from, and a search was made of phones and addresses without results. There was no directory for cell phones. The geeks would have to be put on the search. Frustrated but more determined than ever, the detectives arranged coverage and met Banting at her home. It was a small stucco house in South Pasadena with big pine trees shading a blue tiled roof. Her husband was an Asian, dressed in a long silk robe, not quite a kimono. It was decorated with LA Lakers insignia blazoned across the front and back panels. The guy was at least six two. Protective of his wife, he was home to hear how this would be handled. He wanted more deputies involved.

"Curious about the name *Banting*?" he asked immediately and explained he had been adopted as a three-year-old orphan in Hawaii by an American serviceman and his wife.

Just as Laughlin was going to explore that bit of information, Dr. Banting came out of a back room dressed in Levi's and a royal-blue sweater set. Her black hair and smooth face looked so much better than when it was set in a physician's lab coat.

They discussed the plan and had some nicely flavored ice water. Banting assured her husband that Mason had Franklin's agreement to the switch as long as money came along as well. She would ride with Laughlin and Max in an unmarked car, and they would be near her throughout the time she waited for Mo to show. He wouldn't recognize them or any of the others in the stakeout. Again, her husband interjected, saying he would also go. That was nixed since Mo might spot him and think something was up.

The woman was calmer than her spouse and said that Mo had always treated her with respect, although she added hesitantly, he had always intimated that she should hang around with him more than she ever wanted.

"He could never collect enough followers. I think he resented that I didn't want to be around him. I wanted to get home to George, have some free time, and watch TV in bed when we weren't out jogging."

"It's draining to see all those brain-damaged kids with nowhere to go except back to jail," her husband added. "The bank contributes to a fund for computers at the jail in a rehab program, but most of the young men have trouble even reading. I'd like Beatrice out of the jail mental health, but right now I can't persuade her to leave because she cares too much about the program," George reflected.

"We'll get your wife out of this Franklin Mo situation as soon as we see him, Mr. Banting, sir," Laughlin offered.

They drove slowly across town, taking the 110 down to the 10 and then the 405 to Ventura Boulevard and Topanga. Max questioned why, and Laughlin said he wanted to make sure no one was following them. Taking the 101 might be easier to follow the car, he observed. Max was dubious. Laughlin insisted.

The parking lot was crowded. They were too early for the appointed time and sat in the car for about ten minutes.

"All these people in the valley and LA . . . I wonder if they know what's going on or how this place came to be," Banting questioned.

"Not about this man, they don't," Max responded.

"I mean do they even know about Mulholland and Chandler? The history of the place?"

"More people are like those young guys in jail—ignorant and not even aware of their ignorance," Laughlin added.

"What do you know about it, Doctor?" Max asked off handedly.

"Oh, I know quite a bit. I love history, and this is my city now, so I try to educate myself."

"Are you talking about Chandler, the writer?" Laughlin offered.

"Actually, I was talking about the *LA Times* publisher, but both are important to the city. Do you like Chandler?"

"I always thought maybe I'd be a private detective after I retire from the department—you know, make a little extra."

"Be like Sam Spade, Sergeant?" Max joked.

"Well, Sam Spade wasn't created by Raymond Chandler," the psychiatrist explained. "Philip Marlowe was Chandler's man, and Sam Spade was Dashiell Hammett's."

"I guess we'll need to bone up on these guys, but now we've got to go. I'll walk in after you, but Max will go a little ahead through a different entrance," Laughlin instructed.

"You don't think he'll be suspicious to see men around me?"

"We'll be discreet. Busy yourself with whatever, we'll stay clear."

There were six plain-clothe men and women at the store already. Max sauntered into the Sears department store men's clothes and out into the mall. He liked it that no one noticed him, a black guy in the San Fernando Valley. There were no glances following him or anyone staring after him. He'd come downstairs to look at lawn mowers.

Small and neat, Banting walked to the mall entrance through a California Pizza Kitchen restaurant and was inside in a moment.

Laughlin waited until he figured she was through the pizza place and then strode through the restaurant itself and out into the long hallways. It was crowded, and he scanned the area. He didn't see Banting. He contacted Max and asked if he saw her.

The upshot was that no one saw the elusive Franklin Mo, and Banting never showed at the Sears at all. They traced her steps through the restaurant where a waiter said he'd see the lovely Chinese woman sit down at a booth near the exit after she'd gone to the restroom. A weird green-clothed guy sat behind her, and then she left the way she came, followed by the green guy, through the restaurant's front entrance into the parking lot.

"How could you have missed her sitting at the restaurant? Didn't you have your eye on her the whole time?"

The questions stung repeatedly, and yet no one said a thing. Going through the setup again was frustrating. The audacity of the guy, kidnapping her in front of a secure trap. How had he done it?

The search of the parking lot yielded nothing. How could anyone be found in the myriad of cars stretching out over acres? A review of the security tapes was fruitless, and the waiter's description only emphasized a guy in a green velvet jacket, who walked out behind the Asian lady dressed in Levi's and a nice blue sweater. No doubt it was Banting.

CHAPTER 29

Laughlin swore out loud to the floor and to the roof. Banting had disappeared into the bathroom as he had entered into the restaurant and then strolled out looking for her in the mall hallways. Berating himself for not noticing any green-clothed guy, he was at a complete loss. Max took over and put out a bulletin for Banting and cruised around the area as Laughlin sat in the car, rubbing his chin and continuing to swear. Would she die because of his stupidity?

A call to her husband and a tap on their phone would be the next plan. Then silence for the rest of the day. Max took the whole botched sting as part of the game. "Nothing will happen to her, honest, Sergeant. She'll be okay 'cause he wants money," Max offered.

Refusing to call it a day, Laughlin sat at the station, cleaning out his desk and muttering to himself that he was incompetent and never should have agreed to the meeting. An image of sitting at his bedroom window as a child popped up, and he felt humiliation swarm over him, covering him with bites of helplessness.

Max shrugged, and said, "Hey, it's not over yet," and left. He knew only Laughlin could climb the climb to get out of his mood and resolve to get the suspect.

The big detective felt very humbled. Even his buddy Max was more resilient. It wasn't only that this missing man had outsmarted him but that he, Laughlin, had assured Banting's husband that she would be perfectly safe. Action was what was needed. Berating himself again, he sat thinking about what he could do. He'd been outsmarted for the moment, beaten at the game.

Sudden laughter and some deputies discussing football, a bit of nonsense, brought him back to the present. He decided to go over to Banting's house and wait with the husband.

He drove slowly, planning what to say and hoping to give encouragement when he had none himself. Parking on a side street, he jogged to the house; the place was dark. He banged on the door, still not willing to abandon his plan. There was no answer to his call. He sat on the porch steps. This case had frustrated him from the beginning. No one had cared much for the missing Franklin Mo or whatever his name was—Dolmer or maybe Molloy. No one gave much of a damn for poor Manfred, the bookman, either. Also, there was the crazy guy Gene, his genetics and eugenics and amputations. Who cared for him? Now the decent Dr. Banting was sucked into the void. Where was the rest of the staff at jail mental health in all this?

Laughlin felt the cold slate steps. He didn't move. A full moon came over a house across the street and peered down at him. He felt scrutinized. How long could he sit there, his ass getting cold and his mood getting hotter? Nothing moved within his sight.

Cutting the silence, his cell phone rang suddenly. Max, at two in the morning, informed him of a message at the station that Dr. Banting was with her husband in Carmel. Confused and tired, the detective listened to the report that Dr. Banting submitted.

Mo was sitting in the first restaurant booth by the door, and he told her, "Go to the ladies room and count to thirty, half a minute," and come back and sit down in the booth ahead of him." She'd done just that. He told her to put the money on the seat and leave.

Safe with all the coverage, she'd left him the money and called her husband as she had promised. Her husband was at the parking lot already, picked her up, took her out of the city, and insisted she stay out of this mess from then on.

Assuming the surveillance team was following Mo, she hadn't watched for his car. She described Mo as the man she knew, but with a green suit, no tie, and dyed reddish hair and beard. He claimed his name was Malloy, and whoever Franklin Mo was, he'd only knew that Mo had given him Mason's number. However, he'd had no trouble recognizing Dr. Banting and thanked her for the money he said was "owed" him. He instructed her to walk out the same way she came in. Concluding her report, she asked if Mo was arrested.

Max added, "See, Sarge, I told you she'd be all right. Figure tomorrow we'll get him."

What a fucking relief and what a shameful let down to thoughts of kidnapping, rape, murder, and nothing to compensate like an arrest. Fighting a need to punch something, Laughlin slouched away from Banting's house to his car and maneuvered it through the quiet streets. It seemed as if everyone had outsmarted him, and he was left with his mouth open in a big duh. That was it.

Botched. He'd had reservations about Banting keeping the meet, but she wasn't to blame. He couldn't fault the others either. He had followed her in and missed the whole encounter. He pulled into his driveway and slowly got out of the car. Mr. Winkler wasn't on the porch, and that was a relief. No amateur interrogation to fumble through.

On top of feeling like a fool, he had to acknowledge that he had found those mixed feelings about nothing more decisively dangerous happening disturbing. Chastising himself for wanting action and aware of the dose of damaged pride at no arrest, he unlocked his front door and stepped into the dark.

He dropped down on his big living-room chair, his arms hanging down the sides, his legs stretched out on the slats of the wooden floor, and he took a deep breath and loudly let out a "whew."

Safe at home. He could hide for the moment. He closed his eyes and sat in the silence.

Then oomph! Like an unexpected punch to the gut, the cat jumped up on Laughlin and stuck his nose in the stunned detective's face. He shoved the attacker off, got up to defend himself, and immediately regretted his actions.

"Hey, goddamn it, cat. Remember, I'm in law enforcement. Don't jump me out of nowhere."

He found the unaffected feline waiting in the kitchen for his food.

CHAPTER 30

His cell phone called him again and again, but he lay in bed, staring at the ceiling where he saw some cobwebs dangling and stirring with a flop of his sheet. Too much beer and too much self-pity for himself were his diagnoses. He tried to raise himself, but realized the cat was on his chest cleaning his chin with a rough tongue. It was past ten according to his watch, which the cat had let him glance at. He told the cat it was time to get off and rolled over slowly to get his phone.

"For fucking sake, Laughlin, stop brooding about the stupid sting failing. We've been running around on this assignment over a week and nothing. Let's get this guy," Max instructed his sergeant.

"It's been eleven days and then this. I think I've got to understand how I bungled this major league," Laughlin replied.

"Okay, okay, but don't go Freddie Poplar on me. Breakfast at Denny's now, or I'll come over to your house. Damn it, you're supposed to be my inspiration," Max goaded.

Laughlin frowned. "What kind of support are you, asshole?"

"Now, that's the man I know, nasty bastard on the hunt."

Unshaven and in a T-shirt and Levi's, Laughlin jogged over, stumbled in the restaurant, and ate begrudgingly.

"You pay since you're the failure, smart guy," Max decided. He gathered up his leftover fries and bunched them on the greasy paper next to the ketchup.

Laughlin stood up and took a hard look at Max.

"What's that Freddie Poplar shit supposed to mean? Do you think I'm going to kill myself?"

"Who knows? You're beating yourself up like it," Max mumbled.

"Damn it, what did you say?"

"I'm eating, and I'm going to finish eating at my leisure, okay? I have some rights, you know. Don't get pugnacious." Max took a bite of his burger, one fry, and a sip of his big lemonade. He was not intimidated by his sergeant even though the guy stood a good five or six inches taller. The senior deputy held his own with a knowing confidence. His dark eyes revealed a faith in his intelligence, and his humor rendered him immune to big shots.

Laughlin stood up and waited. Nothing happened. Max took another bite and another sip. He burped. He stared wide-eyed at the standing and infuriated sergeant, shrugged, and finished his pickle. Some chattering teenage kids brushed by, hassling one another, and slid into chairs nearby.

Laughlin walked out and left the noise. He tramped to Max's battered car and sat in it, waiting for Max. He'd been stupid to complain to Max, and Max took it as unproductive. Rightly so, he acknowledged.

So Franklin Mo outsmarted him or at least inadvertently made a fool of him. It wasn't the first time, and it might not be the last in his less-than-polished career. Start thinking, not whining. Now. He glanced in the rearview mirror to look for Max, but there was no one. He waited.

"Okay, okay. Get it together. Start again. We've been hunting this guy for eleven days now," he reflected. He pulled his hands through his hair, feeling the bumps of his skull, and waited patiently. He needed accurate answers from somewhere.

Max opened the backdoor of the car, and sat down. "Here are the keys. Home, James. I'm afraid to sit up front with you. You might crash the car, Sarge," he said and smiled.

"Okay, okay, you've made your point. Don't you ever get down, Mr. Perfect?" Laughlin retorted.

"Well, this time you got something right with the use of the word *perfect* for me. Now what's next?"

Laughlin's cell phone rang as if to reply to Max's question.

"Where? Oh great! He was there all along," Laughlin exclaimed. "Where is he now?"

There was silence as he listened, and then he started the car. They drove to Laughlin's where the sergeant changed while Max petted the cat.

"You might as well come with me if you'll risk it. We'll pick up your car later."

"Before we go, the Mr. Perfect wants to know the destination from the Mr. Fuck Up?"

Ignoring the bait, Laughlin sighed and rattled off, "The big County Hospital again. Eugene or Gene Biskoff is there and had been there all along."

Security Guard Lemont Freedlander led the detectives to the basement; they could hear banging and yelling coming from the kitchens, and watched loads of laundry shoveling off to unknown areas. They finally found the site of discovery of the missing patient in a wide white-painted bend in the hallway.

The young guard had discovered the distressed man in one of the tunnels that formed underground passages from the big hospital to its satellite hospitals. Biskoff camped at one of the junctions. He had quite an elaborate setup, including a mattress, a fat night-light, boxes of raisins, bags of chips, loaves of bread and a big bottle of cranberry juice. Apparently, every night, he ventured out and up to a bathroom and even had a washcloth hanging over one of the makeshift cartons he used as storage.

"I guess he'd stow the stuff on a gurney and wheel it around periodically, so we missed discovering it until now," the guard said with no apology forthcoming. "He'd leave his wheelchair parked with the others since the gurney gave him enough support to hop around is my guess. We found some of his stuff in one of the trams used for repairs, could get around with no problem in them trams. Since the earthquake, this area wasn't used much. Anyways, then he'd pick up his shit at shifts changes and be on his way."

The guard paused for a sip of his coffee held in a LAC-USC mug and finished, "He dinnit give me no trouble. He was real willing about going up to a bed, said he needed a good shower, and whew, he was right on."

"So he's up on the surgery ward now?" Laughlin asked.

"Yup," the guard replied and smacked his lips. "Things like that happen here," he concluded as they walked to the elevator, and Freedlander sat back down at his desk. "We're short of staff, man, and the halls upstairs is like a busy downtown street, so we concentrate there, understand?"

Laughlin and Max made their way from the special elevator up to the main floor and then went to the alcove bank of public elevators to the ward with stable surgical patients. Gene certainly didn't need any more surgery.

Approaching the Formica U-shaped clerk's desk, Max smiled at a young woman dressed in surgical greens, while Laughlin stood, waiting to be recognized. A frazzled clerk sorted stacked charts frayed with use and stuck densely printed forms and mustard-colored separators in new ones.

Laughlin realized she would never ask him what his business was, so he finally showed the clerk his badge. It took her a minute to register. She scratched her thickly braided hair that moved up and down with the scratches, and turned to the woman in the surgical greens.

"This here sheriff wants to talk to Eugene Biskoff. Can you take him or get one of the nurses? You knows I can't leave the desk, Dr. Moore."

Dr. Moore smiled and answered, "Hi, Sheriff. I'll finish with my notes, and I'll be glad to take you gentlemen to the patient."

"You are?" Max inquired.

"The surgical resident on duty, sir," she replied and went back to her notes.

Laughlin and Max waited and watched. The ward was centered by the clerk's desk, and four rooms with six patients per room were its spokes. It was identical to the first ward Eugene had been in. Nurses were going in and out with carts full of medicine cups, bedpans, IV stands, or stacked sheets. Elevators opened and closed shuffling attendants pushing carts and gurneys in and out. The doctor kept writing.

Finally, she looked up, took a five-inch tome, the loosely held together chart, and slid it in front of her. "This is Mr. Biskoff's record for this year," she explained. "What is it you need?"

"We want to talk to him about what he might know regarding a crime," Laughlin replied.

"Well, I think you're in luck. He seems much more with it than the last time he was here. Come on. He's doing quite well with this new psychiatrist and special meds."

The detectives walked with the resident into the far room. Some of the men lying in white sheets sat up and called for her to come to talk with them. "Examine me, Doc. I got the heart palpates for you," and another, "Look here at me. My dick needs handling. Come on," but most were quiet. Their eyes were focused on the intruders.

Dr. Moore ignored the comments and went to the far-corner bed where a quiet, unrestrained Eugene Biskoff lay, staring out through the barred window and its dirty screen. He turned as he heard them.

"Mr. Biskoff, these two sheriffs want to talk to you. Are you okay with that?"

"You can call me Gene or Eugene. Both are good for me. Gene is in Eugene, you know. Now tell me, Doc Moore, am I to be taken away from here? I'm just feeling a little better, and I don't feel the leg so much anymore. The phantom is still haunting me a little. Can I stay a little longer? Please. Eugene needs rest. I've left my man parts alone, and he can stand sometimes on his own, mainly before I take a leak."

"No, no, don't worry. I'll let you know a couple of days before you go to rehab. Don't going running off before you talk to me, okay?"

"Not with one foot gone, I won't."

Biskoff turned his intense eyes to Laughlin, who in turn signaled Max to take Dr. Moore out and get more information. The sergeant moved around the bed, leaned up against the windowsill and related quietly, "Hi, Mr. Biskoff, I'm Detective James Laughlin from the sheriff's department. I talked with you before when you were here."

"Yes, I remember. You can use Gene or Eugene. It's easier than Biskoff and more to the point of me," Biskoff answered, then tilted his head to look up at Laughlin and added, "I was kinda confused then that . . . that—oh, I don't know. I guess that the bad genes were doing bad things. You'd asked me about Jeffrey and who was it?"

Laughlin nodded a couple of times in approval, impressed at how logical Biskoff was. "That's right. I was worried about you and your friends, Jeffrey Faulk and Franklin Mo."

"Jeffrey, is he okay? He was trying to help me."

"Yes, he's safe."

"Franklin, I think he was after something. He was acting on the bad genes, making me drink and stuff, causing mutations. He said he'd find my mama and daddy."

"How was he going to do that?"

Biskoff started squinting and nodding back and forth over and over. Laughlin wasn't sure how much to push him, maybe just one more question. But before he could ask it, the rocking man replied, "He said he was looking and he found a man like a fighter, and he would help us find my family."

"A fighter?"

"A flier. Or was it Mendelssohn? Mendel grew sugar peas, right? In situ is when they grow tissues from genes," Biskoff murmured and wiped his mouth with the corner of his sheet. "I'm a little tired now, and lunch is coming. Thank you for visiting."

Laughlin hesitated. He'd picked up how tenuous Eugene's present state was. Tottering again between wild thoughts and reality, it was risky to ask more of the guy, might set him off in a mess of garbled thoughts. But if the interview was going to get any information that could be useful, now was the time to take advantage of what lucidity the man had.

"One more thing, do you know Dr. Nora Weber, the psychiatrist?"

"Of course, I do. You asked me that before, didn't you? She helped me, but then she was gone. She really believed I could get better. I was at a conference where she asked me about my parents. Do you think the new sheriff, the guy who won the election . . . will he bring her back? He got the job because the old guy died at the time of the election, probably doesn't know much but can learn, can't he? He'll help me with the good gene too. I'm not sure which eugenics caused me to be arrested in my mitotic stage. I've got the Eugene gene and the bad gene."

Laughlin kept still, watching the struggling Eugene with his good and bad gene battle, trying to understand. Biskoff closed his eyes until his tray was set down by the busy attendant, and the patient began to eat the pudding first.

"Thank you very much for your time, Mr. Biskoff. Maybe we can talk again soon."

"That would be very good. I'm getting better every day in every way, good medicines," the hungry man recited and went on with his lunch.

The two detectives took the main elevators out to the street and stood near the wrought iron fence with its beautiful lamps and shook their heads in frustration.

"You gotta give Dr. Moore a hell of a lot of guts trying to make it in surgery," Max mentioned as they started for the parking lot.

"So did she say anything that would help us?"

"About as much as Eugene told you that could help us. Hey, there's a McDonald's. Better yet, what about the little Mexican place down State Street? That's it. Food is on me today, Sergeant," Max exclaimed.

CHAPTER 31

"So what makes me think that Eric Manfred, the obscure bookman, was murdered by our missing Franklin Mo?" Laughlin asked himself and coincidently, Max, who was eating again. Every day he asked himself and every day he failed to get an answer he felt good about.

"It kinda fits together when you realize Manfred wasn't about to allow any more extortion and Mo was vulnerable if anyone found out what he was doing. Of course, you're right. It's only a theory. We need more," Max replied and took his final bite of taco.

"I've had it for the day. I'm not sure why, but it's exhausting to talk to Eugene, Gene, or whatever Biskoff," Laughlin announced.

"Sounds good to me. Lazy as it is. Let's mull it over and I'll see in the morning. Just get me to my car, and I'm out of your hair this afternoon. It's past three o'clock anyway."

Laughlin watched Max drive off, took a deep breath, and sat down in his lounge chair out back of his house and thought about how stumped his was. As he drifted off, he heard a loud meow and saw the cat scratching at the window to get out to him. He wasn't sure if he should let him out and was ticked. Who knew the answer?

Max hadn't asked Manfred's sister yet, and he didn't want the cat lost.

He reluctantly went back in the house and petted the cat, who pushed up against him in greeting. *That's all I need—a cat*, he thought sarcastically.

Then it occurred to him he would call Lucy Tier, the zoo vet, cat lover, and lovely woman. He needed that kind of company. Maybe she was back from her research adventure and they could have some wine while discussing cats and hunting murderers.

She was at home. She would be pleased to see him. He could bring the cat, and she would check it over. It took him a good hour to get the cat in the traveling case. Those blue eyes seem to read Laughlin, and the cat hid under the bed or jumped up on a cupboard rather than be picked up and stuffed in the cat carrier. Finally, the animal succumbed to a piece of chicken and was ready, with loud protests, to be taken in the car.

Laughlin found himself trying to console the distressed cat, saying, "It's okay. Take it easy, you're okay. I'm just taking you for a ride." Sticking his finger in the slots of the carrier, he felt the cat's whiskers against him and a little plea by the cat rubbing his head against the outstretched finger of his capturer.

At Lucy's, Laughlin stood at the door with the carrier beside him, and she seemed amused as he maneuvered the carrier and his bulk through the door.

"I guess I better keep this guy in the cage, or I'll never get him in it again. I can't let him run way."

"Next time, I'll come to your place if you like," she said, laughing.

"I tell you that would be a hell of a lot easier."

He related the story behind having the cat. Lucy took the big fellow out of his carrier and examined him. The cat loved the attention and then parked on Laughlin after the exam.

"How come you weren't afraid to let him out of the cage?"

"Oh, there are too many cages already. I'm against most of them."

"I guess there have to be some to contain trouble."

"I am haunted—the tigers in barred six-by-six enclosures, the elephants in stalls of cement that hurt their feet, even birds caught for display."

"You must have had a hard day. I'm sorry."

"Think about the bears in China with cannulas in their gall bladders, living life in four-by-four cages. Bizarre that humans would treat them so awfully just for a superstition about some stupid erection idea. Or what about shark killing?"

Dylan started to nudge at Laughlin's hand for forgetting to pet him.

"I'm amazed at your cats with their nonchalance stance to another intruder," Laughlin interjected.

"Every day is hard as people enclose more wildlife. These cats were all feral and then jailed in the pound, so they've made a compromise living with me.

"Damn if I'm not learning about cats even against my will."

"Oh, you've had cats before. I know it," Lucy observed.

"Yeah, but that was when I was a kid, ages ago and less jaded ago." His childhood room had been his haven as well as his jail against the abuse. He didn't want to go back there again.

"It seems to me this guy, one beautiful seal point, has done you some good. Look how relaxed you are and how you naturally started to pet him."

"Oh, don't start that cat therapy on me. I know it lowers blood pressure to have an animal, but I'm gone too much, and besides, I think this one will go to his owner's sister. At least I hope so."

"I don't know about that. He seems already bonded to you. How about some wine and crackers?"

Laughlin apologized for not bringing a bottle and settled back, pinned by the cat and Lucy's company. They talked about their careers. She was back at the zoo, allied with Diamond, and he was trying to be successful at detecting.

"Who has the cruelest struggles—you who aim to lock people up or me who aim to free animals?" Lucy asked as she stroked the cat.

"My job is to keep the law and protect innocents, not to lock people up but to find those that do bad things, break the law, hurt others. Then they get locked up. I am a hunter."

"Oh, excuse me. A hunter of bad people. Great. What about all those who are cruel to animals?"

"I can't do it all by myself."

"My goodness, why not, Sir Galahad?"

"Don't get at me with that 'knight in shining armor' guilt trip. Look, I'm here with a cat I rescued from starvation. Doesn't that count?

She laughed and said, "All right. Let's list some things we are happy with, okay?"

"The wine is good, and you start with thoughts about what you enjoy."

There was a whole list. She began, "The sound of footsteps on gravel, sizzling onions, rushes of waves, and tree leaves fooling around in the wind, cats purring."

"All right, how about these? A foghorn wallowing, the disappearing train, and the far-off dogs' barking."

"Those are sad sounds. Let's add Beethoven's music and the pads of the newborn cat, sand, newly cleaned washcloths, eucalyptus bark, mustaches and beards, parchment paper, comforters and, I've got it, hot bathwater."

"You like mustaches?" Laughlin asked.

"At times I do."

"Are you still with that professor, goatee and all?"

"No, but here's some more things. Keep up, will you," she answered teasingly.

Then, while she poured more wine, she went on, "Sunset, sunrise, clouds, blue dragonflies, Munch, Michelangelo's Moses, dictionaries, sleeping children, orange, green, hands."

As he raised his glass to her, he added, "Wine, salt, apples, chocolate, peanut butter, blueberries, mashed potatoes, corn on the cob."

"You must be hungry. That was a good list of food. Don't forget garlic and shallots."

"That's true. Thank you for the observation, Lucy. Speaking to that, may I take you out to dinner?"

She moved over to sit by him, sinking deeply into the cushion next to him.

He put his arm around her to make more room for her, but ignoring his gesture, she took the cat's paws and splayed out the nails. "I think we should cut his nails, and you can learn how for the future. Let me get the clippers." She got up quickly but returned just as quickly, and he put his arm around her again.

"Siamese were temple guards historically. How come you associate the cat with Dylan? Is it the singer's hair?"

"No, that was the name I gave him because of the bookstore owner. I guess after the poet."

"Well, let's ask Dylan. Are you named after the poet songwriter or the Welsh poet?"

Laughlin looked at her and smiled. "Ask Dylan? Ask Dylan." He frowned. "I think you have something with that, Lucy. 'Ask Dylan' could be as simple as that. Boy, do I owe you a dinner and a big kiss."

She clipped the cat's nails, and he gently leaned over to watch. When she was done he took her hand, removed the clippers, and slowly felt each of her tapered fingers. She sat still and then he kissed her, softly brushing her lips. She gave him a more emphatic response, and the cat moved aside.

"Okay then, that was first rate, Sheriff." She sighed. Running one of her fingers over his mustache, she added, "Steady now. I've got to get up early for surgery on a tiger tomorrow, so we've got to put this on hold. Is that okay?

Laughlin sat back and waited to be able to stand and finally smiled. "Sounds like a better-than-nothing plan."

He packed up the cat with her help and sat again to assess his incentive to leave. She stood before him, smiling. "Oh well," she tossed off the phrase with a smile and then pounced on him and filled his mouth with her. Surprised at this gift, he pushed her shoulders away, and his eyes questioned her. She put her hands around his head and pulled him toward her again. She took over and felt him inside his pants, pulled them down, and lifted his shirt. He knew what to do from then on. He stopped questioning and slowly got her undressed, lifting her out of her jeans and panties. She pulled a condom from a side table and waited patiently while he put it on, twirling his hair and breathing in his ear. The moans and occasional prompts were not interfered with by the cats. Then there was quiet. Laughlin lay on the couch, head on a pillow, looking at her. She stroked his hair. There were a few polite murmurs as he dressed, and she went to her bedroom for a robe.

He wanted to say thank you but she put her finger over his lips and shook her head. He left and made it home with hope for more such days. As he dropped into bed, the small kitten he had when he was young crawled into his mind, smooth and loving, and settled down contently. Lucy was like that and maybe like the big cat he had now. His big cat shifted around and pushed up against his shoulder and both slept.

CHAPTER 32

"How in the hell do you ask a cat?" Max complained.

"Okay, okay. It's a little strange, but what's the harm in trying? Remember, that's what Manfred said."

"Shit. All right, I'll meet you at the man's apartment."

The cat sniffed around while the detectives watched. There was a kitty litter tray in the corner of the living area, which the cat decorated and earnestly went about covering up. They walked around the bedrooms, idly looking at books and lifting papers. The cat trotted along. When Laughlin knelt to retrieve a fallen paper, the cat immediately went up to him and butted his head against the kneeling detective, asking for some petting.

"I don't see any photos of the animal, and that cat box is diabolically disgusting—nothing near it or under it. What else can a cat tell us? So that's that."

"Yup. Let's go to the bookstore and see what Dylan might lead us to there."

"You really are going nuts, Sergeant."

"You have any other leads, Deputy Max?"

After giving the cat three pieces of chicken, he was stuffed in the carrier, and they were off to the bookstore.

"How did you spend your Saturday, Joseph? Oh, I watched a cat poo and walked around a dead man's home and bookstore with my crazy sergeant—really fun," Max narrated.

"Take it easy. This won't take a minute."

The bookstore was dark and somber. A relief for Laughlin, the lights came on in the back room when he threw the switch. He wished he could give Eric Manfred his life back as easily.

"I suppose the inspection of the kitty litter is my assignment and I take it willingly, just to get out of here," Max volunteered.

"It suits you, Deputy."

Laughlin sat down on the couch covered with plastic to preserve evidence and called the cat out of the carrier. The cat stood at the wire gate, surveyed the surroundings and jumped out eagerly. He went to Laughlin.

"Okay, Dylan, where is it?"

"What are you asking the cat?"

"For the evidence."

"Oh, this is great," Max retorted and sat on the desk chair.

Nothing happened. The cat walked around, Laughlin sat still and Max swiveled in the chair.

"You win. It was just an idea. Let's go," Laughlin said quietly after about ten endless minutes, listening to humming sounds in the air. Silence was quite loud, he concluded. He'd had enough of dead ends and false hopes. The cat looked at him and brought him a plastic ball with bells in it. Laughlin threw it, and the cat retrieved it three times. The last time, Laughlin saw a key stuck inside the ball.

Dylan got big pieces of chicken and Max a "humble pie," as his dad would say. It didn't take long to trace the lock for the key. A mailbox store was down the block across the street by the movie theater. There was one letter in the post-office box addressed to Manfred, and the return address was Manfred's bookstore.

They went over to Mrs. Porter immediately. Laughlin was introduced to Mrs. Porter and got the appropriate release for opening the letter; she refused the cat, took the letter, and read the contents. Max made tea. The cat wanted out of the carrier, but Mrs. Porter said no, again.

The letter explained why the bookman was giving money to Franklin Mo. Manfred believed Mo could find his son—a son from an old affair with a nameless woman at a book fair in San Francisco.

Manfred confessed he'd been full of intellectual and sexual bravado. He explained that she had written him years afterwards about the child when she needed money, and he sent her letters and postcards to call him, but he never heard from her again. He longed to make more restitution and to help the son if Mo could find him. He paid Mr. Mo dearly and got no results.

He wrote he was frustrated as the time went by and Mo threatened to never reveal anything and destroy any clues he had unless more money was given upfront. Now it was twenty thousand dollars. Manfred decided to report his problem to the FBI and Mo to the vice squad for fraud if Mo didn't stop asking for money with no results. Mo said he couldn't lose his job and retaliated. The threats escalated. Mo said he knew Mrs. Porter's address and no harm would come to her if he got his money. Manfred's last line cautioned that if anything happened to his sister or him, they should investigate Franklin Mo. The signature was preceded by the word *sincerely* and love to his sister, who had a nephew somewhere.

Sergeant Laughlin smiled and reread the letter. He looked at Max and Mrs. Porter. He had some real evidence now, and he had a lovely woman to go to. Was he so susceptible to these variables? Yup, he was. He was something else besides this big mass of lost man. He let Poplar down. He'd stumbled with the attempt to get Franklin Mo. He'd looked around for a woman and found nothing. Now he had a real chance to succeed with the case, the woman, and he had a cat.

With a small teacup in his hand, he announced, "Now we can say unequivocally this man is an extortionist. Why haven't we checked out this guy before he came to the LA jail? Weber said he came from up north. So what if he's been here for half a dozen years? Let's review his background data."

Laughlin revisited the jail's chief psychiatrist for further background, while Max called Stockton. Dr. Brandt had just finished rounds and asked Laughlin to the cafeteria for talk and food.

CHAPTER 33

Brimming with fried chunks of chicken, cheesy pasta, assorted pies and cakes, as well as tossed salads, they slid their trays along the cafeteria offerings, and each ended up with an iced tea and chocolate chip cookies.

Laughlin followed Brandt to a back table and sat facing him. There was a steady murmuring to cover their talk.

"I now have corroborating evidence that Franklin Mo was extorting money from a murder victim. What more can you tell us about him?"

"I'm glad I was on call today to talk to you here. Such a tragedy about Poplar and so unnecessary. Do you think it's related to his confession and Mr. Mo? I just don't know. Both men came before I did and so I didn't vet them. A murder victim you said?"

"Yes, it's ongoing, so I can't say much more, but I wonder how these guys could have been in mental health. Mo was really strange. I can't tell you the details, but suffice it to say, there was a lot going on that didn't fit mental health."

"Detective Laughlin, mental health is a judgment game. Most people are something else rather than readily fitting into a DSM category. Everyone, with or without training, likes jumping to conclusions, making loose associations, off on tangents, and many times fitting the diagnoses to suit themselves."

"Well, give me an idea how you make that judgment."

"If you mean loose associations, try this: What comes to mind when I say the word *pen*?"

"Writing."

"But someone else might say *pig* or *prison* or *train station*, all associated with another function. Or take *pitch*, you might say *catch*, while I might say *Bob Dylan* or *tar*."

"All right, I see that's associations, tight and loose, but how about broader diagnoses?"

"If we're talking in generalities, that's fine. I will not attempt to diagnose Franklin Mo. Let's just say, in summary, I remember the first DSM where—if you were stupid, crazy, or weird in your ways— the diagnosis was demented, psychotic, or neurotic. Now it's more complicated but still much the same. Essentially, I approach a mental status exam in two parts. First, there is the observable nonverbal behavior, including mood. So you'd be looking for appearance and behaviors, like grooming and scars and tics and repetitive movements, for example. You'd be looking for facial expressions or lack thereof. You'd look at the eyes for lack of sleep, yellow sclera, sadness, or fear or whatever. You're playing Sherlock Holmes even before the person talks."

"What does that get you?" Laughlin said and bit his cookie, holding his hand so the crumbs ended in his palm.

"It gets you an idea where to look: taking care of self, neglecting self, distracted with voices, tremors that could mean drugs, a temporal lobe or Jacksonian seizure, cutting scars, compulsive traits, and on and on. Then, you get a sense of mood and how the person relates to you—depressed, anxious, frightened, elated—which you deduce without even talking to them about how they feel. You get the idea without me having to go on listing, right? Of course, you do. You're a detective, and you're watching all the time."

"Okay, that's true."

"So what's the first thing you notice about a person?"

Laughlin was caught with a full mouth and stopped chewing with the question.

"I guess how tall they are, stuff like that," he answered quickly.

"Think about that. What you notice is so automatic, people forget what it is. It's the person's sex and then age—that is, if you can assume these things quickly. If you aren't sure about the sex or the approximate age, that's another clue to what's going on."

Laughlin smiled and remembered many persons of an unclear sex or age. That was LA.

"That's the truth."

"Okay, so then we go to the verbal examination. Three main parts—how many marbles they have to play with, how they align them, and how they play them."

"So you find out how smart they are first."

"Maybe how smart they were."

"We asked the date and their address to see if they're oriented."

"Yes, but that is assuming some basics, like they understand English, for example. You start with an assessment of the vocabulary as an indicator of intelligence and education."

"Yeah, I get it. The mini-mental-status exam tests memory and organizational abilities."

"Exactly. Are they confused, demented, or delirious for whatever reason? Then you got to the person's idea of the history of what happened, the story they tell, and how it's told."

"You mean if it's credible?"

"That and whether there are hallucinations and delusions, obsessive thoughts admitted or displayed. The list goes on."

"Sometimes people don't fit in your DSM and then what?"

"As I said before, the Diagnostic Statistical Manual helps with a diagnosis based on certain criteria. There is always that 'something else' category with traits of this or that not full blown to a disorder everyone would recognize. Humans are varied to the say the least. Agreed, Detective?"

"Hey, thanks. I'll be better prepared when I meet Mr. Mo."

"Good luck. Yours is a hard field too."

The psychiatrist stood then and excused himself to return to his office. Laughlin realized the man assumed he knew his way out and thanked him again with a smile. Dr. Brandt had been cooperative. The detective felt a shift in his original judgment of the guy. Maybe he had been a bit of a fool, and good old Max had tried to point it out. He wondered how often we listen to someone's take on our judgments of others.

He sat there and thought about the case. He'd gotten nothing new about Mo so far, and yet he felt better and mused about being neurotic until a guy with a tray full of desserts slapped him on the shoulder.

"James Laughlin, my god, what has happened to you?"

Laughlin straightened his shoulders to shake off his reverie and turned to see Bill Fies, redheaded and pudgy, in a full smile.

"I'll be damned. What's happening with you, you devil incarnate?"

"Doing my job, buddy, doing my job. I'm up in administration, nosing around safety issues. The carrot man is probing to turn a phrase. May I join you, or are you done stuffing your face?"

Laughlin gestured to a seat, observing the tray full of food. "It looks like you know how to do stuffing well, big guy."

The two men bantered, and then Laughlin described his unfulfilled mission of filling in gaps about Franklin Mo. Fies ate very deliberately and chewed well. It was the manner of a man trying to diet but giving up at the end of the meal; he shoveled his sweets in. Downing his glass of obligatory water, he offered to take the detective upstairs to see whether relevant records were available in the sheriff's files as well as in mental health. Fies figured they had to be in order for Mo to get unrestricted access to the jail.

The din of the cafeteria allowed a moment of reflection, and the two were quiet, settling the last of their food in their gratified stomachs.

Fies took a deep breath and passed judgment on his pie. "Damn if the cooks don't make the best peach pie. It helps get through the day."

Leaving the sally port to the unsecured area, they took the elevators up. The administration floor was an endless, neat collection of cubicles. Within moments, a striking brown-haired woman in a crisp uniform enhanced by her generous breasts pushed a folder in front of Fies. He and Laughlin sat in a corner area with textured half walls sealing them in ersatz privacy. The file revealed nothing remarkable, but Fies suggested the vague letters of recommendation most likely meant there was something to hide.

They talked about mental health in the jail and how much most of the deputies hated either the staff or the crazies. There had been a recent incident where the guy had been brought in, covered with a full head mask, because of his spitting. He was out of control and struggled.

"He got hotter and hotter, literally as well as figuratively, as the saying goes," Carrot Head related, "and, bingo, he got heat stroke and stopped moving at all. Now, shit, what am I supposed to do with that mess? The deputies don't want saliva loaded with HIV or whatever in their faces, and the guy shouldn't cook to death."

"What's the answer?" Laughlin asked.

"We've a review of the case tomorrow, but I've got another one this afternoon—some transgender, whatever that is, being attacked, and the guards supposedly on a break. Last week, a guy ripped his own eye out. We finished the case of the woman stabbing her roommate in the neck with an eyeliner pencil. Imagine the shit that flowed over not giving women their makeup and the shit if someone dies from an assault from a fucking lipstick tube."

Laughlin shook his head. "People are ingenious, you gotta say that."

"And of course, we can't deny them makeup or all hell would start. We've already got the written complaints from the inmates rolling in constantly."

"Like what?"

"Oh god, if you can read them, it's what you and I would complain about too—the stinking food. Next, we'll be hiring a nutritionist. And they put in distress calls about depression and not seeing mental health enough or fast enough."

"You've got to keep trying to fix things, right?"

"Yup, but it's easy for you to say, murder and all. Try living with these incident reports and coming up with an explanation that satisfies everyone. What do I do with a sergeant who won't listen to his deputies when they tell him an inmate is going to be attacked if he's in a certain module and the sergeant says, 'Tough. I got no feelings for the cholo asshole'? And sure enough, the nineteen- year-old kid gets beaten to an unconditional pulp. Who's going to rat on whom and not get beaten up too?"

There was another pause. Fies scooted over to his desk cluttered with kids' photos and got gum for the two of them.

"So what's new with you and your ginger offspring?" Laughlin asked, moving from the depressing subject of unsolved dilemmas to something that delighted the redhead.

"Same old, same old, except we finally got the last one to poop in the toilet. She's four and insists on having 'privacy' now, can you imagine? What about you? Too much privacy, or did you and that woman get together again?"

"Which one?"

"What was her name . . . Madge? Margie? Something like that."

"That was another time and another place. I think I've got a better thing going now, but I've had to neglect that as usual. Damn, it's late. It was great seeing you, but I gotta go now. Thanks for the information. We're following up on Mo, and those letters of recommendation suggest we may find out a great deal."

Laughlin left the top floor and went out into the open. It was sunny and hot, and he was full of food. What more could he ask for?

On route to the station, he passed Ralph's and went in. He found himself looking at cat food, confused by all the little cans and pouches. *"Never thought I'd be shopping for a cat"* was all he could think, dumped a variety of cans for sale in his basket and quickly added bread, cheese and a six-pack of assorted bottled beers including Corona and Modelo. He was pleased that Ralph's allowed assortments and took full advantage of that.

CHAPTER 34

Max had tentative info on Mo. Laughlin listened with repeated sighs. Max went on anyway, undisturbed by the commentary.

"So the rundown is from a sheriff up there in Yolo County, a very friendly guy who remembers a whole lot. He says Mo came to Stockton, which is in San Joaquin County, by the way, from somewhere in Los Angeles. He started working in the Stockton County Hospital as a clerk while studying for his social-work license update accreditation hours. About six years after, he got a reinstated license. An incident was reported about some Tule fog trouble.

"Apparently, this kind of fog comes from the Tule wetlands' grasses and it covered the whole area in December. Mo ran into another car that was parked on the side of the road."

"I've heard of that stuff. Tule fog causes many accidents. What's the big deal?"

"The accident didn't occur on 99 or like the ones on the 405 grapevine but on a small side road in Yolo County. The woman in the car, whom he hit, was banged up badly and said Mo was trying to kill her."

"What are you telling me?"

"The story. Hold on, okay?"

"Okay, Max. Where's this heading?" Laughlin complained and sighed again.

"You know, I'm reporting the info, so relax. It takes time."

"Yeah, yeah. Go on."

"She had put in a complaint about him harassing her when she was at Stockton General. Even though she lived in Yolo County, administration investigated, and the accusation was that he propositioned her while she was being worked up for cancer of the cervix. He asked for sex or money so she wouldn't have to tell her husband that she had genital warts. Mo claimed she was crazy and paranoid."

"Oh great. What was the outcome?"

"The deal was if he transferred out and didn't tell anyone, she would drop the charges. The sheriffs knew because they covered the supposed accident and heard the woman's initial distress."

"So Mo had used blackmail before."

"There were a couple of incidents at the hospital, also questionable. A clerk damaged a chart, catching it on fire with hairspray, and Mo was going to report her unless she cooperated with a blow job. She told her boyfriend who accosted Mo in the hospital parking lot just as another administrator was leaving. There was also an eighteen-year-old woman who had said he felt her up while bending over to adjust her oxygen nasal catheter. She was young and had had an asthma attack. He said she was delirious but the family believed her. What he was doing with the catheter in the first place was strange. The last incident was with a twelve-year-old boy who was found in the janitor's closet with Mo. What went on there was never made clear because the family didn't want the boy to testify in court. Anyway, he got repeated warnings, but the whole thing was dropped. After the Tule fog accident, administration cut a deal to get him out with decent recommendations. The sheriff could do nothing since charges were dropped, but the guy I talked to said it was kinda fucked up."

"Conspiracies abound. I wonder why he didn't shoot her."

"Well, we don't know if Mo ever had a gun."

"There's the gun Manfred was shot with."

"Yup, but it was registered to Manfred," Max answered.

"What do you mean? I didn't see the ballistics report. How do you know?"

"I put it right on your desk last week. Didn't you see it?"

"What the hell! I saw nothing. You're fucking with me now."

"What am I supposed to do, Sergeant? Read your mail to you? You're getting weird, man. It was right on your desk."

"So you're telling me Manfred owned the gun that killed him. Are you suggesting suicide? It doesn't make sense. What else was said about the gun?"

"Nothing much. Wiped clean, which suggests murder. That's all. I traced the gun shop owner and he said Manfred bought it with a friend who matches Mo's description, but who knows? No powder burns on Manfred."

"All right. We were just getting some more motives for murder when this comes up. How the hell did I miss that report?"

"Who knows, but there it is."

"Why did we think of Mo in the first place? Wasn't he connected to Manfred? Didn't we put that all together? Goddamn it! I've got to clear my head. This is a case that is driving me crazy for sure."

"Well, as they say, that's apropos, right?"

"Max, I can't take your horrible humor right now. Let's call it a day."

"Okay, by me, calling it another day but we'll have to talk to the lieutenant one of these other days."

That was that. They went their ways.

Laughlin knew Max would head for comfort and Kim. What was he going to do? He called Lucy and got her voice mail and the message she would be gone for three weeks to a continuing medical education meeting in South Africa. It hurt him she had not called to let him know, but then it occurred to him that he hadn't done anything to get in contact with her after that very warm night—another bust on his part.

He went home and sat in the big living room chair in the dark, two beers with him. He waited for the cat. The big oaf hit him square in his unguarded belly again. "Cat, you have got to give me more warning! I'm just too dumb to get it all," he pronounced out loud, and the cat head-butted him on his chin, purring for food.

After Dylan ate, all was quiet. Laughlin sat down again, this time with a beer resting on his gut.

"He'd fucked up" was his main thought, and it did a good job of tormenting him. Sitting in the dark, tossing thoughts about, he reviewed his carelessness. He was always on the alert, but like some scurrying prey, instead of the hunter, he had missed the devious predator and felt caught and mangled. His own incompetency had done it, and it seemed a recurrent theme in this case. Why had a disappearance of the mental health administrator caused him such a messy approach? Damn. Parts of him wanted to quit, retreat, and just go to sleep. Let the FBI do the work. He rubbed his chin, finished the beer, and closed his eyes. To retreat into nothingness was his hope. Of course, the cat thought otherwise.

Warm and solid on his chest, the animal purred, and Laughlin was aware of the unapologetic demand. The detective rubbed the cat's head and continued his reflections. Here he was without anyone near, without a life beyond murder, and without a fucking clue on how to proceed in this mixed-up case.

The cat purred on, content with the effort made by this man. Pensive. Laughlin became more preoccupied with being lost.

The phone rang. Managing to get it out of his pocket without disturbing the cat, Laughlin answered abruptly and then sat straight. The cat jumped off reluctantly. His mother was calling.

"Hey, what's going on?" he asked softly.

"Well, my dear, I've got a little problem," she answered.

His heart responded with drumming danger, and he asked again, "What's going on?"

"I've decided to have that knee surgery, and I need to know whether you can come in case something goes wrong—power of attorney . . . and do not resuscitate overview matters."

Laughlin tried to suppress his dismay, but he asked, "Why now? That knee has been a problem since I don't know when."

"Well, James," she replied.

She always called him James, not Jim or Jimmy but James. It was dignified attention to him even though he'd peed in his pants many times when he knew his father was coming up to his room. He was four when he could finally hold it, having only a few accidents after that. She would come later and take his wet clothes, pants, underpants, socks, sometimes shoes, and bring new ones for him and just cart the wet stuff to the sink to wash.

"James, are you listening? I am getting old and this knee makes it difficult for me to walk. I just don't want to crash and break a hip. You know, that would be too much even for the stoic person I am, right?"

"Oh, of course. Hey, I'm sorry. I was just thinking about this stupid case."

"I know it's not a good time but better now than when it's too late. Remember, I've dealt with this ever since I fell. You had already gone to LA."

Guilt smacked him. She would not leave, and he had gone anyway. He knew he'd left her to the bastard. His father had hit her, and she'd fallen, breaking and tearing all sorts of things. He knew that his father had caused injury after injury, and he had left her with the nightmare. Ten years ago or more, he'd come home on the red-eye after the last episode and threatened his father. He stood before him, sure of himself in front of the clumsy wasted brute. His father, gray and sunken, spindly and sodden with whiskey, jutted his chin out and said, "This is my home. Get out, you ungrateful shit!"

He'd asked his mother again to come to LA with him, but she had said she'd be okay. Her refusal infuriated him as if she generated the desire to hit her for her stubbornness. Laughlin left rather than rail at her. He admitted he was frightened at his own anger against her as well as toward his father. He left her.

Now she was alone. The old man died years ago, thank God, but she still refused to leave the house. As her son, he helped clean out the mess and settled her and left again.

What detectives have parents? Weren't they free of such ties and could meet women and have intrigues? Still, he cared about his mother and wanted her safe.

He took a deep breath and blew out any exasperation. "So let's plan this. Have you scheduled the surgery or did you call me first?"

"I have reasonable insurance with the job as well as Medicare and thought it best to schedule ahead and let you know so you could plan a visit. What do you think?"

"When?" was all he could say.

"You know, James, I've kept my job and worked hard at being a good teacher. I think you have to give me credit for carrying on and yet you act resentful. I do want to keep in touch with you, you know that, right? Yet, I need to have independence I earned. You know that I earned it."

After his grandparents and then his father had died, Laughlin wanted to leave Detroit behind with or without his mother. Now he would return again. She'd scheduled the surgery on October 15. That gave him time to get things in order. It would only take a day or so and then rehab where she would stay for a few weeks. He could easily come back and forth, but it would be a pain in the neck for sure.

Everything was agreed upon, and Laughlin said he would come a day early to be with her and do any fixing around the house she needed.

"Love you, son," she said. "Forgive this tough old woman, okay?"

"Yup, you and me, tough as nails." He held back his frustration in his voice as much as he could but hated the banalities of her descriptions and said, "See you soon. No worries."

He had a plan now: *Get off your ass. Call Max. Check APB status for Franklin and another interview with Eugene if possible and then request leave for a week.*

Nothing panned out that week except the approval of a leave of absence to help his mother. He saluted Max, who promised to take care of the cat, and went to the airport for the red-eye.

He sat upright and thought about his mother. She was older than he was now when she had him. Late, very late, according to most warnings, and yet at thirty-eight, she delivered a bouncing baby boy of eight pounds eleven ounces, and she was proud she told him repeatedly. Now it wasn't a big deal to be over forty and have babies.

She'd married a cop early in life, and he had been shot dead in a gun battle after eight years of marriage. She devoted her career to teaching seventh graders. She met his father five years later at a survivors' meeting. He was a drinker even then, but he told her she'd be better off with him than alone and she bought it. It was still a traditional world with just a few folk songs saying otherwise. Now her son would be there to help her.

*   *   *

Laughlin drove from Metropolitan Airport way out in Wayne County straight to the Lodge Freeway. The sides of the freeway were green. Green grass and bushes were everywhere. Rich leafy trees made lumpy covers of the horizon. Los Angeles was brown now, waiting for rain to clean and green it. Big rains were still coming.

He concentrated on the well-known road. That was what he remembered as the easiest way to the brick house down from the Market Basket. That had been such a big grocery store in his childhood, but each time he came back, it turned out to be a little more dumpy. Nevertheless, he was able to get some flowers for her before going down the street with its modest but beautiful old houses.

The neighborhood had turned black and then turned old and then turned young with mixed kids and she had held on. Teenagers mowed her lawn and the peonies still came up each year. There were so many clean apartment complexes in Southfield or Birmingham, but she didn't budge. This was her territory, and she'd staked it out for life, rotten and good.

He parked on the grass-divided driveway and went through the overgrown side juniper to the solid brown door with a stained-glass peek window. He rang the bell, a real sounding bell, ding-dong and all.

She opened the door and smiled and then took him in her arms. The living room was the same as always. A cobbler's bench in front of a worn but clean beige couch and two swivel chairs made a little sitting area. She'd put iced tea and cookies out and took her glass immediately. Admiring the flowers, she began, "I'm glad you were able to come. I need to go through some papers with you in case . . . you know, something goes amiss, but tell me about you first."

"What do you mean if something goes wrong?"

"Oh nothing. Just preparation that any surgery would require. Be realistic. Power of attorney, resuscitation advisory—we'll talk about it a little later, please. Now please tell me, how's Max? Do you hear anything from Maggie? There was that veterinarian, Lucy, right?"

"Mom, Max's fine. Maggie, I don't know, and Lucy, she's off some place, so nothing's new."

He wanted this to be a pleasant time, and yet he already felt irritated. Anybody else and he would try to be charming and patient. She'd raise the specter of something going wrong, and that had infused worry in the pale room.

He went to get some ice.

They cleaned out the kitchen after his father collapsed, bleeding from what the doctors had said was Mallory-Weiss or some name as though it were an obvious condition. He knew it now, and it had caused the old man to bleed out down and up the GI tract. Then he stroked out. Always going out.

Laughlin had laid the new tile flooring after scraping off the brown globs of glue from broken linoleum. He moved the stove and the fridge to paint the walls bright yellow and bought a microwave that his mother really liked. She said she wasn't afraid of microwaves since she was a science teacher and not at all superstitious.

He returned and dumped the clinking ice in the pitcher. They both sat in silence after his comment about nothing new, and he guessed she was collecting old images like a deep-sea diver to bring up for that "quiet, accessible old memories" moment. He wanted her here and now attention back.

"I'm investigating a man who works in mental health."

"Now that's got to be interesting to say the least," his mother said, sitting forward with some eagerness.

"It's in the county jail section. The man is missing."

"I've read about all those mentally ill people arrested," she offered.

"Yup, many of them."

"You know, we had some ill ones in our family too."

"Like who?" Laughlin was pleased to get her interest and explore the family history. "I remember about stories of someone eating soap and hearing voices."

"Oh, that was your father's two great, great uncles, I think. It's true too. My side had some strange birds too. There was great Aunt Henrietta who went berserk eating mushrooms and set up a church founded on her visions."

"When was that?"

"About 1852, just after the gold rush and the Latter Day Saints migration. She was a smart woman, married to an itinerant preacher who deserted her. She took up the preaching herself, talked about gold and salvation and Martin Luther to counter all the new stuff."

"What about the guy who hanged himself? I remember Grandma telling me about it."

"Oh, that was the nephew on your father's mother's sister's husband's side who supposedly did that. No one really saw it, but he was found with the bridle around his neck. Some thought he was trying to catch a horse thief and got caught himself instead. Old stories—who knows how true they are? Most of the family was unremarkable, trying to be good and productive. Long history of farmers and then teachers, businessmen, journalists, and scientists throughout; one or two violin players and furniture makers as well. If anyone got killed off, it was with TB right here at Herman Kiefer or with the Civil War or the Spanish American and the World Wars. But you know, they don't get all the lore strange relatives get."

"I always wondered about the guy who rowed off on Lake Erie."

"Yes, I remember that story from when I was a kid. Some sort of brother of Grandmother's father. Your Grandmother said he got messages from spirits. Lake Erie was a good place for eerie adventures, don't you think? He went along the Erie Canal from New York to Philadelphia and out into Lake Erie. No one knew where he wound up. The eighteen hundreds were full of spirit messages, but they sure got killed off in this century."

"What about our own immediate family?"

"Oh, genetically, we are strong stock. Other than Helmut, who I never heard from again, I suppose there was some depression with the depression, no suicides that I know of and the run-of-the-mill sadness with the wars and such. It was hard being of German origins with the wars haunting us. You were lucky the involuntary draft ended. Even though you had to register, you got to go to school. Wars keep coming but all told, I think we've done all right though, don't you? You survived, thank God."

Laughlin wanted her to acknowledge his father's alcoholism and brutality, but he held back. He wasn't going to bring up his own war experiences. They upset her too. She was smiling at him, waiting expectantly for his approval. They would never really talk about his suffering or her suffering or any of it. It was bullshit now.

"Hey, let's go out for an early dinner. I've got a rental and we could go to Greek town. How about it?" He jabbed at his morose thought and hoped to stun it with something happy.

"That is one great idea. Let's do it," she responded.

He looked at her, relieved at the response and said, "Get ready then."

She smiled and stood, pushing herself with her arms and taking a cautious step forward before getting her cane.

He watched as she went across the foyer and down a few steps to the little powder room with its blue fitted-rug-covered toilet. To see her with a cane and a little unsteady caused him to take a deep breath and hold it until she landed.

She was getting old but really in good health, he assured himself. He shook his head at the thought she would never color her hair but made one attempt at plastic surgery when she was over mourning for his father and had had her eyes done. They had laughed about it since her lids drooped anyway, and she gave up mascara even when going to teach taunting pubescents.

He hadn't provided her with more family, but she never complained. Sometimes he told her about cases and she really enjoyed the one about the zoo.

That made him look around for a cat and was going to ask her about that at dinner.

He noticed the rust on her Ford, but she said it still ran well. They settled in the rental, a Dodge. She swung her legs easily into the seat. They wove around Cadillac Square and found the long-forgotten places full of cars and walking people. Dinner was in a cozy redbrick building. Led by a pert little girl in a red jumper, threading her way back through big dark wooden tables, which held fat wine glasses, they settled in at a table for four. The girl swept away the extra flatware. They smiled at each other. Loud laughing and glasses clinking and plates clanking relaxed them both. The slim gray waiter was attentive to his mother as she selected a glass of wine. Laughlin ordered the bottle of Sauvignon Blanc for them.

She made her usual toast to him. "Be good, be well. Do good, do well."

How competent she was and how confident as well. She adjusted her soft blue scarf with silver fingers.

It pleased him that he didn't have to protect her although she was getting fragile. She was like Detroit, worn, struggling, bare bones still growing green thoughts in crevices between sturdy burned sienna brick houses.

The city and she were like familiar strangers; he was sure he was the same to her. They knew so little about each other in adulthood.

"After this, why don't you come to LA again? You were only there a few weeks after he died and said you had to get back or lose your job. You could've stayed. I even had my house then. I have a cat now."

"A cat. That's good. Was it a stray?" She took a sip of wine and continued, "You're right, James. I could have stayed, but I didn't. Let's have dessert. Apple crumble, okay? Even a Greek restaurant should have apple desserts in Michigan."

That was all. He didn't follow up on her questions about the cat. A flicker of fear came to him, and he thought he might not see her for years again. He resolved he couldn't let that happen. The drive home was a quiet one and she didn't complain.

The next day he held her soft bony hand as she went off to the operating room. The orthopedic surgeon was a heavyset, jovial man who reassured them both all would be well. After the surgery, which took a surprisingly short time, Laughlin visited her each day. At first, she slept even when he was there. Her eyelids would flutter; she'd look at him and smile and then go back to a tranquil-like trance from the meds. The leg bandages didn't seem to bother her, and she was sitting in bed in three days and hopping around within the week with a walker. She would be going to rehab soon now that she was up and around.

A few people came to visit her: a teenage boy named Grant with his girlfriend, an old fellow teacher named Mrs. Archer, and a neighbor named Mrs. Tillings with her husband. They shook his hand and related their connection with his mother; each stayed about five minutes and left.

He expected his bed at home to smell moldy, but it was fresh and comfortable although his feet popped out of the blanket at least once a night. The window overlooking the neighbor who didn't rescue him, now revealed three little kids digging in the dirt and piling fallen leaves over a cardboard box.

Before he would urge himself to get out of the house to visit her, he sat at the breakfast table, and the silence let his mind wander. It was a big house compared to her needs, and he was in a big house too. Family members in houses all alone, not together anymore. That was just a fact. How staid this setting was now—still, silent, no roar, no terror. With each trip back, he'd been able to return to the past again and survive. He didn't want any more than that right now. He'd overcome enough.

The rest of his visit, he prowled around downtown and walked the riverfront. He remembered the Paul E. Townsend docked along the rusty belt with the big mushroom mooring bollards. One short street had houses right on the river with gracious grass lawns down to the water and protrusions of ornate shelters for cars to drive under. What were they called in books? Port something? A car park with ivy and brick pillars. He'd run with some of his high school friends past those loud summer parties and put his arm around a girl for the first time in Palmer Park.

Hudson's was gone. He had a Pabst and ate at a dinky burger joint once and at a veggie-only place down the street afterwards. Sometimes he would drive all way up and down Woodward past the Fox Theater and the little upstairs antique shop where he bought a cannon ball for a doorstop.

Beyond that were empty lots and hunched churches vulnerable to the wind skipping and cavorting with white plastic trash. He stopped at the Detroit Art Museum and saw Rivera's muscle men and the university campus, then passed small houses with narrow porches and stores of junk all the way to the Eight Mile Road cemeteries where he'd necked with girls lying on marble slabs. Michigan probably lost many restless souls to the west, and Detroit suffered the most. It was its own cemetery to past glory. Memories like deserted factories could haunt him all they liked. He didn't regret that he had left.

The stress was minimal. His mom didn't die, and she walked slowly but with less and less pain, and he saw her settled at the rehab. Until he could get leave again, when she would go home, she'd have a visiting nurse at first, and that assuaged him of his guilt.

He took the red-eye back. The melancholy hours in the stuffy seat went by slowly. It was an uneventful trip, not even a flirting stewardess. But out on the curb was the balmy wind that greeted him and life was churning vibrantly in the city he now called home.

Phoning his mom after landing, he asked, "I forgot. Do you still have a cat?"

She laughed and said she did. He was named Teddy Roosevelt. The neighbors who visited her took care of him while she was gone.

"Mom, I forgot to fix anything you needed done at the house. Is everything working?"

"Yes, it is. It was just good to see you, James. I love you. Carry on. Bye, I have physical therapy now." She hung up and that was that.

Laughlin paused a moment, trying to sum up the sudden void after the latest interaction with his mother. He'd gone into the past like a therapy patient might do. What good did dragging the past up really do? The room he slept in now had only the same walls. The splintered door was replaced, and his image of himself—a trembling little beast, seeking protection in dressers blocking the door, planning to climb out the window by tying rope to the radiator, pleading to unheard rescuers—was covered over. She had kept his old purring cat when he left, which was the best she could do for him. His mother didn't want to remember anymore, and he couldn't forget, but without her, there was little reality about the past. The cat died at seventeen—lay down and didn't get up. She adopted a new cat a few years later. She moved on. Why shouldn't she? Maybe that was okay. He glanced at a reflection in the endless windows of the airport, out to the taxi. He was grown now and in charge. A good outcome. It was the present now, and he decided he couldn't do any more thinking about old times. Those times merely mucked up his thoughts like polluted rivers. He should be grateful all was flowing smoothly now.

CHAPTER 35

Max was thumbing through a thick paperback with a red cover. He stood up and greeted Laughlin with a big grab.

"So after a life interlude, the boy still has a mom, and he's back in the saddle again."

"Yup."

"How was the mom and the old town?"

"Oh, she was really good, getting better every day. The town not so good and not so bad. What's going on here?"

Max sat down and began flipping through the book on his desk again.

"It's the Diagnostic and Statistical Manual for Mental Disorders, and I was looking to see if I was in it, or, rather, if my fucked-up partner was in it."

"You know, Max, sometimes I wonder . . . Maybe I'm a depressive or have a personality disorder or am somewhere along the attention deficit disorder spectrum," Laughlin mused as he took the book and sat down. "Regarding you, what best describes you—a childhood disorder, mental retardation? Oh, here's a good one—expressive language disorder."

"Now don't be hostile. Remember, we fight antisocial personality disorders, not identify with them. Right, Sergeant?"

"That's true, Max. Look at this. Isn't it sickening that over one hundred pages are about drug-induced states?"

"That's the era of living better through chemistry again. I've read they're planning a whole new diagnoses revision. I think we are what

Dr. Brandt described as 'something else,' and maybe we'll be found in the new perfectly refined DSM."

"I wouldn't want to write that book."

"No need to associate further than the diagnosis called crazy for the characters in this case."

"Ah, now to the update. What's going on?" Laughlin asked cautiously.

"I think the current popular diagnosis is ADD with or without hyperactivity, but narcissistic personality disorder is catching up."

"You sound like you're current on things. Have you been studying or attending classes or what?"

"While you were gone, I thought I'd get a better understanding of schizophrenia and mania. They're kinda mixed in my mind. Anyway, now for the news."

"Do I need coffee for this?"

"Kim and I are engaged!"

Laughlin opened his eyes wide and smiled. "Max, how great. You lucky dog, finally a zookeeper to attend to you. Congratulations!" Laughlin exclaimed and extended his hand.

"It happened when we were looking after Dylan one afternoon and we just sat on your couch and petted him. It felt so comfortable being together, and I just came out with it. She didn't even ask me to get down on my knees."

"That's terrific for Kim and you and for Dylan. Thank you for taking care of him. You'll have to take care of him more often. I'll probably go back to visit my mom again soon."

"That's not all. Here's the good news follow-up on the case. Eugene is really in rehab and is getting better with just one medication. Jeffrey, the drug-addled trainer, is back with his brother, a strict churchgoer, intent on saving his younger brother's brain.

"You won't believe this, but Elvira Moody is living with her in-laws, her actual in-laws. We're looking into them now."

"Amazing, and all that happened while I was gone. What about Franklin? Have you found him?"

"No. That's been a bummer. Dr. Weber's husband died, so we haven't talked to her yet."

"Sorry for her."

"Yeah, and nothing has been done about Manfred's bookstore but Mrs. Porter has continued to pay the mortgage or rent or whatever."

The two sheriffs spent the rest of the day going through notes and making plans for the next morning. They would visit Rancho Los Amigos in Downey and interview Eugene.

When he finally got home, Laughlin plunked down in his chair with a beer and waited for Dylan to jump up. The cat never did, and it bothered him. He questioned how much things had changed while he was away and whether they included the cat's feeling for him.

Relieved at being home, he trudged upstairs, pleased his mom was safe. He emptied his duffel bag, threw his worn clothes into a pile, took a shower, and fell on the bed. It was quiet, and the rough part of the ceiling was still there.

He closed his eyes and began reviewing the case. It was good that Elvira Moody was with the Winklers, even if only temporally. He thought of Nora Weber alone with the waves and Freddie Poplar covered in leaves and Manfred clutching his record book. Tomorrow they'd talk with Eugene and his genes.

A horn blew loudly, and there was the ubiquitous siren way off and the answering dog. He sighed.

Just as he was drifting off, the big cat shook the bed as he jumped up and stepped on Laughlin's chest. He petted the cat to keep the purring. It was a good moment and soon both went to sleep.

CHAPTER 36

Max explained some history about Rancho Los Amigos being an extensive rehabilitation hospital, which had once been called a community poor farm, originally housed polio victims in the fifties and slowly took on more types of rehabilitation. Now it was affiliated with County-USC Hospital. Eugene was transferred to the amputee section to learn to walk with an artificial leg.

"Are they aware of his psychiatric history? I mean, he could do any weird thing there," Laughlin interjected.

"I guess they know."

"Well, I like the poor guy, but that's taking a big risk."

"They have psychiatrists and physical therapists and a major setup as I understand it, Sergeant. I think they must know what they're doing."

They drove across town into the wide avenue and saw the old Harriman Building and an array of different style architecture all over the extended campus. Spacious fields of brown and green grass separated the flat-roofed buildings, and an occasional tower pointed to the sky. Corridors were wide and had arches along the long halls. They were finally guided into the amputated limb section.

"Imagine a section for amputations. I remember a guy from down the street who fell off the roof and was paralyzed from the neck down. They got him to be able to move his shoulder so he could run a wheelchair at the spinal cord injury section, and my aunt's second cousin was here for her diabetes. They saved her leg."

"I hear you, Max. This is a full rehab hospital for all sorts of sadness and hope, I guess," Laughlin summarized quietly.

"Christ, you're getting so philosophical. I'm worried you may climb a mountain and join Buddha." Max laughed and stopped talking.

They were taken into a wide, long room with bright windows and lights shining on long plastic cushioned tables. Laughlin and Max halted and tried to take in the myriad of activities quickly as though it were just another gym. There were bars to pull up on and try to walk along. There was noise as scuffing and dragging, and encouraging words were tossed about. Young men with and without legs or arms exercised about the area, and laughing, yelling, and swearing were echoed back and forth. It was bright and overwhelming because of the loud, energetic activities. Eugene was there somewhere too.

This time, instead of board and care slime bag to greet them, a young, brush-cut guy in a blue dentist-like shirt came up to them and their guide and said, "Hi, I'm Eugene Biskoff's physical therapist. Eddie Dosset's the name. What can I do for you, Detective Laughlin?"

"Mr. Dosset, we'd like to interview Mr. Biskoff and wondered how he was doing," Laughlin began.

"I can show you, then you can ask him directly."

"Is that all right? He was one sick guy when I saw him last."

"Come on and see."

Three tables away sat Eugene Biskoff. He smiled as he saw Laughlin come up to him. Three other guys in wheelchairs quickly moved away from Eugene who laughingly said, "See you guys later. Try to behave." Then he turned to Laughlin and nodded, "I remember you. Sheriff, right?"

"Yes, sir, and my senior deputy, Joseph Max. How are you doing?"

"I remember him too. He went to talk to the nice woman resident," Eugene replied and went into a long explanation about his new leg and how the cushioning was much better and how he didn't get sores on the stump anymore. He praised Eddie and got up to show Laughlin how he could stand.

Eugene's lucidity startled the detectives. Eddie said they could have an interview room off to the side, and Eugene slid back into his chair, wheeled himself to one of the polished blond doors, and ushered them in. They sat at the table and watched him wheel the chair around and position it to face them. He stretched his arm out, shut the door, and asked what could he do for them. His face expressed curiosity, not terror.

"So what's been happening to you? You look much better," Laughlin began.

"I am better. Sometimes I think about the bad genes but mostly I concentrate on being able to walk again."

"You remember about the genes?"

"Of course. Now with the medications, I've calmed down and only take a minimum dose. I've got some sort of schizophrenia, maybe brief episodic, even though I'm a little old for that. In my thirties but young at heart when the good genes are expressing themselves . . . although I am definitely paranoid about sex. What can I do for you?"

Laughlin sat back in relief, and Max took over the interview for the first half hour. Eugene knew about Franklin's disappearance but didn't get upset. He was less worried. He nodded, seemingly encouraging himself, when he described Franklin Mo as always trying to get him drunk and Jeffrey Faulk as going along for the ride. He wasn't sure why they wanted his company. Yes, he was impressed with Mrs. Mo and had given her a book, saying Jeffrey loved her because she would like the big guy better than skinny Gene. He also really liked Dr. Weber, and she had put him on some good meds, which Franklin had taken away from him, saying they would hurt his chromosomes.

"I'm a little hung up on masturbation, but boy, the guys around here think it's the thing to do to help relieve stress and stuff. I'm working on it," Eugene said quietly. "Do you think it's okay and all? I remember you're saying so at the board and care, Sheriff."

Laughlin nodded yes a couple of times. He was taken aback by the directness of the question and maybe that Eugene remembered that day. Finally, he asked something relevant.

"Mr. Biskoff, why was Franklin Mo interested in you?"

"That is an excellent question, Sheriff Laughlin," Eugene exclaimed.

"And the answer?"

"Of course, your questions were good too, Sheriff Max."

"Thank you." Max nodded and looked at Laughlin.

"I think—" Eugene Biskoff paused and rubbed his leg, "I think he was going to find me my parents. Since I didn't have money, he was looking for ways to finance the search. Why he picked me, I don't know."

This line of questioning led to a whole case history from Eugene. How his mother and father were lost to him, how he ran away when he was sixteen from a foster home in San Francisco and wound up in Los Angeles, hoping to find his father but instead was in jail or treatment for years at the county psychiatric clinic.

Elvira Moody had been in his therapy group. He and she would get coffee together. She missed her husband, and Eugene missed his parents.

"I had a couple okay homes up north but they only kept me for a while. When I got older, it was hard to get anybody to give a damn about a pimply, smelly boy. The last foster home I stayed in had chained me to my bed so I won't run. They wanted the money, but I lifted the bed and got my leg free. I just walked off with the whole damn chain around my ankle and removed it at a hardware store. No one said a word 'cause I had money for the saw. I was never going to be shackled like that again. Of course, now I can take the fake leg off and be free. Bet they never thought of that.

"Hey, what about the other—" Max said.

Laughlin smacked Max on the back and interrupted with "Yes, what about the other problem?"

"Oh, you mean the beating myself? Come to think of it, I can masturbate without getting holy hell as well. No one around here seems to pay much mind to it. I'm watching myself and trying to limit my needs. The old pecker ain't what it used to be, but it works, thanks to the surgeons.

"The staff looked for my family. The one thing they found was a damaged birth certificate with no readable date, which indicated my father was a no name from LA and there was an old postcard with this request to help pay for the kid. It had a Westwood postmark but only was signed with the letter E. Weird, huh? I wonder if they were religious about natural functions or what."

With Eugene's permission Laughlin reviewed his chart. Nora Weber had traced his background through child services and had found out that Eugene's mother had been killed when Eugene was only three. There was no contact for the father, and his life began with the typical awful foster kid scenario that the detectives often discovered after the child was dead, not before. As a runaway teenager, he'd worked for a Japanese gardener in Pasadena and then held a job with another hardware store until he would get too paranoid about being discovered or "got urges that were too sinful."

Recent progress notes indicated structure helped Eugene remain stable now and he liked his group therapy with the psychiatrist and social worker.

The two sheriffs said they'd visit again later and left Eugene so he could have his group therapy session. He shook hands with Laughlin and Max and didn't seem to have a problem using his index finger like a funny thumb when he signed the release form to investigate further.

Assuring Dosset that they could find their way back to visitor parking, the detectives strolled out. It was a warm balmy day with trees making long shadows. They were ready for lunch. The rehab structures were scattered throughout the dry fields and shone in the sun like random beige building blocks.

As they walked, Laughlin spoke first. "So it wasn't that hard to put together. Franklin Mo was going to make Eugene Biskoff the bookman's son for money."

"You think that's it, Sarge? Could it really be his son?"

"Well, we'll find out. Either way, it was extortion on Mo's part. I just couldn't tell Eugene yet. He was doing so well. He still thinks he can find his father."

"Thanks for stopping me from telling Eugene he had another ankle," Max offered. "Also remind me to be a nicer guy to crazies."

"Amazing what the mind puts up with and survives. I always wonder how."

"I say big loaded burritos and beer, okay?"

CHAPTER 37

After eating, they wrote up the reports, presented to the lieutenant, got yelled at, and were told the FBI was going to handle the whole damn case soon enough. Neither of them wanted to do anything else and they split for their cars. They both knew where Max was going.

Laughlin drove down Sunset, its meandering was relaxing, but he still was dismayed when it ended with two gas stations. The pale gray restaurant's parking lot was okay but not what he thought the legendary street might have ended with. PCH was jammed as he headed for Zuma, seeking solace.

There were all these 1930s oases built way out from the city in county territory to put away anyone who didn't fit. There was Rancho Los Amigos and the County Hospital and Camarillo, north of Zuma, when it was the mental health hospital of no return. Now it's part of the Channel Islands University, bell tower and all. It was about five years ago when Camarillo closed the few remaining wards, just after Laughlin had helped escort one crazy guy there. The guy was probably on the streets in Ventura now or in men's central jail right downtown where, long ago, civic planners had tried to store all those undesirables far away.

He stopped at Malibu Seafood to take out clams and fries and then ate oyster crackers for the clam chowder while he drove into the big beach parking lot. It was his island away from what fit and what didn't. He rolled the windows down and dined in the car. It was great. Then he went for a run, barefoot, in the bubbling surf.

The evening lingered. No end to daylight savings yet, only when Halloween came, then early dark. He flopped out on the dry beach and rubbed his toes together to get some of the wet sand off. He'd been tempted to strip and swim but was too lazy now that he'd eaten. The run was good enough.

Drifting back to pressing thoughts, tomorrow he'd try some more interviews, to complete the first round. Too bad, he shouldn't see Nora Weber now, but one had to have some discretion. Then he decided to call her anyway. Why not? He was close by.

The lifeguard truck came by, and Laughlin got up to return to his car. He dusted his feet with his socks and put on his shoes and drove toward home. It was after eight, and he felt good. She answered her phone right away and invited him over.

He'd said he would only stay a few minutes and asked how she was doing.

She opened the door before he's even finished wedging his car in by the bushes. They walked slowly into the house and were greeted by the waves.

"How are you doing yourself, Detective Laughlin? It's been a sad autumn with the loss of Freddy."

"And your husband," he added.

"Yes, that's true, but with Larry, it was mixed with relief."

"How's that?"

"Oh, I think, in long illnesses, grief gets mixed with relief for the person dying and for the person watching. Drink?"

"No thanks. How are the goblin clouds?"

She smiled. "Merely a drink of iced tea or lemonade, okay?" she assured him and went into the kitchen. "The clouds have been capricious fluffs. The dark and foreboding will probably come around on Halloween."

He followed her to the deck, and they sat down with their drinks held firmly against the wind.

"I just came back from seeing my mother. She had knee surgery," he declared and was immediately puzzled why he was telling her this.

"Oh, that's stressful. Did it turn out okay? Where did you have to go?"

"Yes, it's fine. Detroit. How are you? How's Mrs. Poplar and their children?" He didn't know which subject was more ill-suited to discuss.

"Well, glad your mother did well. The Poplars are coping as well as can be expected. And you?"

"Yes, she'll do well. Sorry about your husband. I still think about Dr. Poplar. I wish he had listened to me. He was a young guy for suicide, wasn't he?"

"I think so. Both of them were young," she answered. They each took big swallows and looked out at the waves. The sunset was fading to the dark blue night.

"We still haven't found Franklin Mo."

"Missing or dead seems to be the lament this month," she added.

What more could he say? He wanted to console her, but she seemed resigned to sadness. He stood and placed the glass on the table.

She followed him to the door. Standing close, he turned to her and hugged her, and she stood, leaning on him, crying quietly. They held each other closely. A comfort for both, and then the porch light clicked on. Slowly she let go, and he opened the door, gave her one gentle bow, and left her with the waves.

Getting in the car, he shook his head. The sensation of her against him lingered, but he didn't want to figure out what that was about—let it linger and fade rather than be tossed and trussed in why.

He gunned the car out onto the highway to home. Smelling the leftover food, and switching thoughts quickly, Dylan would wonder where he was. There were a few clams left; maybe the cat would like them.

Pulling the car into his driveway, he saw a lighted candle flickering on the porch railing. There, sitting on the steps, were Mr. Winkler and Elvira Moody. Rosie the cat was nowhere to be seen.

"Good evening, Sheriff Laughlin," Winkler said.

"Good evening and to you too, Ms. Moody," Laughlin reciprocated. "What is going on with the visit and the candle?"

"Good evening, James Laughlin. We were trying to conjure you up. It was getting late and we wanted to talk with you," Elvira said with a smile.

"Please, let's go inside."

Elvira blew the candle out. The little group half stumbled and half sauntered into the living room and each took a chair. Laughlin looked at the two visitors. Mr. Winkler was relaxed in his usual chair. The old man's eyes were still eager and his loose-fitting suit was still clean.

Elvira Moody wore her green scarf but her hair was darker and combed back. Her face revealed a freckle or two on the pale smooth cheeks and full lips. She was a relatively good-looking woman in a healthy way, belying what he knew about her and considering what could have happened to her. She'd lost some weight, which made her look even more pleasing.

"I've been told you have a cat now. Isn't that an advancement?" the old man said to Elvira.

"It's the cat's meow, Pa. Maybe Rosie and the Sheriff's cat can play together."

Laughlin was damned if he was going to ask how Winkler knew he had a cat and decided the old guy had looked in the window and saw Dylan; that was the probably explanation. He replied, "Understand that Ms. Moody has moved in with you. Is that right?"

"Aren't you the smart one, and here we came over to give you the news. Elvira was sweet enough to help me with the house and all since Rosie is in the hospital again. The wife should be home soon, but I am hoping Elvira will stay and help both of us."

"Let me get everyone a drink. Ms. Moody, what will you have—beer, Pepsi?"

"We'll both have sparkling water if you have it," Winkler announced.

Laughlin fussed in the kitchen. Dylan ate the leftover clams and some dry food, and then both came out with the tray.

"On the wagon too, are you, Sheriff?"

"Just being polite for my guests."

"So first, before anything else, I would like to apologize to you for my absolutely obnoxious behavior. See, I was on a manic kinda of high, maybe from drugs, maybe from the wonderful phrase, quote, chemical imbalance, unquote. I finally listened to the psychiatrists and a really sweet social worker. That helped me decide to help Pa here. Of course, you understand that doesn't mean you aren't one hell of a guy. I mean that wasn't a drug-induced problem. I just get a little bit carried away and can't stop my thoughts, and they come spewing out like a geyser, kinda—you know, those water things that come out of the ground, not like sprinklers but more like fireworks, Fourth of July like it really is. I really am sorry—"

Laughlin held up his hand to stop her and interrupted, "It's okay. I'm really glad you're better."

"Okay, okay. Wow, that was hard. Okay, now, let's get on with it."

Winkler reached over and patted Elvira's shoulder. "You did really fine, my dear, really fine."

"So here is what I think you need to know. Pa told me you're trying to put things together about Eric and Franklin, right?"

Laughlin nodded and waited for some real information.

"I was working at Eric's bookstore because he was sweet. I would pal around downtown or walk along Caesar Chavez to the frilly dress stores and party places after group therapy, and then I would take the bus to Eric's store. He'd put an ad in the newspaper and on the bulletin board at the clinic and let me help in the store. He was so sweet. He knew I'd lost my husband, and he said he'd lost a son."

"Did he know Franklin Mo?" Laughlin asked.

"I'm not sure. How do people get to know people? I know once, Dr. Poplar dropped a letter off for Mr. Manfred. Didn't he work with Mo? Could've been through books. It seems weird. I mean I never saw Franklin with a book at group meeting. Oh, hey, maybe it was through Franklin's wife. She loved books and would sometimes call up and asked if Mr. Manfred had any new finds. You know he would go searching for collections. Most of the time the big places like Heritage would get everything but sometimes at estate sales and stuff Mr. Manfred would score. Anyway, Mrs. Mo would beg him to come over, but he made her come to the store. She smelled good for sure, something like lilac or maybe closer to whatever a violet would smell like. I used to like jasmine and rose water . . ."

"Did Franklin Mo ever attend any of your group therapy sessions? I wonder how he got to know Eugene Biskoff."

"Dear Eugene, how is he? Are his genes treating him better? You know what? I'm going to visit Eugene. I miss him and our talks."

"Yes, he's much better. I'm sure he'll contact you soon."

"Well, I know, once Eugene was in jail for sleeping in a garbage bin behind this classy restaurant, three times he did it before they finally arrested him for vagrancy. He was young then. I told him to go to the Midnight Mission instead, but he said everyone was afraid of getting TB there. Mr. Mo must have met him in the jail. I heard Franklin liked to look at young boys. They had group meeting there too and of course, he could have heard the case presentations."

"I've got the possible connection between Franklin Mo and Eugene Biskoff, but how did Franklin meet Eric Manfred?"

"Oh, that's easy enough, right?"

"Yup, like I said, it was through his wife. Manfred had to have come over to see Mrs. Mo about some books," Laughlin concluded.

"Isn't that possible, Elvira?" Mr. Winkler questioned.

"Oh, maybe, but he usually made her come to the store."

"I was shown a book at Franklin's house Eugene had given Mrs. Mo that was from the bookstore."

"How did you know it was from Eugene?"

"Mrs. Mo's mother told me. She said Eugene gave it to her but wrote on it that Jeffrey loved her."

"What a tangled web we weave when first we—" Winkler interjected.

"Oh, Jeffrey, he probably stole the book from the store to sell, and he gave it to Gene instead. Jeffrey was like a little dog wanting his biscuit of money and nothing else mattered. He's kinda brain-impaired, don't you think, Detective?" Elvira suggested.

It was close to one o'clock when Laughlin walked the two visitors home. They invited him in but he declined.

Jogging home leisurely, he took in the silence and was pleased that all the connections had been made. All fine and great, but where was Franklin Mo?

In the morning, he heard a rasping sound and realized the cat snored.

CHAPTER 38

When they met at the station, Laughlin saw Max's smiling, handsome face and mused that faces didn't indicate if the owners were crazy or not. "I could tell race and sex, speculate on height and weight, even guess on smarts, but many times crazy was not discernible. I'm hoping my guess about you is that you're sane."

"Unless the face was painted like a warrior or something," Max added, laughing and mugging. He took the good news that Elvira Moody was found with known relatives safe and apparently sound. He didn't much care about the bully Jeffrey but agreed it was a pleasant surprise to talk with Eugene when he was less crazy.

"We've got to find Franklin Mo."

"No shit."

"Any news from Mrs. Porter? I wonder if she would be interested in having a nephew like Eugene," Laughlin speculated.

"She hasn't done a thing about the apartment or the bookstore according to a message she left me. Feels she has to wait until after Halloween for some reason about black cats being safer then. I don't think you have to worry about Siamese."

The day was spent writing up reports and speculating about the whereabouts of the illusive Mr. Mo. No doubt he had to come up with more money, but whom was he going to tap? No one had caught sight of him at bus terminals, train stations, or airports and not in Chinatown or Little Tokyo. The FBI figured he's split for other cities but Laughlin was convinced he was in LA. Why? It was in defiance. Franklin Mo thought he was too clever to be caught, and he had certainly pulled a good trick at the Topanga Mall. He was still in Los Angeles.

At four o'clock, while arguing with Max, Laughlin got two calls. One was an unknown number that turned out to be from a construction company that offered their services at a discount, to which Laughlin said thanks but no thanks, and one showed up from the Franklin Mo residence. It was Bowed Flower.

Of course, she insisted the sheriffs come over, and both men were happy to do so. This way they had somewhere to go.

The tiny lady was alone in the quiet, polished house. Her daughter was not back from Hong Kong. No servants were darting in and out, and she led them immediately to the kitchen stash at the bar.

"Matter of fact, I've heard from Franklin," she stated. "He left me a message when I was out getting another colonoscopy. They are such a pain in the ass to say the least. However, my doc is a real pro and he said I had only one little polyp this time. I mean I've got to die from something, and yet everyone wants a piece of me for posterity. I've told my doctors that I'm done now. This old woman is going to just wilt away. What do you guys think about dying?"

Max jumped in, "Franklin Mo left you a message. What'd he say, Mrs. Flower?"

"Sheriff Laughlin, will you please tame this partner of yours. I'm talking about dying, the great dragon of life, and he talks about a fool."

"You see, it's this urgency we feel about the case and the missing man," Laughlin added.

"I'm talking about dying first. I asked you about it."

Max took a bottle of water and said, "Yup, we're going to die. I don't know anything else about the rest of it, afterwards and all."

"Also, you don't seem to care. Is that right?"

"Look, Mrs. Flower, we've got a job to do, and so when you called, we were more than willing to come over to get the information you had. I think you're well aware we aren't here for a discussion of the end-of-life philosophies," Laughlin said firmly.

"Oh, very well, I just wanted your take on it all since you see all sorts of horrible things."

"I appreciate that, but the immediate horrible thing was the death of Mr. Manfred, and we think Franklin Mo was involved. Please tell us what you have."

"Yes, well, he left a message about two o'clock this afternoon. He said he was a salesman with an unpaid bill and he'd like to come by for collection. I knew his voice. It was him. He couldn't fool me. I remember when he'd call from Stockton all those years away from us and whine for money. All he wanted this time was a paltry six hundred and forty-two cents. Bet he thought he was fooling me. He said he'd be by around six or so."

"Do you have the recording? It would really help," Max offered.

"Oh my, I erased it. I needed the recording time for the results of my tests. I can tell you he wants to come by tonight. I was a little intimidated, so I called you."

They went over what Mrs. Flower remembered and decided to set up a stakeout. Laughlin was somewhat discouraged since Mo could have been observing them when they drove up, but they left with the plan made and assured Mrs. Flower she wouldn't be alone. They told Daniels's team to enter the house from the back where the mudroom was, even though it had probably never seen mud. Mrs. Flower left the back door open and said she would go into the living room and wait for the doorbell. Daniels was to call Laughlin and Max the minute he heard the doorbell. They'd be in front observing.

They waited. Daniels called to say Mrs. Flowers was on the phone three times, but no one saw Franklin Mo. At one in the morning, Laughlin went in the house. Max stayed outside.

Mrs. Flower was asleep on the couch. She looked like a wilted flower wrapped in a silk yellow dress with green slippers sticking out on the floor that she had envisioned for her death. Three glasses were beside her, all empty. He tapped her tiny veined hand, and she opened her eyes immediately.

"Oh, Sheriff Laughlin, how charming to see you again. What's happening?"

"To put it plainly, nothing. Nothing at all."

"How extraordinary. People just don't keep their word anymore. Franklin could at least be expected to collect money. I told him you'd be here. He called twice to ask if it was okay to come for the money. I explained he could get the fake bill settled, but I was safe from him, and he couldn't take anything from the house because you were watching out for me, and you were more clever than he was."

"Great. You tipped him off we were here, is that right?" Laughlin sighed and sat down on a long couch with orange pillows.

"Oh, did I? We chatted so long on the second call, but last time, he said something had come up and to give his regards to the sheriffs. He said he hoped they found dear Mr. Mo and he'd collect the bill later. Wasn't that a hoot?"

While Laughlin filled everyone in on another disappointment, that very evening, Franklin Mo had approached his former paramour Mary Mason who gave him seven hundred dollars, afraid to refuse him this time. She'd left a message at the station. She didn't remember Laughlin's cell phone number and wanted him to know Franklin said he wouldn't bother her again if she came up with money.

Calling her at home, she was hesitant to talk much because her pulse was still up, but she said they met at a movie theater. She couldn't explain why she went other than fear. She described him as still having that scraggly beard but no mustache, aviator glasses, wearing a brown corduroy jacket over a blue shirt.

"He begged me to give him money even though he claimed he didn't remember me when I finally agreed to meet him. He said he found my card in his pocket. He's weird, and I tried to push him away when he came at me to grab me. Imagine trying to touch me when he said he didn't know me, just like he did before. I was afraid of him even though my pulse was only ninety-six. Why haven't you found him? He's going to hurt me one of these times. I'll never leave this house again. He can't make me!" she screamed. On further questioning, she had not marked the cash and gave it to him in twenties. Refusing to have the sheriffs stop by so late at night, the frightened woman stopped talking loudly, said her husband was coming downstairs, and muffled goodbye. Laughlin said he would come over whether or not she liked it.

After explanations and apologies, he felt he had to make to the stakeout team—that was that. Everyone cleared out of the unrealized Bowed Flower drama. His mood sunk low with another beating by this smug bastard.

Driving over quickly, he ran the bell at the Masons and found only the husband home. He was a pale man with dark-framed glasses, a perfectly pressed light blue shirt under a black suit and, incongruously, only stocking feet. He sat on a hassock, rubbed his feet, and related that he had taken his wife to the emergency room and come home about a half hour ago. She'd become paralyzed and needed a workup. He had found her slumped over a chair with her legs askew. She flopped around when he tried to pick her up and wailed about some guy from work stalking her. Mr. Mason shrugged, "I just decided to take her to the emergency room for her own protection. I couldn't watch her all night and be ready for work too."

Pressing for more information, the engineer stated that a psychiatrist had been called in and the conclusion from what he could gather was his wife had some sort of an electrical malfunctioning of her brain that didn't meet normal pathways; the husband related calmly the diagnosis was named a converted or conversion disorder, something like that. What that meant was puzzling to him, but the ER staff told him to go home and they'd observe her for the night.

Mr. Mason went on saying this was one of many times his wife had visited the ER and he wasn't distressed. His face showed nothing while he slowly intertwined his hands, talking in a monotone. After a few minutes of relating Mary's history of nerve problems, he requested Laughlin leave so he could get some sleep to be alert for work tomorrow.

Driving home, the detective felt as empty of ideas as the engineer was of feelings about his wife. The somber streets were resting for the night. LA was not a city that never slept. Many little enclaves were tucked away by nine at night. He'd driven Malibu when it was deserted. He'd looked at South Pas when no one else seemed awake.

Northridge might easily be slumbering after dinnertime. There could be peace and quiet even as the disturbed minds planned their crimes.

A lack of traffic didn't soothe him enough and didn't quell his awareness that Franklin Mo outsmarted him again. There was the direct challenge, no doubt about it. Was he really going to be beaten by this criminal?

This searching had yielded nothing; the traps had yielded nothing.

Mo had money again, and he'd been successful at hiding right in the city. How?

In bed, with the cat crowning his head, Laughlin struggled between blanking out in sleep or finding an answer to where Franklin Mo was hiding. He turned on his side, and the cat slipped off onto his face. The two of them finally settled comfortably, the cat spooning and Laughlin not aware of anything anymore.

CHAPTER 39

Morning was warm and quiet. His first thoughts were the same as his last. He kept his eyes closed. Inhaling deeply, he felt a pressure on his chest. Men got pressure on their chest from heart attacks but this was more difficultly breathing than pain. He opened his eyes and staring at him were the beautiful blue eyes of the Siamese.

"Goddamn it, cat, get off. I have to breathe." He lifted the animal by the scruff of the neck and deposited him on the floor.

The cat stood for a moment, seemed offended, and tried to jump up again.

With this successful attempt, Laughlin glared at the cat, gave him a gentle push to the side of the bed, sat up.

"Why did I wind up with you?" He put his hand on the cat's belly and rolled him back and forth. The image of the cat coming out of the door with Manfred popped up. "Yup, you were there from the beginning. Too bad, you can't talk to me about it all. Tell me why Manfred died and where Mo is. Maybe we should go back to the bookstore and look for some more clues in the kitty litter."

Then the idea flashed before him—the bookstore was where Franklin would hide, where he'd stay and no one would think to look, old but true, and where he could be arrogant and assume this sheriff was oblivious.

"You rest, you big chunky cat. Guard this temple of mine, and we'll see about your old haunts."

When he called Max, he heard a slew of words but not yes.

"Sergeant, you're headed for the loony bin. Jesus Christ, man, you must be deranged. Did you just wake up, or are you still bombed?

I mean, where the hell did you pull that theory from—MJ, Ludes, DT's?"

"I thought of the cat and his connection with the bookstore."

"Ah, come on, give me a break. I've gone along with the feline informant once, not again. I can't buy another wild association. Give me some real reasoning. Tell me, you're not going insane, bonkers, nuts? Have you got the cuckoos?"

"Enough with your synonyms. Shut up for a minute, please. Listen, let me explain."

"Off your rocker, bananas, loco."

"Max, please shut up! Shut up, we've got to get this guy."

."It's six in the morning. I was having fun. Why stop me?" Max complained.

"Give it a break and listen."

"I'll meet you for breakfast and then see if you have a grip on reality or you've gone gaga, crazed, off the deep end. Man, I could associate you with nuts, for sure."

"Damn it! Cut out the insults. You think you're so clever, a big narcissistic personality disorder. See, I can sling the bullshit too." Laughlin yelled back.

"Truce, truce. See you for scrambled eggs, not brains."

Munching cantaloupe after pancakes, eggs, and biscuits, Laughlin explained his theory about the cat. "It popped into my mind that Mason said Franklin Mo was wearing a corduroy jacket, further association with the bookstore. Mo was wearing one of Manfred's jackets. I'm sure. Why else could he be so brazen?"

After finishing half a dozen hotcakes and three mugs of coffee, Max was finally sold on at least going back to the bookstore. Franklin Mo had been cocky, and he deserved to know he wasn't going to fuck with the sheriffs any longer.

The crew took the collections from the garbage men to the lab and shorted through the debris in the adjacent big dumpsters. They found lots of take-out containers but nothing definitive about any camping in the building, no fingerprints and no Mo in particular. All that didn't deter Laughlin, and he reasserted the plan.

The FBI reported a sighting in Indio, but Laughlin stuck with his hunch. Stakeouts across the street revealed nothing unusual. It didn't deter the detective. No attempt to go in the bookstore was indicated, so Mo wouldn't be spooked. It was a long day.

Max decided to take a leak twice while cruising around, and that ticked his sergeant off.

"Hey, I'm not letting this guy ruin my kidneys," he stated firmly and suggested Laughlin go to the McDonald's and get coffee and take a pee. "The break will give you something to do while we wait and your pants will stay dry, Sarge."

Laughlin gave an exasperated laugh and did just that. He'd always wondered if most stakeouts had urinal bottles with them. They certainly couldn't concentrate on the subject with full bladders on twelve hours or longer shifts.

The whole approach arranged. The detectives made sure there was not an exit behind the bookstore that was not covered. They had a car and two men in the parking lot area as well as all doors from the other stores covered when they would make their move.

Laughlin figured about eleven at night was good, less dangerous for innocents. Everyone agreed with his decision. Waiting was frustrating, but the sergeant justified it by emphasizing the reduced risk for injury. He was in charge. The team watched the bookstore all day. The other stores had minimal customers, and the bookstore was quiet. There had been no activity but now there was a light escaping through the back door slits. Franklin Mo was there. He had to be.

The raid was on.

Opening the bookstore's front door quietly, Laughlin and Max led with their guns. Instantly a fierce blinding light assaulted them. It flashed, it rotated. It banged their eyes shut and worked continuously with an ear shattering buzzer. Another light and buzzer started up in back of the first to further the pummeling.

Max jumped to the side wall, Laughlin dropped down on the entrance floor. He chose to lie flat rather than bunched up. Shots came. Guns were firing from the back of the store. Stray bullets smashed glass. He heard Max swearing. Squinting cautiously, he saw an outline of a figure in and out of the light coming at him to steal out the door. Laughlin was spread out like a road block to the shattered exit. He grabbed, caught a leg, and held on. A gun butt repeatedly smashed his temple but he held on. The leg shook and twisted as the captive struggled to get free of the trap.

Soon the lights were shot out, the buzzers were dead, and only shuffling, scuffling sounds remained in the dark. Laughlin held on. One of the deputies switched on a flashlight. Laughlin was still holding tightly even as the beam of light caught him and his bloody face. A wiggling figure was down next to the detective, trying to pry the gripping hands loose. The gun was tucked in his shirt.

"All right, Franklin Mo, stop struggling. Detective Laughlin's got you. Stand up and put your hands behind your back. You've been trapped like the scumbag you are," Max grabbed Mo's gun. Reluctantly, the caught man took his time extricating himself from the tangle, distain for the sheriff evident.

Laughlin stood slowly and wiped his face. He smiled.

It was an unglamorous capture, and Max made the most of that, but it was a capture and arrest and advisement. Franklin Mo was handed over to be booked.

Paramedics applied some Steri-Strips and dismissed Laughlin's brain injury as nonexistent. He refused to go for observation. Max tried to contradict them about brain damage and they all had a good laugh at the bleeding and bruised hero.

After all the sirens faded, the two detectives remained behind with forensics for a fast look at the bookstore, the gunfight aftermath, and the setup that had confronted their senses. The photos were taken quickly, and that was that.

The back room held a small teakettle on a Coleman stove that was turned off. All the wall hangings were intact. The couch had a lush quilted cover of bright red shiny material like silk, and the floor had a woven yellow rug with patterned animals on it.

"This guy had to have been bringing this stuff in for days. Where in the hell were we?" Max complained.

"We were being smart asses trying to catch him in a sting." Laughlin pulled drawers open and reexamined a packet of papers. He sat down and picked through them, finding receipts paid in cash and bills dating a week after Manfred's death, camping equipment vouchers, an instruction sheet on the installation of rotating eighty-six-millimeter LED flashing lights with stud mounts and those damned buzzers, and a plane ticket seat assignment from Miami, Florida, days after the shooting. Evidence was packed up, without bothering what it meant, to be examined later.

Finally, the detectives were alone.

Quiet remains of the store's assault laid out piles of books burst open, pages exposed like gapping tongues, strobe lights morose in their shot-out shells, wires hanging everywhere but making no connections. Broken shards crunched as they walked on the wooden floor.

"He must have just gone in the back like nothing was wrong, and nobody gave a damn about the cordon tape and trespassing. We were so busy chasing him and ignoring the obvious."

"All right, I already gave you and the cat your due. We sure missed any evidence of him being here when we brought the feline detective."

"Probably hadn't settle in yet. Too bad the place got wrecked."

"Damn, we were lucky he didn't hit us."

"I think he emptied his gun right away, so instead, he had to whack me with it. He probably thought he would eliminate us through shock or shots to get away again."

"What a mess to leave Mrs. Porter," Max observed.

"Yup, it was an okay little bookstore. Goodbye for now," Laughlin said remorsefully. He took the Advil the paramedics had left, and the two detectives went to hear the suspect interview.

*   *   *

In the holding area, claiming he was guarding the store against intruders, the full-faced, wispy bearded man sat causally, checking his nails. Taking off an ill-fitting dark brown corduroy jacket, draping it carefully on the bench, he rubbed his leg and said he was going to sue the sheriff's department for damages to his leg and his store and racially motivated harassment.

His story was elaborate, and he recited it repeatedly. He owned the bookstore and was afraid of break-ins. He didn't know who Franklin Mo was and said he was Mr. Frank Dolmer, born in Los Angeles, actually in Alameda. He immediately requested a lawyer.

Laughlin and Max listened to the recitation. They showed him photos with his mental health badge and his driver's license name. He curled his lip and said they were fraudulent. He had no recollection of this Franklin Mo person. He had no idea who Freeman Malloy was either. He claimed this was all absurd, and he again demanded to talk to his lawyer.

CHAPTER 40

Laughlin and Max went through the routine of organizing notes for their reports, slumping back in their chairs and reflecting generally on the case and the charges. The lawyer would not be a public defender but some big private defense lawyer, where so-called Dolmer would probably get the money from Franklin Mo's coffers.

"How do we explain the connection if Dolmer claims he didn't know Franklin Mo? Should be some clever bullshit is my guess," Max expounded.

Now it was a waiting game for arraignment, trial, testimony. Max decided to go to Kim's and wait for the next assignment.

Laughlin had no definitive answer to what he was going to do. At four-thirty in the morning, what was there he could do?

Max lectured him not to neglect the cat, go home, and change the litter. Laughlin knew it would have been nice to celebrate toasting the waves.

The void of no comfort and no pursuit was a letdown. While driving home, Laughlin found himself lost in reviewing the case. The brass should be happy with the arrest. The rest was up to other forces he could not control.

His house had a few paper ads held together with rubber bands and one glossy magazine haphazardly thrown on the steps. It was too late for Winkler, but Dylan was waiting at the door.

"How the hell did you get out?" That remark was greeted by a rub on the pant leg and an eager trot inside the house to food. Laughlin followed and had a toast and some apple juice. Upstairs, he found an open window that made an easy access to the garage roof and freedom. He didn't shut it but made his way to the shower and hit his bed in ten minutes.

A few hours later, just before noon, he sat at his office desk, reviewing his report, and the lieutenant came by to ask him how he was feeling and tell him that his case was even weirder than before. Franklin Mo, a.k.a. Frank Dolmer, or the other way around, was claiming some sort of mental disorder. The lawyer he called from a number in his Dolmer wallet recognized him as Franklin Mo.

Furthermore, the prosecutor's office was not sure what the charges would be.

They could present the attack on the sheriffs at the bookstore and probably extortion, but to justify murder, more evidence was needed. The Miami airline ticket could mean he was gone when the murder occurred.

Max made things worse by telling him he'd seen on the news some of the firm representing Mo and asking if that wasn't the same firm that included Maggie's present boyfriend. Max was sure Maggie had been in the photo of a yearly law firm party in the *LA Times*. He asked if that was the guy she'd dumped Laughlin for.

So she'd moved on to a lawyer. Swearing quietly, Laughlin acknowledged the news and told Max about the prosecutor's concerns.

"What the fuck?" Max pronounced loudly. "Hey, maybe you could get the cat to testify."

That was all. Laughlin walked out.

"Ah, come on, Sergeant, lighten up," Max called after him.

What was he to do when he didn't want to stay at the station and didn't want to go home? The beach. Punching radio stations, looking for company, he drove quickly. KUSC, not 88.1 Jazz, his day station, soaked the silence with soulful music. Now by himself, the minor key spoke to him, distracted him, occupied him, soothed him. It turned out to be Schubert. Laughlin hadn't known that but he'd liked the piece.

At Malibu Seafood again, he wolfed down the fried clams and coleslaw in the car tucked in the back parking lot, and then cut under the tunnel to the beach. The low tide exposed black rocks crowned by big mussels like praying hands.

Off went his socks and shoes to jog at a leisurely pace. Thoughts moved along in his mind too. He knew mental illness was a common defense for alcohol and drug addiction, now called diseases. No one said Franklin Mo drank or used. What would he claim? Not ADD . . . although more adults seemed to give attention to that diagnosis now. Maybe split personality or, what was it that was so prevalent in the eighties, multiple personality disorder. That was a good one with a surplus of drama.

How strange it would be to see Maggie again with some lawyer jerk undermining the case against Mo. Maggie—hadn't she been with some accountant? He wondered about her kids.

He wondered if she'd read about him being one of the detectives on the case. Probably not much said or shown. A dead bookseller wasn't sexy, but maybe a mental health administrator suspect from San Marino might warrant more coverage. He wondered if he would meet her again.

He checked his cell phone, hoping for some sort of call. The message transferred to his cell phone from the station said that Mary Mason had completely recovered from her paralyses when she found out Franklin Mo was in jail. He shook his head, wondering about going crazy too.

He drove around the block before pulling up to his house. A heavy rain fell. He was looking for anything suspicious; it was his routine now if he remembered.

When he got home, the cat wasn't there. It was raining cats and dogs, he mused, but his roof wasn't falling in. He'd be damned if he'd call kitty kitty. He trudged upstairs, showered, and went to bed. At about three, there was a thump on the floor and a trill. Purring, the wet animal took his rightful place on the bed, and Laughlin was relieved.

Maybe Lucy would be back soon, and he would have her come over and check the cat. Women intruded on his thoughts and sleep.

CHAPTER 41

At Trader Joe's, Maggie came up to him. He was struck again by how lovely and tall she was. He had never really forgotten. They exchanged greetings and she smiled while doing so.

"Are you all right? I saw your name in the *Times*, the assault by that guy, and Lester mentioned how tough you were too."

"Oh."

"Looks like you're healing quickly. Another interesting case for you, don't you agree?"

"I supposed so," he said and looked down on the display of ready-made sandwiches.

"My, you're reticent today."

"I apparently am reticent today," he repeated and fumbled around the sandwiches.

"James Laughlin, come on and have a coffee with me for old time's sake."

"What for? You don't have to get case information for your boyfriend, do you?"

"Hey, that was below you."

"You're right, I'm tired and ticked," he replied and looked at her directly.

"Well, that's what the coffee is for, silly."

Across the street were a small doughnut shop and a sushi restaurant. She picked the restaurant. He fussed and said they probably wouldn't have coffee, but she said green tea was better. Like a pet puppy, he followed her and was now mad at himself instead of her.

They sat down on thin steel-legged chairs at a shiny black table. Other than the sushi chef on one side of the neat bright room, there was nothing else suggesting Japan. The waitress handed out laminated menus and waited.

"Just two green teas, please," Maggie ordered for both of them. "So you're free this afternoon, is that right?"

Laughlin studied the menu and ordered some cucumber rolls as well, saying, "It's almost dinnertime for me. Finished at the station and came to pick up some supplies."

"You've got to know Lester is a member of the firm but not really involved in your case, don't worry."

"So I thought you'd dumped me for an accountant, not a lawyer."

"Time flies when you're having fun."

"How are your kids doing with rotating men in your life?"

"You know, I don't have to take this shit from you. Why aren't you being civil?" she responded in a harsh whisper.

He quickly raised his arms above his head and opened and closed his hands.

There was a slight flinch on her part, but when she saw he was just stretching, she picked up her teacup.

He lowered his arms and nodded. "Yup, you're right. So how are the kids?"

"They're fine, living with their father right now. Lester and I are thinking of moving in together. He really is a great guy and confidentially doesn't think much of the mental disorder plea the client is claiming. What do you think? Could that be a real reason for his strange behavior? Lester won't say . . . confidentiality issues and all."

Laughlin took some tea and listened to the take on Lester. *What a stupid name*, he thought and wondered about Maggie telling him all this stuff. What was the real agenda?

"So Lester is delightful. What mental disorder are you talking about?"

"What did he plead, some dissociating thing. Wasn't it on the news?"

"I don't watch the news much." He ate two rolls. "What's this socializing about, Maggie?"

"Just a friendly hello."

"Well, it isn't working. I gonna go. Good night." He got up, grabbed another roll, threw a ten-dollar bill on the table and left.

After finishing at the store, he drove slowly through the traffic and cursed himself for being so lame. She was approachable. He was even more angry with her for her "Aren't we friends?" attitude. She was over him, and there was no residual. He pulled over to a curb with big trees and ate one of the sandwiches. He'd always been told he got irritable if he was too hungry. All those voices were right.

Thinking about meeting Maggie did nothing but create a turmoil of need. Nevertheless, against an urge to smash slow-moving cars, he made it home and there on the porch was Mr. Winkler. Alone. A little barnacle on his steps.

Laughlin left the car in the driveway and walked over to the old man.

As the lump struggled to his feet, he said, "Good evening. Well, almost a good evening, Detective. How are you?"

"Tired, and you?"

"Wet. Do you have a new case?"

"Yup," he lied. Then he asked, "Where's your companion Ms. Elvira? Out misbehaving?"

"How did you know? It's sad. She had a relapse. It's Robert's birthday, and she goes bananas every year about this time, probably got some amphetamines to counter the depression," Winkler lamented.

"Hey, I'm sorry," Laughlin offered. "Come on in for a beer. Where's Rosie?"

"Rosie one is still in the hospital, and Rosie two stayed home from the rain tonight, probably misses Elvira."

Laughlin was aware of his unerring tactlessness. The visitor was lonely and needed good company. He scolded himself and resolved not to be a sarcastic asshole.

Winkler was eager to fill the detective on the news and downed his beer, commenting on his preference for Karl Strauss beer, while petting the Siamese and noting his brindle.

"See, in cold weather, these temple guards get slight stripes on their thighs as well as darker ears and paws. Such a great cat. You must be proud."

"He tries."

"Oh my, dear detective, this cat doesn't have to try. He is."

"So what news do you have?" Laughlin asked while going for another bottle.

"You want another one too, Mr. Winkler?"

"No, thank you. The news about your case against Franklin Mo, and in remembrance of Eric Manfred's not dying without some retribution, is mixed. The man calls himself Dolmer and pleads dissociative fugue. I have my collection of DSM books and it's something added after the last manual update. It used to be akin to psychogenic amnesia. Amazing how diseases keep popping up and changing names. I remember when we all thought the world was solved with labels of loony or not, and when . . . when penicillin killed all bacteria. Now we've variations on variations, viruses, and retroviruses and mutations and all sorts of stuff."

"Yes, sir, the world is a complicated mess," Laughlin added.

"Please be more imaginative than that, son," the old man suggested.

"I'm not a goddamn poet, you know. Only a cops and robbers man."

"Come on, get some better images. You've got the brains. Anyway, to the point, a person who gets dissociative fugue is like a lively zombie, contradictory as that sounds. He changes life roles and doesn't even know it, runs around with a new identity but without the FBI witness protection program. It's not dissociative identity disorder, you know, multiple personality and such.

"Great idea, all on his own, loses himself. Isn't that merely a big bluff to avoid responsibility? Just another mental illness ploy by a psychopath?"

"It sure seems probable, but who can prove it? They said on the news that people may have some sort of horrible trauma or merely drop out and then burst into a new identity half-assed or all the way."

"I'll look into it, but it sounds smarmy to me," Laughlin offered.

"I wonder how many others will use the idea to avoid charges of extortion and murder."

"That's the way of a defense," the detective decided.

"Yes. 'Hell is empty. All the devils are here.' Clever ones at that." Winkler sighed and added, "I guess the rain is still not done even after a hell of a wet spring."

Laughlin walked Winkler home about ten, an early time for both. It was still raining in sprints. There were rain rivers jumping curbs and mud on the sidewalks everywhere. An El Niño year, not yet turning into a La Niña, did its thing. Soon it would be too dry and the rain would be missed. El Niño and La Niña—the climate twins.

Walking back home, Laughlin was bombarded by distorted images of Franklin Mo posing as crazy, and Maggie being a hypocritical Ms. Gracious. Yet, the world was being washed and freshened. Rain pounding and sliding down his neck, he also recalled Winkler still philosophizing. How was he to put it all together? How could he? He was trying to be mature, face disappointments, barriers, but he wasn't that well equipped—just a dumb, eager plodder.

He prescribed immediate bed rest for himself and followed his orders rather than getting blotto.

Chapter 42

Mrs. Porter called Max. She wanted to know if she should let Jeffrey Faulk come over to apologize and would the deputy be there if she agreed. Laughlin and Max went over that next morning. It was still raining. A half hour later, Faulk drove up in a once shiny red pickup truck splattered with mud. He had on a bright multicolored checkered shirt and baggy pants covered by a plastic garbage bag against which he carried some yellow sunflowers carefully. Dripping water, he nodded repeatedly, seemingly rehearsing his entrance.

Shocked to see the sheriffs, he dropped the bunch of wet floppy flowers and stooped to pick them up. "I wanted to bring you a momentum and ask yur forgiveness. I'm much the better now, honest sheriffs. Here," he added and dumped the gift in Mrs. Porter's lap on top of the stuffed cats.

"Oh my lord, well, thank you, I guess, and I hope you never frighten anyone again," the chalk-white woman replied while wrapping her shawl tightly about her and letting the flowers drop. Faulk bent down and picked them up again. He put them on the table.

"That's probably better until they dry, huh? I-I-I'm really a reformed person. Honest. Probation has helped. There's a goodness about you that makes it hard to lie to you, and my brother will kick me out like a rat in the silo if I do wrong," Faulk continued and looked to Laughlin and Max for approval.

"I think it's a good thing you apologized, Jeffrey," Max said.

"Yur's right, sir."

"After this, it would be best if you leave Mrs. Porter alone from now on," Laughlin added.

"Sure, sure, but I brought this other thing for her. It might help. Mr. Mo—he give it to me to keep. Now he's in the pokey, ya know, jail and stuff, I thought maybe you, being Mr. Manfred's sister, could keep it for him, seeing he was always getting these messages from yur brother and all. Me, I never gonna come back to LA, no more. Just this one time. See, I've still got some brain left, my brother says, and I've got to protect it, right?"

There was immediate silence as Faulk took out a small manila envelope from under his shirt and handed to Mrs. Porter.

"Well, that's it, ma'am."

"Jeffrey, one thing more, when did Franklin give you this?" Laughlin asked.

"It was about the time me and him and Eugene became buds. Seems so long ago now. I'd been rooming with Eugene at the board and care. He was a little loony then, but he'd not cut his thumb off yet. He was a good guy, all told. Met Mr. Mo at the jail when Eugene was held for vagrant dumpster living. He done it at least three times. Then we all became friends when he cut his thumb off in a diner. People didn't want to eat, seeing that, and the owner called the police. He was in jail, mental health then. Something like that. After he went back to the board and care, Mr. Mo would bring us over to his mansion and we would partee. Something like that." Faulk sighed and looked at Laughlin. "I remember you too. Yur'd talked to me after this deputy punched me and stopped me from getting away. Hey, it's okay now."

Mrs. Porter opened the envelope and took out three pieces of paper. One was a postcard and two were folded letters. She read all the documents, squeezed her eyes shut, and reached out to Laughlin to take them.

The postcard was addressed to a Vicky Vonn Biskoff, PO Box 1023 in Stockton, offering help with the child. It was signed Eric Manfred along with his store address. It was posted on February 12, 1973. Laughlin understood now there had been two postcards, not just the one that the psychiatrist had found.

One folded paper was a duplicate of the complete birth certificate listing Eugene as a seven-pound baby. Eugene was now officially twenty-five years old, younger than everyone had thought. The third paper was a list of instructions for Jeffrey if Franklin disappeared.

"I dunno what that was all about. It dinnit make sense to me since they was pals, but I thought it better if you carry out the list. Youse could've taken care of yur brother more easy than for me to do," Jeffrey added.

"The list included burning any notes about money, and if Mo didn't have time, I was to be taking care of Manfred if he began to talk about Mo asking for money. I didn't quite understand it all. See what I mean? So that's why youse could help," Jeffrey concluded.

"He put a one-hundred-dollar bill in there too, but I spent it to come down here, sorry," Jeffrey explained. "I gotta go now. My brother will be waiting at the truck stop. Goodbye."

Mrs. Porter, Max, and Laughlin watched quietly as Jeffrey Faulk nodded and quietly shut the door like a remorseful child.

"My goodness gracious. I think this means I'm an aunt of some sort. Is that right?" Mrs. Porter exclaimed and looked back and forth between the detectives for confirmations. "Deputy Max, I need some tea. This is extraordinary, to say the least. Is that boy alive still?"

"It also means Franklin Mo contacted your brother after he returned to Los Angeles to get money from him. Then he wanted your brother killed to prevent being exposed as an extortionist," Max concluded as he went to the kitchen.

"First things first. I want to see this boy, right here, right now."

A few days later, they were all in the hot square living room in a circle.

Sitting on the hearth, Laughlin was to the right of Mrs. Porter and her cats; Max was to her left on the hearth as well. Dressed in olive green hoodies, Mr. and Mrs. Winkler were on the settee, Elvira Moody Winkler wearing dark black hair was in one of the two big chairs, and holding her hand was Eugene Biskoff in Levi's and a

Rolling Stones T-shirt and red tennis shoes on foot and fake foot in the other chair.

"Hey, this is really special for me," Eugene began.

"I'm glad you think so," Mrs. Porter answered.

"I mean, this is like the group therapy gatherings. You've got me in the twenties, those officers in the thirties, I'm guessing, Elvira in the forties, Mrs. Porter in the fifties, and Mr. and Mrs. Winkler in the sixties or so. All ages except, of course, for young, really young ones, or really old ones, but this is still really good. The genes are quiet," Eugene exclaimed.

"So let's hear about you, Eugene. How are you doing?" Mrs. Porter inquired.

"Everybody is always asking me that because of what a butcher I was. It's hard to explain what I did. I wouldn't have come here if it weren't for Elvira. She brought me books and talked to me about life. It sure was a surprise about you, Ms. Porter. I thought it was a con, but these sheriffs kept on telling me it was on the level, and then Elvira said it too. Imagine that."

"I need to know what your plans are now."

"My boy Robert—he should have been here too. He got destroyed. I miss him," Mrs. Winkler piped up like a talking shroud, loud and clear.

"It's so true, Ma. I miss him too," Elvira said and started to cry. She grasped a brown vial from her pocket, shook some pills, and quickly cupped two into her mouth. Sobbing, she wiped her tears with her sleeve and covered her face with a swoop of her hair.

Winkler struggled up, handed her a handkerchief from his big sweatshirt pocket, and quickly plopped back down, startling his wife.

"He did 'rush into the secret house of death,' for that is what a soldier must risk. He was brave," Winkler pronounced, grasping his wife's hand.

"Let me get this straight—you don't have genes in common, but you act like you still care. Let's see, Elvira, you married the son and don't have any genes from them, but you call Mrs. Winkler Ma.

That's kind thinking," Eugene began to elaborate. "Me, I have some genes with Mrs. Porter, right?"

Mrs. Porter nodded.

"My genes come from your brother, and your genes come from my father's and your mother and father. That would be my grandparents. Somehow I got other genes that didn't work as well."

"You've got your mother's genes as well," Elvira responded.

"My boy was so smart. Why did he die?" Mrs. Winkler began again.

"Elvira, you have to get Rosie to be happy while you're here, for my sake," Mr. Winkler pleaded.

"But I'll never know my mother and her genes. Maybe I have a mutation."

"I know depression can be inherited," Elvira moaned.

"Schizophrenia too, but it's not a split personality. No, it's a split between the feelings and the thinking. I think that's what I read. Genes can cause it. I have those genes," Eugene lamented.

"Rosie, Rosie, we're here now. Let our boy go. He needs to rest," Winkler whispered to his wife and, crazed with grief, turned to all the room and said, "You see her eyes are open. Ay, but their sense is shut. Help her to be here now."

"What good is that, Pa? Let her be lost. Oh, I wish I could be," Elvira cried.

"They can get genes from bones, and we could dig up my mother and your son, sir," Eugene added.

"He was my good boy. Where is he now? He played soccer. Is he outside now? Where is that boy, always running off?" She clutched her hands together and twisted the intertwined fingers.

Winkler started shaking his leg up and down while Elvira bowed, hiding her face in her hair.

Eugene frowned and started counting his shirt buttons over and over.

The agitation, the craziness, was escalating like an orchestra's dissonant tuning but never playing the music. Suddenly, standing up, Laughlin, imposing his full size on the room, caused everyone to stare at him. He wanted this Tower of Babel stopped. He looked at the shocked faces and ordered, "Let's try to deal with Eugene today and now. Okay? Got it?"

"I lost my brother and you a son and you a husband and you a father," Mrs. Porter finally entered the fray, picking up the idea, pointed at everyone, and proceeded in her orderly fashion. "This is about something good now. We must look to Eugene and his future," Mrs. Porter said firmly. "I don't have room you could stay in, but we'll figure out something, you being my family and all."

"Yes, let's help this man find a better life," Laughlin added, continuing to stand like a monitor.

"Mrs. Porter, may I get us all some tea, please," Max offered and went about the preparation and brought the now silent group the cups and muffins.

The tea party went on for another hour with Mrs. Porter keeping control over the subject matter. The focus was on the here and now again. Then Laughlin and Max excused themselves. The little group nodded their goodbyes and resumed talking about Eugene and where he would live when he was discharged and how Mrs. Porter would give him an allowance and manage his SSI.

Getting out of the hot house, Laughlin rubbed the back of his neck and walked slowly to the car as though he were carrying the grief and hope along with him.

Max shook his head. "This was one mental health circle jerk. I don't know how psychiatrists stand it," he concluded.

"I understand Eugene has written Dr. Weber to tell her what's happened. I think she would like that. She'd done extensive work to find Eugene's father. I bet Franklin Mo didn't want her to find out he'd lifted valuable documents," Laughlin concluded. "Damn, though, I couldn't help thinking about poor Freddy Poplar. He's the one who rushed into that secret house of death. Sad, considering how well it all turned out."

"Hey, I'd forgotten about him. I don't know, Sergeant, I can't get around it all. Mental health and all sorts of deaths are awfully messed up. I understand taking the new evidence in. That's straightforward, but all this dying and crying—too much for me."

"I wonder if it all doesn't boil down to how we process death in any form," Laughlin offered.

"Exceptionally profound for a sheriff. However, Freud baby, our job is to investigate murder," Max concluded.

That remark brought up the still pending murder trial, and after finishing reports and leaving the station, Laughlin sat in his car, staring at nothing. He finally ran his fingers through his hair, scratched absentmindedly, and then held his head between his hands for a moment. He yawned. He'd learned about the jail and its toll. There were fucked-up people in this case and a lot of them outside the jail as well as in it. Their minds plastered with sticky labels called schizophrenia, mania, delirium, cutting, conversions, depression, grief, dissociation, suicide, and his own paranoia. What did it mean? In the end, it all winds up nothing.

His cavalier remark about processing death had been more to the point than he initially recognized. Maybe it did all boil down to that—how to process death, crazy or not?

He thought of that distant Lake Erie adventurer. Row off to oblivion might not be a bad idea.

There he was stuck in a boat, investigating death by murder—victims who didn't want to die, murderers who didn't care. It was shitty work. What was the saying? I can't go on; I go on.

CHAPTER 43

Bowed Flower called as one of the last of the case characters wanting to say goodbye. Her daughter and grandson were home for the trial, although no date had been set. She suggested the detective come over because she had some news that Franklin might plead guilty or no contest to lesser charges. How did she know? Laughlin would have to come over to find out.

Max came along reluctantly, but there was such a paucity of murders at the moment he reasoned the visit was easier than sitting and stewing. Laughlin was relieved he didn't have to face that house and its inhabitants alone, but speculated she might have evidence that added credibility to the incriminating papers Jeffrey had given to Mrs. Porter.

The dangling wet sycamore leaves and the soaked stone walk with dropped lemons led to the open front door and Bowed Flower. She stood in the frame like a carved wooden maiden who had been warped by time. Still, her smile reflected the inlaid glitter in her eyes. She beckoned them in with a light blue scarf trying to escape in the wind and a bracelet covered arm. She jangled as she walked.

"Sheriffs, into the kitchen, please."

They followed docilely. Max took a seat away from the bottles of booze and at the end of all the other stools. Laughlin stood until Bowed Flower gestured for him to sit next to her.

"Although I'm sure you get inside dope from the prosecutor's office, my information is even more inside. I've seen the accused man, and he woke up when my daughter confronted him. She agreed to pay the bail monies only if he stayed home with her. That woke him up in more ways than one. He came out of a trance and said he didn't remember anything."

"So is he Mo again or still Dolmer?" Max wondered.

"Oh, he's Franklin Mo again."

"Just came out of it with no prompting, right?"

"Not quite, you said Mrs. Mo confronted him," Laughlin interjected.

"Now he's 'Mr. Yes, Dear,' thinks he'll be put in the jail hospital so he doesn't wander off from here. It's hard to stomach since I found out I haven't much longer to live."

"What do you mean?"

"I am dying, that's what I mean!" Bowed Flower exclaimed.

"No. What about being in the hospital?" Max said.

"That's great, Deputy Max. Still no concern, just a little something for me? Some concern, some sympathy, some condolences—what's the matter with you? Didn't you learn anything?"

"Mrs. Flower, we are here to listen to you. If you are ill, we could come back at a more convenient time," Laughlin offered.

"There is no convenient time for dying. I have pancreatic cancer, a silent killer, and I refuse any treatment. I figure, at my age, if vessels don't clog you up, then cancer will. All that chemical intervention would make me sicker, and I would rather die healthy."

Laughlin waited. He didn't want to point out her contradiction. He was attached to this outspoken woman. She helped him find Biskoff through Faulk, way back at the beginning of the investigation.

"I am very sorry. I hope you don't have severe pain," he finally said quietly.

"I'm very sorry too," Max joined in.

"Well, that's better than last time. Now let's have a drink to life, liberty and the pursuit of happiness."

They picked Pepsi, Seven-up, and bourbon straight, Pappy Van Winkle Bourbon. Laughlin longed to get a taste and tentatively smelled the cap. Then she began talking.

"Oh, go on. One sip won't get you kicked off the department. It's after hours already anyway, right? It's my private reserve. I get the stuff from my contact in Kentucky, a Chinese engineering student from San Francisco who travels down from MIT. He's good to me because I put him through school each year."

Laughlin and Max each took a sip and sighed with pleasure.

"The tongue's taste buds bloom and throat mellows with the slithering of the brown liquid," she said. "I love how that feels on the way down. Isn't it great? Now listen. I overheard him talking to his lawyer. They ignore me like I were some vase or a pillow or a rug. I haven't decided which yet. I thought it was supposed to be a fly on the wall. Nothing significant. My daughter, she sits by and is amused while hating Franklin intensely. He is going to ruin either her reputation, her business, or her free time to meet with her true love. My ever-missing grandson stays out all night and is about to return to Hong Kong. They merely want Franklin paid off and disposed of quickly, while he wants to stay out of jail. How to accomplish both goals? Easy. Pay the lawyer to plead a mental disorder."

"Yes, we heard that. I think it's in the news again."

"Franklin, my dear daughter and the lawyer are all in the living room now. Of course, my grandson has run away already.

Suddenly, a brown-haired man with a stiff sharkskin suit and orange leather shoes rushed into the kitchen. His black briefcase covering his chest was tightly held by his stubby fingers, two of which had gem rings sticking out like colorful warts. He looked around, his whole torso quivering, and, below a perfectly trimmed mustache, shouted, "How do you get out of here? Where's the back door? Damn it!"

Mrs. Flower shrugged and pointed to a hallway.

"He's gone berserk, threatening to kill her and me if I say anything. Get in there now. Somebody stop him! I'm leaving." And with that, he ran down the hall.

Laughlin and Max shouldered Mrs. Flowers through the kitchen into the living room where Mrs. Mo sat on the couch with a pillow over her stomach. Franklin Mo was standing over her with a strange pointed weapon.

"I'll stab her if you come any closer. Don't attack me. Where's that fucking lawyer? I need him to witness what they've been doing to me."

"Hello, Sheriff Laughlin, and you must be the kind Joseph Max. My mother has told me about you and your excellent care of her when she was in distress," Mrs. Mo smiled. "By the way, pointing at me is the husband you were so diligently seeking and I was so diligently avoiding."

"What's going on?" Laughlin demanded.

"This is my decision, you uniformed lackey. I'll stab her if she doesn't confess she set me up. You guys are always after the wrong people." Franklin Mo howled, while jabbing this poker-like object in the air and stabbing at the pillow Mrs. Mo clutched.

"Go away, Franklin! Go away and leave my daughter alone." Mrs. Flower screamed.

"It's okay, Mother. He thinks he's a warrior. Look what he's got. He took my exquisite dagger-axe off the wall, over two thousand years old, it's the Ji I brought from China. Imagine, it's from the Qin or maybe early Han dynasty. Be ever so careful, Franklin. Of course, he didn't let me take the crossbow or even a shield to protect myself. Brave, isn't he?"

"Look, this is simple, you sheriff guys get out of here. Emerald and I will settle this by ourselves. God has made me in charge."

"You're threatening her. Put down the weapon now," Laughlin commanded.

"Yes, put down the weapon, Franklin. You can't get away with it, and I'll be damned if I'll give you more money than I already did for bail."

"I need to get away. I was not myself. I've found my true voice. You know that."

"Incredible that you convinced that lawyer about the fugue business. Ask him for money, not me. Imagine, free on bail with a murder charge."

"Mr. Mo, put down the weapon." Laughlin turned slightly to nod to his deputy. "Ready, Max? Approach from the other side on the count of three."

"Damn. Why did I leave my gun just because the house is first class? All right, Sarge, on three."

"I'll stab her if you move." He thrust the spear at his wife and tore the pillow and tried to slice her neck. Laughlin lunged at him.

"Not waiting until three, huh?" Max circled the couch and pulled the woman over the back of the couch and on to the rug.

Laughlin grabbed hold of the weapon and twisted his body around, trying to rip it away from the desperate man. Mo began thrashing. Blood dripped down the shaft of the dagger.

Both men fell on the velvet couch and then onto the floor in a tangle of limbs. Each held tightly to the shaft, and Mo slashed the air with the ax end. Laughlin swore and then lifted Franklin Mo along with the dagger-axe straight above him, rolled and threw the body and ax. Mo dropped with a thud and the weapon skidded away. Red pillows absorbed the blood making dark splotches.

Max exclaimed, "Nifty bench press," and bent over the stunned attacker. Both sheriffs pulled him up and onto a chair. He didn't resist. His right hand was cut deeply and bleeding. Laughlin's left shoulder was slashed and bleeding through his shirt.

Bowed Flower pulled off her silk scarf for Laughlin.

"Get something for Mr. Mo as well, please," Laughlin requested as he compressed his shoulder wound. The old woman ran into the kitchen and came back with a pile of dishcloths.

While she was returning, Emerald Mo stood up from behind the couch. Her neck was leaking blood. Mrs. Flower screamed and went to her daughter. Both woman collapsed on the far couch and hugged each other. Mrs. Mo held a towel to her neck and started to laugh.

"You've done it now, Franklin. Whatever mental illness you want to use, I'm filing a complaint. Attempted murder is a splendid way to keep you away from me and in jail. Two sheriffs for witnesses should really seal the charge."

Inclining his head on the back of the chair, the subdued man cried, "Oh, Emerald, Emerald, this is not right. I was just upset over all this torment. I never would have hurt you. This is turning out all wrong. Can't you see how unjust you are? Help me."

"The gall you have is incredible. You're insane. My god, you are insane. I'm dumbfounded. I helped you when you had to leave here because of the incident with the boys in juvenile hall. I helped you when you were in trouble at least three times in Stockton during our separation. I helped you meet bail in this fiasco, and now you asked for more help. Go straight to hell!" Emerald Mo yelled and walked out of the room, holding her mother's hand.

"Let's go, Mr. Franklin Mo," Max said and hauled up the now quiet man by his wrinkled shirt and dragged him along while giving him his rights.

Laughlin picked up the strange dagger-axe, wrapped it in a towel, took another towel for his shoulder, and pushed Franklin Mo through the front door and into the car. Franklin Mo was going back where he'd started but this time on the other side of the sliding steel doors.

CHAPTER 44

The newspapers showed colorful pictures of dagger-axes and detailed how the user would take the ax stab and slice or slice and then stab the victim. For a few weeks, there were running accounts of the mental health issues, and the *LA Times* presented a precise summary of the known case and background articles on the incarceration of the mentally ill.

Jail staffers were unbridled with accounts and anecdotes about all the things Mo did, supposedly did, and was going to do. Two deputies and three old inmates registered complaints against Mo. Ancillary personnel would tip off information to the reporters. Florence MacBride was besieged by others wanting to know all she knew. She gave an extensive interview behind a steel desk with her new position on display to a local valley paper, describing Franklin Mo as a ruthless manager who tried to have his way with her and how she was able to resist. She discussed his nefarious practices, including photos of children and dogs. Rumor had it she was paid five hundred for the information.

Dr. Mason's husband filed for divorce, and she began to give paid lectures on getting involved with strange people.

Through all the publicity, Franklin Mo remained in a single cell on the medical mental health ward at the Twin Towers jail. His hand had needed tendon repair done at the LA County General Hospital. While recovering, he was moved from the county hospital jail ward on the thirteenth floor, back to the Twin Tower's medical mental health ward. He would pace his room and peer out into the hall through the thick glass. He'd swallow his antibiotics, refuse psychotropic meds, and asked for Vicodin. He changed lawyers, and no one visited him. Concern for his safety was high. He awaited his appearance at Superior Court 95 for the mental health hearing.

A flood of opinions poured out of state experts. Morning shows had hours of material. Discussions revolved around subjects such as whether this really was a dissociative fugue state and what that was, why it was different from dissociative personality disorder and all the other dissociative categories.

One expert from an Ivy League university was quoted he thought the defendant had been malingering, and one from another upstate school reported to the *NewsHour* it was a factious disorder.

Laughlin sat with Max at the station each day, discussing cases, and they were stymied by the deluge of terms and no date for the trial for the Mo case. News was apparently sniffing elsewhere, and time went by in the orderly fashion of clocks and calendars. Halloween and the Day of the Dead came and went, and Thanksgiving stories took over. The moon and Mars probably had water, Clinton was paying for his cigars, the Tigers had won the pennant, and Leonardo DiCaprio was still drowning in adoring fans.

"Nevertheless, dead as it is to others, I care. Manfred died, and Freddy Poplar died. Franklin Mo was the cause. Whatever the big honchos finally conclude, I'm voting for antisocial personality disorder and pure prison," Laughlin opined.

"It's frustrating that this guy could get away with murder because of reasons of insanity and no one gives a shit," Max complained.

"Was this all a sham? I'm trying to make sense of it all. Connect the associations, the relationships, diagnoses. I understand from the DSM, *malingering* means faking illness to get out of something. But *factious disorder* means faking illness to get in the hospital. Which is he?"

"It's fucked-up, Sergeant," Max replied, and, "It's sure as hell all fiction to me."

"You're right about that. It's all made up."

Finally, there was rumor of a new case. An emergency room technician had been found dead wrapped in a dead boa constrictor. However, it appeared he and the snake were both dead before they were wrapped together and had been frozen in a meat locker for months.

Max and his sergeant bantered on, and Max concluded Laughlin should go for post-traumatic stress disorder and get some more time off rather than get another bizarre assignment.

He declined. He knew veterans who really suffered.

His temple wounds were healed; stitches from the shoulder had been pulled weeks ago, and he felt fit for duty. Begrudgingly, he began the task of reading through his pile of papers. It was all anticlimactic and tedious. There was no quest until their new assignment was official.

Sorting the mess quietly, he reflected on the jail and the mental health dilemmas. Franklin Mo had used the jail setup for his own gains, breeding animosity or counting on disinterest, concentrating on exploiting others' grief.

All those inmates lingered in limbo and vulnerable to drug laws and sentences of lost time with no benefits. Dumb bastards. What a waste of their lives and everyone's money.

The stifled, insulated staff of the jail mental health, gossiping about transgressions and yet attempting to improve the situation for themselves and the inmates, were as vulnerable as the inmates. There had to be better ways. Captured shouldn't mean capitulation of hope.

Laughlin threw down the last pile of forms to clear him for active duty and turned to Max. "Hey, buddy, it's late and I'm ready for lunch. I want to go somewhere good and stuff myself. Does Philippe's sound like the answer?"

"Right on. I'm ready," Max agreed.

This time Laughlin drove the two detectives along Alameda and past Men's Central and the Twin Towers. The detectives sauntered into the casual restaurant and ate their full and then went on to other things.

Returning to the station, they read their reports and signed out for the day. The senior deputy was planning his wedding, and the sergeant was planning another visit to his mother.

On his way to Zuma again, Laughlin saluted Nora Weber's house and thought about the last few weeks. The surf was flat, taking only small breaths and exhaling gently on the sand. He jogged easily on the foam. The day died quickly now that daylight saving was over, and the cold water signaled to his feet, it was time to go home.

This case had never solidified for him. It was full of ill-defined places and amorphous people. Franklin Mo was as much a symptom of all the chaos as he was a perpetrator of corruption. Now it was up to others to judge.

No one was on his porch, only throwaway newspapers and glossy magazines. It was all a letdown. He went in and got his beer and half a leftover cheese sandwich, plopped down on his chair, and waited for the cat. He had a buddy in that big fur ball, as Lucy called him, and that was good. Soon Lucy would be back again and he'd call her for sure. That would be good too.

Taking the pile of mail off the floor, he put the bills on one side of the end table and threw the rest on the floor. He was behind in bills even though he tried to sign up for automatic deductions, but that still didn't cover everything. More shit to do even when there was a lull at work. Who knows what his credit rating might be and what difference it made.

A high-pitched meow came from the big cat as he trotted down the stairs to greet the irritated detective and jumped up on the arm of the chair and then onto his cluttered lap. Laughlin stroked him and, in between gratifying the cat, continued opening mail. He came upon a manila envelope. He opened it and pulled out a note from Eugene Biskoff. It surprised and pleased him.

It read:

I got a message from Dr. Weber at the rehab hospital after I wrote her of my family, and she sent me a card that said to find this poem. She said you were interested in poetry and might like it too. I found it in a collection of British verse. Apparently, it's pretty famous.

I think Dr. Weber means I am a one of the "counter, original, spare, strange" things who can be okay with help. It doesn't matter if it be God or Nature or good genes, it's all about being thankful.

Mr. Winker says only Shakespeare counts, but Elvira and I are going to get some other poetry to read too, and I can live in my dad's old place with all the books I want. I include the poem and send greetings from my Aunt Isabel and the Winklers.

Thank you and Deputy Max for all your help.

Pied Beauty
by Gerard Manley Hopkins

Glory be to God for dappled things –
For skies of couple-colour as a brinded cow;
For rose-moles all in stipple upon trout that swim;
Fresh-firecoal chestnut-falls; finches' wings;
Landscape plotted and pieced – fold, fallow, and
plough;
And all trades, their gear and tackle trim.

All things counter, original, spare, strange;
Whatever is fickle, freckled (who knows how?)
With swift, slow; sweet, sour; a-dazzle, dim;
He fathers-forth whole beauty is past change:
Praise him.

*　　*　　*